The Secrets We Take With Us

By

JAMES J. HILL III

This story is a work of fiction, created to entertain my readers. Any similarities between the characters and real people are purely coincidental.

The Secrets We Take With Us

James has also published other novels, including "When the Dandelions Sing," along with "Phoebe's Heart of Stone," as well as "The Gift of Life, Plus One," and, "The Forgiving Path to the City of Springs," and most recently, "Big Ish."

This Novel is dedicated to my daughters Taylor, Sophia, Sadie Grace, Scarlett and Stella, as whenever times are toughest, I continue to see your smiles.

To my sister Jennifer and brother Joe, for the times we spend apart, and for the times we don't. I appreciate you both.

For my nephew Joshua Michael Daywalt. You left this world too soon, but for a much better view.

Special thanks to the following people who continue to help with my editing:

Amy Wolverson
Flora Poloway
Amy McCormick

As life is full of difficult lessons, we have but two choices: to grow from them or to stay still in them. Both decisions grant very different views, so choose wisely.

— James J. Hill III

Contents

Mistakes are made every single day, by people who are ordinary at their core, and by those who are more than ordinary. It seems that we are born to fail so often that when we succeed at something, it can come as a surprise, even for ourselves. But success is a funny thing. You see, it can bring someone from the depths of rock bottom all the way back to a complete comfort they never imagined possible through either sheer dumb luck, or an insatiable will so many shall never taste in a lifetime of trying.

It can also be born from something that it was never meant to grow from, just as a weed grows through an imperfect crack in an old dirt covered concrete sidewalk in the front of your home. And the measure of success is different for every human. Getting a promotion at your job after years of slaving away and trying to get noticed would be considered a huge success to many people. Saving enough money that you could have that long off retirement you always dreamt of, certainly can be seen as success in many eyes.

But what about a mistake that was never meant to happen, that granted a unique change to the lives of not just one person, but many from one side of a mountain to the dip in the valley far to the west? Something that on any given day would be viewed as a common failure to an incestual world that is so used to seeing others fail and fail hard. Yet, many would be wrong to assume that it was as they had heard it, or been told about it through second and even third hand accounts over generations of both good and bad.

There's a story about a man named Tarvis Michael Richards. I didn't know all the origins of the story growing up, but my parents knew it all too well. My mother grew up not far from where everything took place, and she remembered her own mother reminding her to be cautious whenever she was outside of their home. There was a fear throughout the small quaint town of Falls City, West Virginia, that shook an entire generation of people to their bones, instead of allowing them the ability to decide how they wished to live their lives out. Simple people that minded their own damn business and kept their nose to the grindstone to get by without ever being noticed by outsiders.

"But things happened sometimes and that was that," as my father would say to me. He wasn't from the same area as my mother, so he never felt the impact that my mother or the people from her town and the surrounding ones knew as a part of their upbringing. He had grown up in Scranton, which was in Northeast Pennsylvania, and although I'm sure the tale carried the miles to where he lived through word of mouth, if not much further, he didn't care much at all. It wasn't affecting him directly, so what did he have to be concerned over?

Me? I didn't know what I do now about Tarvis. I had heard a little of the monster he was from others, and at times my parents talked about what happened all those years that are now so far removed from the chaos we see today that it really didn't matter. Why would it? It was in the distant past, and to be honest, a lifetime away from where we all walked freely, even if the dirt on which it took place on was the same. There was enough going on today in the here and now to not be worried about something that was long over and now just a lost story that old people rarely ever brought up. Most that did talk about it had a lifetime of not much else to discuss anyways, and so people really never paid them much mind.

The fact I learned as much as I did about Tarvis Michael Richards seems important to me now, but if you would have told me before I saw his name in writing and stumbled upon the lost story of a man that the devil himself would cast from hell out of fear for his own safety, that it would change my life in ways no one would see coming? I would say not even remotely possible!

He was in a jail cell an hour or so from where I lived, probably serving a sentence beyond what any human could rightfully finish, and I was just a freshman at Tuft County High School doing whatever it was girls should be doing at that age. Not researching and learning about dangerous criminals and their excuses and lies they built their lives around, and that much I knew.

But that's not how it was, at least for me. A simple handwritten letter, a project meant to help us understand a lost art in written communication, give hope to someone reentering society, and perhaps add a bit of inspiration and purpose that kids our age apparently lacked. Nothing more, and nothing less.

When our teacher, Mr. Reynolds, handed out the assignment, no one was excited, least of all me. I'm not a writer. I have no desire to pull out a sheet of paper and write word after word with a pen in hand, pretending to be remotely interested in some poor idiot's life that will learn nothing from a 14-year-old about life and its ultimate purpose. If they haven't learned to adult yet, they aren't going to with my help. That time has come and gone, as my mother said often enough.

We had rules to follow for our homework. We had to always stay positive in our words and could not ask them about the crimes that landed them behind bars. We would not use our real names, so we had to develop individual nicknames in order to write, and those nicknames had to be approved by the teacher first. The letters would all be sent at the same time, from the school's P.O. Box so that we would all remain anonymous and no one would ever be in any danger. At least the school got that part right.

I chose the name Olive for myself. It was so far from my real name, Rain, and I figured it was as if one was extending an olive branch out as my Mee-maw would say. It just seemed fitting, and so I became Olive, with no last name. I sat down to write my letter, not knowing who would receive it, nor what to expect back. Not anything life-changing, for sure, and simply a grade I needed to avoid going to summer school.

But that is where simple ended. The months to follow were anything but what they should have been, and fear, doubt, frustration and finding the meaning behind one of the most horrendous acts of crime became such an obsession for me, I just about forgot who I was. I placed myself into the center of a ferocious storm so powerful and unpredictable that finding my way back would take everything I had, and more.

And so it began with a simple introduction,

"Dear sir...."

Chapter 1

* * *

The state of West Virginia is beautiful, and yet so many people don't get the chance to experience the hidden small towns tucked away in the deep mountains, that are almost as if they have stood still in time as the rest of the world moved surely around it.

We have a different way of seeing things here, but eventually, everything catches up with us. The joke is that we just learned within the past year about the internet or have finally had indoor plumbing installed which made us no longer needing our outhouses, and we hate when people say stupid things like that. Or that we all marry our first cousins. I don't know a single person who married their cousin ever. And my favorite of all, do we hear banjos playing in the woods as we walk through them in overalls? No, I've never heard a banjo play through the trees, and the only thing I know of that movie "Deliverance," is, "Squeal like a pig, boy!". Which is gross.

We have great award-winning schools, just like anywhere else. Our styles come from the same places as the rest of the country's do. We use social media and honestly, I'm tired of explaining to simple people why West Virginia is just like any other place, with the exception of the geography of its location, which does seem to be tucked away on a map.

Now my Mee-maw? She may be the exception to the rule. If you talked with her, you would think she is exactly how outsiders view us. She had my mom when she was in her late forties, so she is much older than my friends' grandparents. She is smart as a whip, but she's feisty and can be a bit cold at times. How my mother ever grew into the soft-spoken woman she is living with that woman, I will never understand. That trait did not trickle down.

Her husband was even older, but he died well before I was even a thought, so I knew very little about him. I don't even recall his name, but Mee-maw said if he were alive, I would most certainly call him "Pappy", so that is how he is referred to the seldom times he is brought up in our conversations.

But times have changed, and it feels weird to call someone I've never met—someone who died long before I was born—Pappy. I don't know. Maybe it's a name reserved for someone closer to you. I never knew him and he never knew me, but at the end of the day, whatever makes her happy I guess is alright by me.

Anyway, there was school, and I'm actually a pretty good student. I missed the honor society by a very small margin, but that was my own fault. At the end of the summer, I was messing around when I entered freshman year and didn't get on track for almost a full month and a half. Now that I am realizing what a different school expects from me, I should have no issues getting back on track.

"Okay, settle down. Settle down. The assignment is pretty clear, but if any of you all have questions, now's the time to ask," Mr. Reynolds said.

Of course, Bobby Davis and his ever growing ego made him ask the dumbest questions just to show off and get a rise out of everyone…

"What if the killers find out our real names, and let's say they get out, stalk us at home, and, well, you know. Do we still get a decent grade for at least trying, despite our ultimate death?"

"No one is going to come looking for you. I've already explained that no one will use their real names or home addresses. Nor will anyone send a letter to anyone who is in prison for murder or anything like that. These are people that have made mistakes for sure but nothing so serious that we would worry for any of your safety. Okay? And before you ask Bobby, I will need to approve the names you all use, so if you want to drag this on with names you know I won't approve, it will simply come off your grade," Mr. Reynolds said back with a smirk.

We had to open our computers and fill out the form so that we could be placed with someone to write. I entered the nickname I had chosen, and the information about what I hoped to gain from this, which was basically a good grade. We would keep our nicknames private for now, so that no one knew who was writing which letters and to whom they were writing to. The idea was to keep this anonymous and even though the initial letter was going to be read prior to sending, we didn't know if they all would be.

Once the names were approved, they showed up on the teacher's screen in front of class.

"These are the names that have been accepted so far. Congratulations to those that have followed the rules and created those acceptable names. You may now start your letters, and I will place a box up here in front of the room for you to drop them off. Once we initially read them and send them out, a man or woman at the prison will be selected at random from an approved list, and they will be your person. Remember to be courteous and understanding as some of these prisoners have few people in their lives who write them. This may be the most important letters they get while serving their time," Mr. Reynolds explained.

And so, I went home and sat down at my kitchen table, placed my bag against the wall so it was ready for the morning, and placed a sheet of blue lined paper on the counter along with a pen. All I had to do was write a basic letter, be careful to not include any information that would: a) identify me, and b) offend my "person," as they were called in class.

"Mom? When is the last time you had to write a letter to someone and send it in the mail?" I asked.

"*Had* to or *wanted* to?" was her reply.

"Eww, who would actually want to? Wouldn't you just send a text if you wanted to share something? That's a weird answer," I snapped back.

"Rain, watch it. I was answering your question. I've

written letters on occasion to Mee-maw as she doesn't use her cell phone to message, nor does she have an email, but she still prefers I send them. It's been a few months since the last though, so I guess she is due," mom said.

She walked into the kitchen to spy on what I was asking for.

"Mom, stop! Why are you looking at my things! It's a blank sheet of paper with nothing on it. It's not to a boy or anything. Mr. Reynolds has us, never mind. It's for school. I was just asking."

I didn't mean to be mean, but sometimes adults just bother the hell out of me. They don't understand what we are going through in today's world and all the pressure we are under that they never had to face. Life is so different from what they experienced, and so it frustrates me when she tries to help. I can manage my life just fine on my own.

I snacked on some carrot sticks and peanut butter, walked around the room a little, and texted with Brit about her boyfriend who seems to like someone else now, only she isn't seeing it. The rest of our school can, but she is blind for some stupid reason. I think it's more denial than anything, and I have no idea what she sees in him. He's not even that cute and he's really short.

Eventually I get back to the letter, but it's now almost 8:30 at night, and I am annoyed. Annoyed at my mom, and annoyed I must write a letter about things I don't even care to deal with, and honestly I would be shocked if anything came back that would make a difference in my life. What, are they going to say, "Stay in school and listen to your mama?"

Or maybe "Don't do the things I have done that landed me here in this God-awful place"?

Yea, thanks dude but I know this already. I don't need an incarcerated idiot to tell me not to do stupid things just because they had. And if I did anything stupid, it would never be dumb enough to land me in jail. That much I know.

"Dear Sir, I will tell you my name is Olive, but that's only because we aren't going to use our real names. It's nothing against you, but just the rules the school has for us."

Okay, finally a start. Something to get me going. I'll get back to this later though. I have a week to get the letter done and tonight doesn't feel like the night to rush through it. So, I'm going to trust my gut on this and wait a few days.

"Mom, I'm sorry I was upset earlier. I just have a lot of schoolwork to do and didn't feel like a lecture. Did you write Mee-maw?"

I think my mom likes it when I sit with her and apologize, which seems to be often lately. I don't even know that I need to really, but it makes her feel good when I do. So at least she gets something from it. She can be ultra annoying, but she's still my mom.

A few days go by and the letter just sits there. It appears to be staring at me each time I walk by it, as if it's telling me to stop procrastinating and finish the damn thing. "I know. I know," I tell myself.

I decided to pull out another sheet of paper and completely start over. I can do much better than what I have barely done thus far. So I will.

Dear Sir,

My name is Olive, and I'm currently a freshman in a local school. The reasons for my letter are interesting. To start, I can honestly say that I've never sat down and physically wrote a letter even once. So, this is my very first attempt at writing one. Please give some grace when and if you reply as I have not a clue what I am supposed to be doing. I also wanted to let you know that if you have any words of advice for me, I am willing to listen to those. I'm sure you have experienced a lot in your life and probably can tell that I have not seen what you have. That's not to judge you, mind you, but just a fact of life. You are clearly older than I, and so naturally you would have more experiences to share. Plus I've never been to prison, and again, not judging you at all, but I would be interested in learning about what it is you see when you are there. All I know is what I see in videos that are shared online. Do you get to go online there? If not, is there anything you would like to learn about that I can maybe send to you the next time I write?

I think that is it for now. I'm not sure what else I should be writing in this, but I think for my first ever handwritten letter, this isn't so bad. What do you think?

Olive

Chapter 2

* * *

My initial letter somehow made it through the inspection by Mr. Reynolds. Which is good because if I had to rewrite it, I doubt I could make it any more interesting. Not that the first was fascinating at all, but a second attempt after hearing what I did wrong would deflate me.

The letters eventually came in from the rest of the class with several having to be corrected. The class was told which nicknames had to redo the letters, and you could easily tell whom some of the students were simply by the way they reacted when their fictitious names were called. The idea was to remain anonymous and creative yet normal but telling high school students that was a senseless task.

I, on the other hand, wanted to remain anonymous. I had no desire to have my letters exposed to the other kids in class for good or bad. I wasn't a writer at all, and although I am certain I did better than some of the other boneheads, I wanted to keep my words, my words.

But because of the extra time needed, the letter I wrote had to wait longer than it should have. They were all going to be sent at the exact same time, so that we would possibly all get letters back at roughly the same time, depending on when the inmates wrote back of course. It made sense, but the unfair part was that Bobby was a child with the mentality of an infant looking to be the center of attention and didn't care if his letter passed through or not. He simply wanted all the focus on him and to be funny when he really wasn't. At least he was not in my eyes. He was simple. That's exactly how I referred to him. As a simple child. One that if I had to guess, could end up marrying a first cousin and making those outsiders proud to have been right.

I forgot about the letter for the next few weeks because they had to still get the last few corrected ones in and I had finished mine by the deadline when it was first expected. But then one arrived back. Not for me, but for another student. Because everything had to remain a mystery, the letter went into a box that Mr. Reynolds had made. It had the nickname written out on the front, but since no one knew the person behind the fictitious name, only they could get it and keep it that confidential. He had a curtain set up so that you could walk around the back of to where the large box sat, and grab the letter without anyone else noticing. But to keep it a secret, we had to wait until all the letters were in.

It got to the point that letters were coming in daily, and eventually, all but one was in so we were going to proceed. For the one not returned, we were told that the student would still receive a passing grade if it never arrived, but to be patient as it still may find its way here.

Because of that one missing letter, we were told each would go around the back of the box and behind the white curtain, one at a time, and see if we could find our letter. If it was there, you would take it and place it in your bag. Because the made-up names we picked were known to the teacher, he would place that name on an envelope with a blank letter inside for the one that did not find its way back yet so the class would not know who didn't get one. It actually made sense to me.

One by one we all walked to the front of the classroom and grabbed an envelope from the box. No one would know which one had an empty message within as we could not open them in class. So I could not tell if mine had anything written inside or not. I saw my name, Olive, grabbed it quickly, placed it in my bookbag, and returned to my seat.

As school finished, I found an interesting curiosity to open the envelope but figured it best to do at home and not on the bus where it could be exposed to others. I kind of liked the secretness of all this, as it had a mystery-esque feel about it.

When I returned home, I could wait no longer. I had to see what this inmate, assuming it was a man (and hoping I didn't call a woman, a sir), had to say. The front of the envelope simply said "Olive," and so I opened it up, pulled out a single sheet of paper, and saw that it was entirely blank. Are you freaking kidding me! All this built-up excitement and my inmate can't read or write? I'm the idiot that got nothing back? This sucks. I was excited about one thing, and here I am feeling let down by a convict who apparently found better things to do with his downtime. You would think he would at the very least write something or draw me a picture of something, anything, in all that spare time he has.

I tossed the envelope in the trash and walked over to grab a bite to eat. As I nibbled on the carrot, I could feel the let-down come over me. I was kind of pissed off to be completely honest. And that made me wonder a lot. Why would I be let down? I didn't even want to do this at first. This was stupid and if I was going to get a passing grade for doing nothing at all, I should be very happy to not have to do anything. But I wasn't. I just wasn't.

The next morning I headed back to class, and figured if the letter ever came, we would all need to walk up again, and all but one person would have to act as if they were really looking for the letter. The reality is that I would be the only one still in need, but I would play it off as if it wasn't me. I didn't want to give my identity away.

But it did not. There was no mention of it, and the other kids were already writing back their second letters in response to what they got the first time around. My closest friend in the world, Addie, ended up telling me about hers.

She had a woman who was serving a twenty-six month sentence for stealing from the Walmart of all places, for the fifth time. Even though we weren't allowed to ask them what they were in for, I guess some of the inmates had no problem letting others know, or if they could not understand right from wrong and were in jail, they probably didn't care all that much about the rules anyway.

"Rain, what the hell is wrong with these women? You would think she would learn to steal better by now if she's been caught a hundred times already," Addie said.

"Or maybe not steal at all and get your life in order?" was my reply.

Addie laughed, knowing that I was probably right. These people were in prison not just because they weren't very good at their crimes, but because they had decided along the way that the rules did not apply to them. It wasn't that hard to follow the laws set forth, well unless you were Bobby. Who we all expected to end up in prison at some point anyways.

"What did your inmate do? Anything better than that?" she asked me.

I didn't want to tell her that I was the one without the response. That my letter was the only one either not opened, not read, or not cared about by the inmate selected for me. So I just nodded and replied,

"Yea, just stupid stuff you know," and left it at that.

Chapter 3

* * *

After a few weeks, I no longer cared about the dang letter. In fact, school became pretty busy and I had a ton of work and studying to do, so this was a blessing in disguise and I was just happy that I didn't have even more work to stress over. So I let that all go and got focused on what truly needed my attention.

The teacher eventually moved the curtain and box to a corner of the room where it would be out of the way, and fewer letters appeared in the weeks that followed the first round. Either the students lost interest in the project, the inmates maybe were getting released, or somehow along the way, people just gave up and didn't find it of any use to continue writing their thoughts.

But then, when everyone was moving on to other projects and talking about new goals for the upcoming semester, Mr. Reynolds announced that a letter had arrived, one from the prison that somehow either got lost or who knows what. He said he would move the curtain and box back to the front of the classroom, and each student would come up, backpack in hand, and repeat the process we did weeks ago.

A collective sigh was let out, as students were already over it. They had no desire to go up and fake as if the letter could be their letter. I even followed along with the sigh. Not to hide that I hadn't received one. Just because now, while everyone else was basically done with theirs, I had to start all over and write more. I had no desire to do something that should have been finished already, had he or she followed the rules.

The students all got up, stood in a line, and each walked up as instructed. Some of them went as far as to open the zipper on their backpacks or bags to make it sound as if the letter might be theirs. But I knew better. I knew it was mine, because I was the only one without a letter.

As I walked up, a curious suspicion formed out of nowhere. I saw my name, or the name I made up, Olive, on the front written neatly out as if they were taking their time. I felt the envelope, wondering how short or long a letter it may be, and placed it neatly in my bag. As the rest of the students went up, the 8th person knew one of the first ones owned it, and the next knew it was one of the ones below them because there was nothing left in the box. But I don't think anyone cared about who owned the actual last letter by this point.

They eventually all finished and we were all seated back down at our desk. Back to classwork for us. But for me, I was now itching to open mine, as truthfully I deserved a letter in response. I had earned at least an explanation of why it took so long to finish a single written letter. Either he was just rude, or mentally slow. One or the other I thought to myself.

But I had to be patient for just a little longer. The letter wasn't going anywhere, and who knew what was even in it other than the inmate himself. A few hours and I would be home in my kitchen, snacks in hand because I just *have* to have snacks every time I return home.

Finally, after hours of finishing up classes, listening to Bobby tell stupid jokes that only he found funny, and a bus ride through the rolling hills of brilliant leaves changing all different fall colors, I was on my front porch, unlocking the door, and walking into my house.

I placed my bag onto the table and unzipped the front pocket. There inside was the letter, with the name "Olive," written much differently than when Mr. Reynolds had done so to ensure each student at least had one.

I placed it on the center of the table and went over to grab some round crackers from the pantry and some cheese and red grapes from the kitchen drawer. I love red grapes and cheese more than anything, so mom makes sure I always have a healthy amount of both. Maybe she does that for me, or perhaps she does that for her so that I am not arguing with her about yet another thing. Either way, I have them so it makes no difference what the reasoning is.

The envelope is sitting there, as if it's daring me to open it. I let it sit some more. I don't know why, really. I guess getting a letter from someone in prison seems a little bizarre. I mean

I am only 14, and to think some man is writing for inspiration or to make himself feel better because it'll save his soul or something, just feels weird.

As I take another bite of my cracker with sharp cheese and a sliced grape on top, I start to imagine what my inmate did. He probably robbed a liquor store for booze. Maybe he is homeless and just wanted some wine or whatever he drinks. Isn't that why they are called winos?

Or maybe it was something simple like what Addie's criminal did. He probably shoved some shirts down his pants and thought no one would notice as he wandered out to the front of the store. But because he's so heavy, the shirts were very noticeable and he could not run as fast as he needed to in order to escape the police.

What if it's for tax evasion? He's one of those "white collar," types that has no business being in a jail with all those tough guys there. He could write back to me with a cryptic message that spells out "HELP," in some strange way because he realizes he won't last another month there if someone doesn't bust him out.

Not my problem, I say to myself. Whatever he did, he got caught. And when you get caught for a crime, you do the time. That should be the slogan on top of the prison. "If you do the crime, you will do the time."

Alright, I'm finished procrastinating long enough. It's time to just open the damn thing and see what happens. Not like anything is going to jump out at me. Stop being such a wimp and get to it.

Dear Miss Olive,

To say I was shocked to receive a letter from you is an understatement that stretches beyond words. I receive many letters, but most of those are from people far stranger and more selfish than you or I. So first things first, thank you for such a simple letter.

I am not sure why you felt the need to reach out to me, but I am not one to complain about the good graces that are granted to me now and again. If there is one thing I will grant back to you in return, it is grace, as you wished.

I remember being a freshman in high school, and although it's been many decades, I can still see the halls and the wooden desk I sat at. I can smell the musty odor of textbooks we once used and hear the sounds of my own teachers clapping one eraser against the other to clear off the dust as they prepare the next lesson for us.

I am happy to give you some advice as requested in your letter but remember that this old man has been gone for many years now. The boy I was once is no longer a thought in the minds of anyone of importance, so take what I say as a lesson for both now, and also for later on in life.

Live your life free. Listen to the simple sounds around you with just a little more intent. Let the soaring birds, and the babbling brooks that lead to greater bodies of water sing to you. Let the noisy crickets at night be your solace when things weigh heavy on your mind. Let your loved ones know that you are there for them in their time of need and remind them to be there for you when you need it back. Hold on to 14 as long as you can, Miss Olive, and don't be in a rush to hurry this life on. Remember that life is unfair more often than not, and justice? It is rarely just. But whatever you are faced with, whatever happens along your journey through this life, you are only responsible for how you show up. That's it. So show up with a smile on your face. Someone breaks your heart? Smile. You lost a job you had always wanted? Smile. You break an arm slipping down a soggy moss-covered hill because you lost your footing? Smile.

You can lose everything in your life, but it's how you show up that will make a world of difference. So smile through it all. It's the one thing they cannot take from you. And I promise you this, Miss Olive. If you can smile through pain and grief and struggle, you win.

I am blessed that you have chosen to write to me, and hope that if I do not hear from you again, you understand that you made a difference in someone's life, even if only for today.

So thank you for that young lady.

All my best that I have left to give,

T. Michael

Chapter 4

* * *

It was pouring outside, like a gully washer, as Mee-maw often said. I hadn't the faintest idea of what a gully washer was, and nor did I care enough to ask anyone. She had all sorts of crazy sayings that only she seemed to understand, but spoke them plain as day as if everyone around her knew exactly what she was talking about. Maybe a few old people knew, but that was about it.

We were going to visit with her in a weeks' time, so I had to pack a few things for the night, as she would hear none of us heading back home after dark. She was a worried woman all her life, even for someone so strong willed and rough as a bucket of rusted nails.

Her home was slight, built almost into the side of an actual mountain with an old wooden outhouse still in use, although she did have a bathroom inside that one of her sons had installed after years of the children complaining. She saw very little need for modern amenities, but still, she relented so that they would bring the grandkids around and stop all their damn nagging.

I was packing up, and decided to read the letter from inmate Michael, as I called him, once more. My father was heading out of town for business he had up in Ohio, so I wanted to ask him a few questions before he left for his drive north.

I read him the letter and asked him what he thought about his response.

"Well, Miss Olive, not sure what you are asking from me. Seems like a decent enough letter. Are you required to write back?" he asked with a smirk on his face.

Dad was always focused on work and rarely sat down to discuss life's issues or things we had going on in school or our personal lives. He left that all to Mom, but I wanted his opinion on this and not hers. I don't know exactly why, but I was curious about what he thought. As I read the letter, I noticed a few things that stood out more now than I had the first time I opened it.

For one, Michael was very well spoken. Seemed obviously educated, and unlike the letters some of my classmates had received and let slip out, he seemed genuinely interested in giving me feedback on how I should live my life. The advice was simple at its core but had me thinking about the times I had let others get to me for no good reason at all.

"Smile through it all," was such basic, simplistic advice but had a deep note of power behind it. If I had smiled when Chase decided to talk with that girl behind my back at the football game last fall, instead of confronting both of them and losing my temper in front of so many others watching the game, I would have appeared much stronger. But I was weak that day. Pissed off at what they thought was okay to do to me. It hurt, and I reacted as such, embarrassing me for weeks.

Or when I struggled with my braces the first time I had them done. I hated my braces, and everyone knew it because I stopped smiling. Mom would always remind me to smile because she loved when I was happy, but I wasn't happy. I wanted her to know I hated them. Hated everything about them and just wanted the metal to be ripped off and my teeth all straight without the hassle of waiting. I had little to no patience.

But had I smiled, I would have thrown everyone off. I would have probably felt a little happier, even if I was mostly faking that smile. Which lead me to more questions. Did Michael smile while in jail or was he just giving me advice he could never follow himself?

I mean, he was in prison surrounded by walls and steel bars. I doubt one could find a positive reason in that type of environment and smile through the daily nonsense they must deal with. I'm sure the food sucks, and making friends is probably not the easiest task. Wait, what if he had to join a gang to feel safe? I saw a video where these guys were bullying another inmate and the only way he could get protection was to join a gang that would protect him. It was sad, because the guy was clearly scared out of his mind and had no other options. Just a tiny man who had no business being in with all those animals. Did Michael have that same experience? Did he smile through that? Doubtful.

I decided I would write him back, but I wasn't sure how to respond just yet and clearly dad was going to be no help.

I think when I visit with Mee-maw I will ask her for some advice. Not that I enjoy talking with her, but she's a decent listener and unlike my parents, she will hear what I have to say and at least make me feel heard. Maybe she really just let me talk long-winded and tended to her duties without hearing much. Hard to say honestly, because she didn't always respond with words I could understand.

We drove an hour or so through the Allegheny Mountains to a town seemingly without a name. There were no traffic lights for miles, and one run down store off what you could call a main road if you didn't know any better, where you could buy a few things to get you by until you could make it to the Walmart, which was probably a good hours drive away.

She had no street sign directing you to where she resided, and I know she enjoyed that.

"No one has any business up here for no reason no how unless I says they do," she squeaked time and time again.

I sometimes felt an embarrassment that she was related to me, but deep inside I had a sort of sense of pride that this mountain woman from a different lifetime away, was still going as strong as she was at her age. She didn't let a day's hard work go undone. I can't remember ever a day when my mom said that she had to visit her mother in the hospital. She probably had mom in that worn-down excuse for a home and instead of calling a doctor, delivered mom herself with whatever tools she had lying around.

Mom reminded my brother and I to mind our manners and to not take anything Mee-maw said to heart. Yea, easy for her to say. She had a lifetime of living with her and had developed thick skin for her lack of charm. Me? I felt scared anytime she walked into a room and looked at me and said, "whatcha think this is a resort? There's things to get done, so get going on them."

Half the time we had no idea what things she was talking about, so we would just go outside and pick up sticks or whatever and act as if we understood.

But she was getting older and mom said to just not worry so much about her. Life was finally catching up to that old woman and she was starting to understand that. But she still would never leave that home. It could fall down all around her and you would just need to wait until she died and bury her in there. That was all she knew, and she was going to die in that house one day.

Still, I wanted to share my letter with the woman to gain her thoughts. She would tell me like it was, and not mince words, as mom always said about her.

So as we unpacked and set up the tent in the back of the property so we could have our space outside of her house, I grabbed the letter and placed it in the back pocket of my shorts. When the time was right, I would take it out and ask Mee-maw for her thoughts.

That moment came just after our first supper with her as I was volunteered to help "clean up the dang dishes and throw away the rubbish into the pit out yonder in the yard so the coons could eat healthy the scraps," or whatever it is she said.

"Whatcha got on your mind midget?" she asked.

"Nothing really. Just wanted to ask you if I could read you a letter I got from an inmate at the jail is all," I responded.

The way I asked nonchalantly got exactly the reaction I should have expected. If I had taken a minute to hear my words before I spoke them out freely, I could have stopped myself.

Who leads with something like that without giving the background information? A 14-year-old is messaging a man in prison and I expected her to think that was perfectly normal for one to do?

She just looked at me. Gave me a glare from the supper table as she grabbed the last remaining items to put away. Her eyes were glossy, and the lines around them showed the years of hard living that seeped into her skin like a river through the valley does. The dark, spotty patches of skin that formed on her face were proof that life was brutally harder than it was not. Just as Michael had said. But she forgot one thing through all that living. She forgot to smile through it all. At least that's what I was told to do.

Instead of judging me right off from the start, she ordered me to read the letter. Her eyes were not as good as they had been yesterday, she said, so I would need to be her eyes for this one. Nothing about why this man and I were messaging, though. Just a matter-of-fact, do as you said you were going to do.

And so I did. I opened the letter, leaned against the counter to where the dishes were stacked neatly and ready to be placed back where they belonged, and began to read his words to her.

Chapter 5

* * *

Falls City was one of those insignificant little towns that somehow had a strangely significant population for the area it covered. To drive through it now, you would see nothing of what yesterday had to show of it.

The noise and chaos and the eerie, chilling sounds that used to plague the air all around the streets was now covered in a quaint blanket of mostly the small conversations of shoppers along the tiny local establishments currently lining the streets. You would think you were somewhere a million miles away from the original backdrop of the town.

Back in the early 1800s, men logging the area discovered that the location of this town, with its access to water from the New River, provided a perfect place to set up camps for those that needed a place to rest their heads after long hours at work. They quickly made makeshift homes using extra timber and whatever other materials they had handy, and while these places were serving their purpose, they were anything but ideal and comfortable.

Men struggled to find the comforts they had known at home, and tempers often flared with ferociousness and precision. If you weren't able to fight and fight well, you quickly would succumb to the Falls City boys who did not have an ounce of fear or care in the world. Especially for the mountain boys that came down from those hills high above the dirt below, who were just built differently from the rest of the boys in the country. Those boys knew of very little in life that you or I would consider a basic comfort. They had nothing to their names but the worn ragged clothes on their back, and an ability to find food whenever and wherever they went.

As time went on, not much changed in the town. It stayed a place for men to rest their bodies, but eventually some of them brought their families and made more permanent homes there so they did not have to travel as they once did. It would simply be easier to have their wives and children close by, instead of traveling the distances back and forth to wherever they originated.

Then, in the 1980s, a town that few had ever heard of — one mentioned on printed roadmaps only because it had to be— gained national attention for all the wrong reasons. It placed Falls City at the top of every newspaper that one could find, giving attention to a place trying to stay as far from the spotlight as an old town could, and to resist growth that most of the rest of the nation seemed to beg for.

For the first time in dozens of decades, people were drawn to Falls City. They were captivated by the horror stories they read, and curious as to how anyone could get away with such a tragic tale of crimes in a city that must be no larger than a few country miles. But it wasn't as small as everyone thought, and as tragic as it was, whoever was responsible for the missing souls popping up, was obviously good at keeping things off his trail.

I was born in 2011, so far removed from anything that happened 3 decades ago, but my mother had been an 80's child and knew the stories her own mother told her about. The local people, although tough and certainly able to handle matters themselves without outside interference, were a scared bunch and confused on what needed to be done.

After the first disappearance, no one seemed to pay much attention. But then a second came just a few months after, and then another, and another. There were no suspects in a place where everyone knew everyone's families for generations. People seldom said more than a hello when walking by but now stopped to see if they had a hunch about who was doing all that foolishness. It was a lot of "did ya hear about that poor sap the other night? I bet it was one of those so and so boys."

There were guesses as good as any as to where all those missing people had gone, but no one had anything solid to go on. It seemed whoever or whatever was responsible was able to slip away in the darkness of the night as a shadow does once the sun goes down over the horizon. Somewhere doors were never locked, it suddenly became a practice everyone thought more about doing.

It also seemed as if the kidnappings were random and had no connection to each one before that anyone could see. A young lady whose family was relatively new to the area just up and gone.

Then an old man who had spent his entire 75 years in town being the second to vanish, clear on the opposite side of town. A third was a soft-spoken man who lived at home along with his sister and brother. They were spared, but why? How did the victims get chosen? Was it random or was there a sign that no one was seeing? One that could easily tie them all together and could prevent them if they just saw what it was that made them all similar after all?

The State eventually got involved after realizing this was more than the small local police department could handle on their own. It wasn't that they didn't try, but they were ill-equipped to handle an investigation of this nature. And time was not on their side as the missing people seemed to pile up.

By the end of the year, there were 7 confirmed missing, all within the town's limits, and all disappearances seemingly with very little to go on. Even after a witness spotted what they thought was a figure running towards Barnes Hardware Store, they could find no trace of anything out of the ordinary.

The mayor of the town had basically given up, and begged the Governor of West Virginia to send more help. If they could just catch a break, and have some hotshot detective crack open the case with the slightest of leads, maybe it would deter whoever was involved, have them pause for a while, long enough for him or her, or them, to slip up and give themselves away. That was all one could hope for, because clearly this was the work of someone much smarter than a drunk who ended up killing off someone in a fit of rage.

During the winter of January 1984, an 8th issue had come

about. This time, something was left behind. The body.

The victim was 68-year-old Winnie May Haftner, who lived alone after her husband left her some years before. She kept to herself and would only venture into town when it was absolutely necessary. She had been dead for some time. But because she was alone and had no children in the area, no one thought of checking in on her. It wasn't until someone from the church in town went to drop off a dinner that they realized something was a muck.

The door to her place was wide open, despite the temperature outside being in single digits. When they called out her name and got no answer, they decided they had better at least check in to ensure all was okay with old Winnie May.

When the couple entered, they noticed a radio on in the far left room of the main level, which was where she slept at night. The radio wasn't set to a station with music or any talking, but rather static.

They again called out her name, hoping to hear some type of response, but still nothing. The thought was they should call the police, but they also wanted to be sure one of their own was safe, so they continued into the room cautiously, where they found Winnie on her bed, in a pool of dried blood, and clearly no longer alive. As they stood there stiff from the site, they quickly glanced around the room, unsure if what had done this was still in the home.

Eventually, they found her phone plugged into the wall and quickly called the police, who told them not to touch a thing. They decided to get back to their car and locked all the doors as they warmed up from the terrible crisp chill in the air.

As the couple looked at each other, they could each see the panic and fear in each other's eyes.

"God almighty, you don't think the killer is still in these woods do you?" the wife cried nervously.

The husband wanted to calm his wife's nerves but was looking all around the car for a sign, any sign, of movement in the fading daylight. Every noise and gust of wind that lent it's power to the exterior of the car was a concern. The police would be at least twenty minutes away from her home as she was just on the edge of town higher in the woods.

Those brutal twenty minutes felt like hours in the approaching night. As they were about to give up hope of staying there any longer, they could hear in the distance the sirens coming up the long dirt drive which was covered in a fine coating of powdered sugar-white snow. Suddenly, they felt a sense of relief.

The rest of the night was spent combing over the entire house and surrounding area. The couple that discovered the scene were quickly taken to the police station to report anything they could regarding what they encountered when they arrived at her residence. Even the state police came in on this one to offer their assistance.

Enough was enough, and the Governor finally stepped up with his authority, moving officers from several neighboring counties and towns into Falls City, hoping the extra manpower would make enough of a difference to capture this killer or killers and bring West Virgina away from the negative spotlight. To this point, they had still never found the bodies or any signs of the missing seven.

The following 2 years saw 5 more go missing, each within the limits of the town, for a total of 12 missing and one confirmed deceased. And then, for reasons no one knows, and without any apparent signs of regret or fear of being caught, they just ended.

Falls City could, for at least the time being, breathe a sigh of relief. It took a good many months for folks to finally let their guard down some, as the residents were temporarily happy but feared the "what if they start again?" questions. But they did not.

In the latter part of the summer of 1985, without a lot of information and with no large media presence which the towns-people were getting used to, the police made a statement that they had caught the person responsible and hoped to give new information on the whereabouts of the missing 12 which everyone had been waiting for.

Chapter 6

* * *

After reading the letter to Mee-maw, I placed it carefully back in the envelope and turned to where she was standing. At first I wasn't certain she had heard a word I read as she was still acting busy in the kitchen moving things and placing things where she had grabbed them from earlier. But then she turned to me and opened her mouth.

"So what did you take from this Michael fella?" she asked.

"Me? I don't know. It was for a class project but he seems so at ease with being in prison. Maybe he is getting out soon and happy for that, but what if he is in longer? How could someone be that happy and okay with it?" I responded.

It did make me think, though. We weren't allowed to ask about their crimes, the reason why they were there, or anything about their sentence they were forced to serve. In fact, we were discouraged from asking anything that had to do with prison life. The idea was to not make the inmates feel bad about their situation, but rather happy to give back to someone else and hopefully, when they were released, an idea of a better way of life that would not lead them back to where they had just left. But that was going to be hard, because I felt like I needed to know more about Michael and how he came up with his, "smile through it all," theory.

"Well, he certainly seems like he's accepted his position. That there is what life is about. You must sometimes accept that the bread you baked burns, and while that isn't what you set out for, it ain't all bad now is it? You still eat the burned bread." Mee-maw said.

I had no idea what the hell she was talking about accepting bad bread as good, but she talked strangely everyday I've known her, so I just let it in one ear and out the other. Lately, though, I thought she was losing her mind more than usual.

She left the room and then returned after a moment.

"Here," she said handing me something.

It was an old, cracked pocket watch, missing the glass bezel on the front, stained and damaged all about. The black hands still moved, but nothing else about this watch was remotely worth a copper penny. Why did she have this broken, trashed clock, I had no idea, but it should have been tossed away in the burn pile behind her house years ago.

She could tell by the look on my face I was puzzled, but that didn't stop her from giving it to me anyway.

"I know whatcha thinking. It's broken and useless and busted to all hell. Ain't ya? Well, let me tell you something about that fancy life you live with your momma. Fancy ain't always better. You have that fancy phone of yours in your purse that tells you the time, but guess what? That there watch does just as good a job. Better, in fact. You know why?" she asked.

"Yea, course you don't know why. It doesn't need to be charged. This piece of old metal that I've had for, let me see, fifty or more years now, tells the time just as it did the day Pappy had it. And ain't no one needed to plug it into a wall and charge it ever. It may not be perfect, hell it may be a dang busted mess, but you can still trust it just as you could the day it was made," she continued.

I looked at it and realized she was right. It wasn't pretty, but it did in fact work. Now, I wouldn't want to wear it around or anything where others could see it, but all the same, it could still tell the time in a pinch. Maybe that is what she meant by the bread still being bread. It could be burnt some, maybe lost some of its softness, brown color and delicious flavor because it was left in the oven a little too long, but you could still eat it if it was all you had. It was still good enough bread, even if not perfect.

I'm not sure what this had to do with the letter, or if it had anything to do with the letter at all, but it was interesting to hear her explain things in a long roundabout way. She never seemed to be able to just say "things that are broken still have a useful purpose." No, instead she went on about half broken dishes and crusty old bread that was burnt or watches that told time without needing charging and anything else she could think of to tell her story.

Funny thing was, as hard and rough as she was, I was appreciating the time she was taking to give me her advice on life, even if it wasn't the normal way people expected it to sound.

I went to hand her the watch back and thank her for sharing that with me, but she abruptly turned away and said,

"I didn't give it to you to see. I gave it to you to keep. It was Pappy's. And even though you ain't ever seen him a day in your life, he would be good with me giving it to ya. Keep it. This way you will never be away from the right time. It won't ever let you down. Besides, I ain't got no time to be any place, so I don't much care what time it is anyhow."

I thanked her and placed it in my purse, careful not to screw with the hands that still worked. I had no idea what I was going to do with it, but this woman who barely said much to me at all, seemed to have found a soft spot for her grandchild, or at least a less rough spot than usual.

With that, she said one more thing before leaving the room,

"When you write that fella back, remember that even with him in there, maybe he ain't as broken and useless as you think. Be fair but be careful. Don't be getting yourself in any bad spots like that fella did. And when you get the next letter back, you read it to Mee-maw. Deal?"

Chapter 7

***

School was going as it always had, and every now and
again a letter would come back to a student, showing
that for the time being, a few people were gaining
something from this project. Most students had accepted
they did just enough to get the grade, and that was that. For
them, even if the inmates wrote, the chances were high they
would stop sending responses or if they did, they would be
short in reply.

I decided to write a second letter to see how Michael took
it. Although at first this wasn't anything I was particularly
interested in, his first letter meant a little something to me.

Dear Michael,

*Thank you for the response. I'm a little confused about why
you did not expect a letter. It was our class teacher that
arranged all this, and so I just assumed everyone getting
a letter knew. Do you not talk to other inmates there and
share what goes on in your lives? I'm not sure I understand.*

Perhaps you can share a little about your days and how you spend your time while incarcerated. I know we aren't supposed to discuss that, but a little bending of the rules never hurt anyone.

There's a lot of mystery to this all, but I guess that's to keep everyone feeling safe and to protect both you and me. I mean I know my story and my real name, and you know your story.

I was visiting my Mee-maw this past week and she gave me some sound advice about bread being good even when it's bad. Well, I don't remember her exact words, but it made a little sense once I sat with it for a while.

She also gave me a pocket watch that has seen much better days, but it does tell the time still. And the good thing about it is that it never needs batteries or to be plugged in, so it's always useful.

I'm not sure what else to say, but I hope something good and memorable happened to you this week. It's always good to have a moment to look back on, and as you say, smile through it.

My best,
Olive

I hesitated sending the letter for a few reasons. One, I asked a question I was forbidden to ask, but maybe having a nickname would save me from any trouble. No one but me knew that I was Olive. The box was now in the hall, so I would just need to be a little more cautious grabbing or placing a new letter there.

For second, I felt as If I was getting personal with the inmate, but what else would one talk about? I had to be a little personal in my writing, or the letters would be filled with a bunch of space and words that mean very little to anyone and this would just die off. So again, maybe I was okay with doing so.

I had no idea of the address to mail him to, so it all had to stay within the schools power, which was probably a good thing. I meant to ask my mom what prisons were nearby enough to be the one where my inmate was living.

The next morning, Mr. Reynolds tells the class that out of the 24 students who started this journey to save the lost art of letter writing, there now stood only six that still found something in this.

He was amazed about both sides of this. For one, he had not expected so many students to stop so quickly, but on the other hand, there still were six students who found that what he set out to do was a good, positive thing. This was proof that while the art of letter writing was dying for certain, it was still there in small numbers if you just let it happen. And those small numbers were strong enough to make an impact for at least six lives on the other end of those letters. They probably had little in the way of something to look forward to, other than their release date, if they even knew when that would come. It wasn't about the masses of letters, but more about the impact of which those few letters that continued had on another human.

I spent my week hoping that Michael would get his letter sooner than later, but I did want to at least let Mee-maw know

I mailed it. When I was home one afternoon, I asked mom if she could give me her number so I could call her. It would be the first time I called her in forever, but she wasn't much for talking on the phone anyways.

"Hey Mee-maw. It's Rain. Just wanted to let you know I mailed a new letter as promised," I said to her.

I could hear in her voice that she was trying to be her normal gruff self, but she somehow managed a hint of approval for what I had done.

"Well, that's good for you. Let me know when ya get another reply from what's his name, that fella you write to. I got things to do around here, but let me know," she said before telling me,

"You did a good thing," as she hung up the phone before I could even reply.

She really did not like to talk much. It wasn't her thing. My mom said that Mee-maw always told her growing up,

"I'd rather do than to talk about doing."

She was a busy woman, for someone retired who had nowhere to be. All her days were filled with finding choirs to tend to, even if everything was completed. She felt that if she sat still and allowed herself to rest, she may end up resting for good. She meant dying of course.

But she wasn't afraid to die. That wasn't the issue. She saw the world as a work in progress, and that there was always a lesson to be learned in anything and everything she did. She just didn't want to leave anything on the table, my mom said.

Another week came and went, and each day I checked

the hall box for a sign of a letter. There were two in a week left there, but none of the had the name "Olive," on the front.

We got into November and were preparing for Thanksgiving with a few relatives coming in. Dad was tasked with driving down to grab Mee-maw as she had recently lost her license because she apparently hit three park cars in town, two mailboxes on the way home, and didn't see nor hear the police sirens behind her for six miles until she pulled into her driveway back home. The funny part was that the officer knew her car so he just figured he would talk with her whenever she was eventually tired of driving. It wasn't like she was driving over the speed limit to avoid capture or anything like that. She just kept hitting parked things.

Mom said she was "madder than a box of frogs," because she swore, even with the clear damage to her car, that she had hit nothing of the sort. She had no idea how the long scratches and deep dents on the side of her car got there, and for them to take her license was senseless and prejudiced against old folks with much more sense than they ever had.

I kind of felt she was growing on me in a way. While I found her to be harsh and cold most times, she was funny about it. I don't even think she meant to be funny but telling people that she had much more sense than any of them, when they were simply doing their job, and of course had dashcam footage to prove it, made me laugh.

"Hey Rain, wanna go with me for a ride?" dad asked.

He did not want to drive her back here by himself, listening to her complain about his driving, the weather no matter what it was and that he had no control over, the other drivers on the road picking up relatives as well or heading to their families, or the fact that she was heading to see her own family for a holiday, when she could be back home feeding the 'coons that needed her more than these people did.

It turned out the day before school let out for break: there was an envelope with Olive on the front. I decided, even with my curiosity, to open it when Mee-maw arrived, but this would be even better. I could open it and read it to her on the way back, and we could talk about it while dad drove and didn't have to nod every second, agreeing with "whatever that woman says," as he told me.

On the way, I asked dad about Mee-maw and what he actually thought of her. His answer was surprising,

"Well, Rain, I like her as a person. She can be a sore pistol most times, but when I first married mom, she was good to us. She wasn't the type of person to give her approval or disapproval of people. She told mom that she was marrying me, so she had to be the one to do the approving. She said if it were up to her, she would never approve of anyone, and that would do no one any good. She knew mom was happy, and that was her way, I guess, of telling her she approved."

My dad and I don't really have talks anymore, so the time spent with him was nice. Although I'm not about to tell him that. Maybe I have a little of that mountain woman, as my dad calls Mee-maw, in me. I kind of like it. It's almost like a badge of honor that was passed down, skipping mom and landing on me.

When we arrive at her house, she's on the front porch which has seen better days, with a bag in each hand. She looks at my dad as he gets out and walks towards him as he reaches out for her bags.

"I ain't crippled. And I ain't a lady in no damn distress. I can carry my own bags just well enough. Hell I can drive all the way to your house and back if the dang idiot cops would stop being up my ass," she said.

I missed her. Her feistiness was slightly contagious. Her raw, uncorrupted energy was unique. That I could tell. This was going to be a fun car ride back, and I could see in my dad's face he was hoping for a long letter in that envelope.

Chapter 8

* * *

"Dearest Olive," I read the letter as we hit the interstate heading home. Only this time, the words he strung together were different. There was something very strange and confusing about how this letter began. The first one was simple, offered some words of advice, and didn't really add much as to who this man, inmate Michael as I had called him repeatedly, was.

I could see as I finished the letter, Mee-maws face drop. She was sitting in the front passenger seat, being more attentive than I could ever remember seeing her. She was focused on what I was reading, which meant a great deal to me because I wanted to share this with her.

"Rain, give me that thing," she said reaching her old, shaking hand towards me. She never turned around to acknowledge me. Just pushed her hand back, waited for me to hand her the letter I had just read to her, and then abruptly took it to her lap. She didn't even look down at first, and honestly

I started to feel a bit of confusion and some fear ran through the middle of my chest and down to my stomach. I had no idea what she was so upset about as I had done nothing wrong that I could think of. All I had done to this point was to follow the rules set out by our school. Well, mostly follow the rules. I had bent them just a little, but what was it that set this woman into a harsh tizzy?

Even dad looked as if he saw a ghost, turning his face a pale, milky white, while peering over to Mee-maw with his eyes, but head still straight on the road ahead.

Mee-maw looked down at the letter, and searched it over. I assumed she was rereading it to find whatever it was that made her grab the letter from me in the first place. But I still couldn't understand what it was and she wasn't offering any words to help her cause.

"Who in the hell gave a 14-year-old gal a pen pal that the entire state of West Virginia had nightmares about at one time or another? What in everything that is holy did that fool of a teacher think he was doing when doing this? I'm fixin to pay a visit to him and knock the lard out of his head, that's what I'm doing," Mee-maw snapped.

What was she talking about the entire state of West Virginia having nightmares? I was hesitant to ask anything with the rage she was casting out. I've always had a fear of this woman in one way or another since I was a young kid, but over the last year, I grew out of that because she seemed to have a weird respect for me as I grew on her. Now, I was wondering if I somehow set that back again.

"Mee-maw, did I do something wrong?" I asked quietly.

"It ain't you, Rain. It ain't you. I'm sorry," she responded.

The rest of the ride was quiet. She didn't elaborate, and dad, well, he probably enjoyed the quite coming from her. He had wanted an easy ride back and seemed to have that. Even if it was filled with questions and possibly some concern on both of their parts.

I wasn't going to ask her for the letter back, but I desperately wanted to have it. I wasn't sure if at some point Mr. Reynolds was going to ask for us to finally give up our nicknames, and maybe even read aloud the letters we both sent and received to see how we did and what others thought of our homework. I knew we were ghosts basically for now, but maybe that was part of the test. To be so for as long as we could, and to see who could last the longest writing to their inmate, or just how well we could follow the directions handed to us. With which I clearly failed, but not in a way bad enough to cause any concern.

We arrived at the only home I've ever known and exited the car after a mostly silent ride. Dad looked at me as he exited first and gave me an awkward smile as if to say sorry but without words. I just gave a half smile back and dropped my head some in an almost defeated manner.

Mee-maw got out and grabbed her things before Dad could ask. After being shut out when he asked at her home, I don't think he would have tried again.

"Rain, give me a few moments to settle in. I'll talk with you about this letter more. Sound fair?" she asked.

I was taken back a bit because she sounded both sincere and as if she really wanted my input on her asking instead of her usual telling. It put my heart at ease and I smiled but only for a moment. I wasn't sure what that smile would do for her, so I kept that mostly to myself.

"Yes, Mee-maw. Whenever you are ready is just fine."

Everyone was making their way to our house, and the noise of pleasantries filled the air. Not everyone gets along, but for the moment it seemed as if they all were capable of letting grudges go, if only for a few days.

My uncle Waylon, for instance, hadn't spoken to Mee-maw in almost twenty years now. They had a falling out over some land he felt should have been his to build a house on, but Mee-maw said he had to earn it to build on it.

Uncle Waylon was one of those uncles everyone has. The one that doesn't really ever work but somehow gets by just enough to survive and bother others. He's a little strange, but mostly harmless. I say mostly because my mom and he argue a lot and he's always telling her she thinks she's better because she's married and has kids and he has neither a wife nor kids. It makes her cry most of the time, so I'm not sure why she continues to talk to him, but she reminds me he's family and hasn't had a good go at life.

He's always been nice to me, but almost with a non-trusting attitude about him. Not sure why as I think I've always been a trustworthy person, but to each their own I suppose.

I'm glad to be off from school, and if I write a letter back, it'll be the early part of next week that it gets out, so I have time. I can't imagine not finding out more, but I guess the first step is to see what happened in the last letter that I am somehow missing. Soon as Mee-maw is ready, she can tell me and I can decide from there.

We all sit around and people are talking about their last year. Dad is helping mom with the place settings, while I'm sitting near Mee-maw, not bugging her, but certainly there for when she's ready to open up. I figure with me near, she won't forget what she wanted to talk about. It seems to me though, with the seriousness she had, it won't go without an explanation.

"Rain, come here," she finally says at last.

I'm a little hesitant, but I do wish to know. So. I go over and sit down on the floor in front of where she has rested. I rarely see her sitting still, but she looks a bit tired. Perhaps she finally realizes that a break is okay. Or maybe being in someone else's home has her pinned down to the couch as there really isn't a chore for her in sight.

"I know I snapped like a turtle back there, Rain. It ain't anything you did that made me do that. It's Michael, Rain. I want to talk to you about him," she replied.

"What about him, Mee-maw? Is this a man you knew?"

Chapter 9

* * *

"Ashes in the Hills."

That's what people think about anytime the legend of Tarvis comes up.

They never found those missing twelve, but there was a tale that someone burned the remains of those poor desperate souls, removed their teeth so that no dental records could be obtained, and spread them throughout the dense mountains that overlooked the town below. But those were folk tales, as best I could tell.

My mother said they were like faceless ghosts looking down over us as we continued on, just as if they never existed long ago when they were once very much alive. Mee-maw told her she would hear their cries for help late into the night; from the moment the sun began to play hide and seek with the horizon up until the morning rise. Mom said the noises she heard were just baby deer begging as they tried to get their mother's attention, who had run off in search of food so they could provide nutrients to their young, but that's not what Mee-maw said she heard. She was convinced that those lost souls were somehow still alive, looking for either help, or possibly revenge that was ready to be delved out to those that had caused their demise, or forgotten them altogether.

Dad said everyone was just crazy after those disappearances. He heard stories about old men walking in the trees high into the hills and hearing whispers of,

"I need your help. Please don't go. Don't leave me here."

Some men even refused to go back into those woods, but dad assured me they were men that had some mental issues due to their age, or from drinking the hill's moonshine they made in those very same mountains. Or maybe it was a bit of both. Whatever it was, those stories kept me up at night on more than one occasion as a small child, but I had forgotten about them for years now.

I bet Halloween was an interesting time for a few years back then when all of that first happened. Any little sound through the wind and trees probably scared the bejesus out of people. I know by the time I was trick-or-treating, it was just a faded, distant memory and no one wanted to dress as missing, soulless people.

But Mee-maw lived it in real time. She never discussed it with me, but I knew her life was affected by all she lived. She was worried about her own kids and had to assure them that they would be alright, even if she wasn't sure they would be.

It wasn't until a few years later that a suspect, Tarvis, had finally been pegged as the one responsible. It finally eased people's minds, that is until the rumors started up about the screams in the hills, and the dust that traveled with the wind, with words traveling miles as if the souls had an ability to fly with that same wind they begged for help from.

I didn't believe any of that, but the nightmares still came here and there when I overheard someone talk about those days. It was long before I was born, but I don't know. What if there was some truth to those stories? I mean anything is possible, so I guess that could be as far-fetched as it seemed now.

Mee-maw had mentioned to me that the letter was an issue for her, but up until this moment, she had not given me a sign of why she suddenly turned a shade of green. That was about to change.

"Rain, remember long ago I told ya about those disappearances that happened when your mama was just a spit of a child? Remember that?" she asked.

I didn't right away, but after some thought, I knew what she was referring to. I remembered them, but what the hell did that all have to do with this letter? This man was in for some stupid, petty crime. We were only allowed to message with those that were getting out in a few years, and not those that had a horrible manic past, tied to one of the biggest mysteries in all the state of West Virginia.

"Member his name?" she then followed up with.

One of my favorite things about her was that she didn't always speak as properly as people around me. In fact, rarely did she ever. "Member," was her slang way of saying, "remember." I asked mom about it once and all she would do is say,

"Oh honey, for years she has said that. I asked her about

it once and she just said she said it exactly the right way, so I stopped asking."

Mom rarely stood up for herself, and when it came to Mee-maw, she still had a healthy respect, or maybe it was more fear of daring to challenge her mother. Even with so many more years behind her than ones left in front of her, that woman could strike fear with just her natural ways and the look she displayed when she did what she did. And her words? You just let it go. Maybe she's earned that right to speak as she chose. Either way, it never bothered me, as it was her way.

'I remember. Michael is his name, Mee-maw," I returned.

She looked at me, wondering if it was my innocence that didn't pick up on what she had. Whatever it was, I just hadn't a clue as to what she was after, but she did and she would tell me in her way.

"Michael. T. Michael Richards. That's how this man signed that dang letter, Rain. You notice?" she asked.

I had not really paid any attention to his signature. I was more focused on the words he placed on the paper. He seemed so eager to give those to me and share the wisdom he found while lost in a prison. Words he could not find for himself but could for a complete stranger. A stranger doing a school project to earn a grade and nothing more. But Michael, as he was to me, signed it "T. Michael Richards," which still, meant nothing to me.

Mom saw me sitting there looking confused and came on over to check.

"Rain, everything okay? You doing alright honey?" she asked.

Mee-maw didn't even look at mom, but she answered for me.

51

"She's fine. Just catching up, is all, ain't that right, Rain?"

Mom looked at me and I shot her with a reassurance with my smile that we were all good over here. I know she was worried about me, but honestly over the last year or so, I've really developed a decent relationship with Mee-maw. Who would have seen that coming? Not me. Not my mom. Definitely not my dad. He didn't think anyone could ever find something kind to say about her, but I don't know. She was growing on me. Her openness and brutal honesty, I respected that in her.

As soon as she walked away, Mee-maw got up and walked outside, and without having to mention a thing to me, I knew instantly she had wanted me to follow, and so I did.

"Mee-maw, you know Michael?" I asked confused.

She sat there, looking out over the newer homes that lined the street where there once was nothing but land. It was so far removed from where she had been most of her life, and although the name of the state was the same here as it was there, it was a lifetime and a million miles different, maybe even two lifetimes and more miles than that. Nothing was remotely similar. I don't think she enjoyed change much. Her life was set in those hill's and she had her routines that kept her moving along with a purpose she respected. She would never do well in a place like this.

"I know Michael," she said pausing again.

I didn't interrupt her though. She clearly was deep in thought about something else that only she could see, and I had no desire to interrupt that. I wanted to just wait for her to continue, whenever that may be.

The air was growing crisp. I felt the need to grab my jacket, but I dared not move. She was in an old pair of blue denim jeans and a button down, black flannel shirt. The cold did not bother her at all. She had thick skin, and one could see that even the harshest of conditions would not get through her skin enough to cause a chill in her bones. She was just a tough mountain woman, built resilient through years of hard, backbreaking work and an even harder life. But she would have it no other way.

"It's been many a years since I'd talked about him. Many a years. I had hoped to never hear it again, but it ain't your fault, Rain. It ain't your fault none," she said.

I thought for a few moments, and though it was not coming to me, I knew something about Michael was very, very wrong. What exactly had he done, though? And why was he only in prison for a short time if he was so bad a man? Mr. Reynolds assured us all that each inmate we would be writing to would have records of mostly harmless intent. On their way out of jail in a short time as it would be, and that was one of the reasons for writing to them. A little hope for the ride home to freedom, so to speak.

"Well, he may go by Michael now, but he also goes by another name. Tarvis," Mee-maw said plainly.

I stood there frozen, as if I was hearing the worst news of my life for the first time. I knew who Tarvis was. I knew the stories and I knew the name from other people mentioning him over the years, but there had to be some type of mistake. No way I was mailing the same vicious man who had been arrested and placed in prison many years ago, for the disappearance of those twelve people that just vanished in the air. The same Tarvis who the courts said had killed a defenseless and elderly, church-going Winnie and was sentenced to death for the crime. Hadn't he been put in the chair or whatever it is they do to inmates facing a sure death? Surely he wasn't still allowed to breathe the same air as the free, was he?

Chapter 10

* * *

That day felt like the longest one. People sat around to eat, and most talked of fond memories of the past year, while a few others spoke about politics and family matters better suited for another occasion. But that's how it always was. We rarely had what I would consider a normal family dinner when we had mom's extended bunch there.

I sat in dead silence for most of the evening. It wasn't that I was upset with anyone or had little to say or anything like that. I had a lot to say, but honestly it was better to just sit there and keep that to myself for now.

Tarvis Michael. How did that even happen, when we were told specifically that the inmates were simple, common criminals and had done nothing too harsh or out of the ordinary? What Tarvis had done was far from ordinary. As far as one could get from ordinary. I had no explanation and neither would my parents. I made Mee-maw promise me that she would say nothing to my mom for now. I wanted to process this and knew if she told her, she would panic and worry so much more than she needed to, and I did not know what it was that I wanted to do just yet.

She understood and knew I was able to make educated decisions about my own affairs in life. At least I suspect she understood, because she agreed not to tell my mother.

The problem was that a part of me was ready to close the door on this project and no one would fault me in the least. Especially now. But then there was this side of me that had a curiosity beyond one I've ever imagined. I felt this desire to see what, if anything else, Michael would tell me. But what would I do? Ask him about the murders that only a monster could commit? See if he was indeed the same Tarvis I was told he was? What if he got angry and wrote back to stop judging him or else?

My other thoughts were why had they not fried this man long ago? You commit a crime, go through the motions of a trial, and if convicted, go to prison to serve out your sentence. So how is it he was serving only part of his? He was convicted and sentenced to death, yet here he was, living and breathing in a jail that was only meant to hold him long enough until they shot electricity through his veins, or whatever they did to rid the earth of terrible humans.

That night I told my family I was going to my room to get some rest. Mom of course wanted to be sure I was okay, but I told her I just wanted to be alone.

"Mom, it's a girl thing. I just want to talk to my friends for a little, okay?" I snapped back.

I immediately felt sorry for doing so, but I was already on

my way up the stairs and heading into my bedroom for my time, so I would just tell her I was sorry for snapping later.

As I arrived, I sat down, turned on my computer and typed in the name, "Tarvis Michael Richards."

There were articles, news stories, and older photos of not only a man named Tarvis, but also of the victims that were part of the story. It was weird seeing photos that were decades old of people who no longer walked the earth. Their smiles were forever cemented in those final shots, but I imagined how they looked and felt when they knew their lives were about to end.

I found myself morbidly obsessing with everything I was seeing. Clicking the articles, the photos, hoping for more and more things to read and see as I did. It was a strange fascination but I was caught up and knew I had to read everything I could find despite the hesitation.

Some of the articles were short and to the point. Those were ones that came from faraway states that covered just enough to share, but not being from the area, those writers clearly did not feel what the more local ones had.

The articles from the immediate area were long, detailed and full of fluff. "A dangerous soulless man has been positively identified as the brutal serial killer that somehow eluded capture for nights on end, as he terrorized an entire state." They painted Tarvis as a troubled man, who had a life of good in front of him but chose to listen to the demons that rested deep within his spirit.

A man who wrestled with not only good and evil, but with the unilateral decision of life and death for others, as well as himself. I mean he had to have known that eventually he would be found, tried and convicted of the heinous crimes they spoke and wrote about. How could one get away with those with all the technology they have now? It wasn't like he was Jack the Ripper, who we had read about in a class I took one summer.

In that class I signed up for, they spoke of DNA, the uniqueness of fingerprints and even hair samples leading to the capture of many criminals that would otherwise never have been caught. DNA is left everywhere we go, and on everything we touch or breathe on. Scary in a way, that we leave a roadmap of what makes us, us, with the simplest of movements in our daily lives, but we do with every step.

Except for Jack. Because he had committed those murders before anyone knew of this way of tracking and finding people, there was doubt that the true Jack would ever come to light. I don't even know if there would be a reason now, other than to prove that we could and would find anything we wanted to if we tried hard enough. But Tarvis? Apparently he left something strong enough that his trial and conviction was a formality at best.

And now I had that same DNA of his, laced on the paper he used to handwrite me those letters from prison. I, Rain, had something that only detectives and prison guards had for the last few decades. The actual DNA of our states most notorious killer, at least that I am aware of.

But what did that matter anyway? I had no use for his DNA. Maybe there would be sick people in this world who would pay for something like that, but outside of them strange, deranged beings? I could think of nothing that would come of it for me.

Maybe I could sell his autograph online, and profit from the school's and jail's stupid mistakes. I mean, it's the least they could do, considering they put the life of a young, innocent child in grave danger at the hands of a stone-cold killer without having the safeguards in place to avoid such a thing.

But not yet. I hadn't decided on what course to take. I could end this all now. Simply not write back and ignore any letters coming in. He's not getting out, so not like he could hunt me down or anything like that. But what if he wrote to me and I didn't respond? Something about that didn't sit well. He probably has no friends or family left, and if he did, did they ever bother writing to him any longer? He may be a loaner with nothing to look forward to other than death, and that was hard for me to accept.

Yes, I know what he did. And I know common sense would say to let this die as surely as he will, but I still have the letters he wrote to me, and in those I sensed a different human than one that would go on a killing spree just to kill. A man who was handling his punishment as a man should, and still, somehow, willing to help a kid learn what life truly was all about.

I decided I would write him back, but I needed a little time before doing so. I wanted to think this over and ensure that whatever my heart told me to do, I did it with compassion. Just because he lacked it when he took those people's lives, didn't mean I had to lack it as well.

"Rain? Honey? Everyone is finishing up. Come back down when you are ready," my mom said from the bottom of the stairs.

I heard her but decided to pretend as if I did not. Besides, I was tired. I felt like I just wanted to sit in my thoughts, close down the computer and close my eyes. That's exactly what I did and then I passed out into the night, dreaming of the letter I knew I had to write.

Chapter 11

* * *

The following morning, I rose much earlier than I expected to on my break from school. I had slept like a baby, as they say, and eventually my body told me that enough was enough.

I opened my bedroom door and listened to see if anyone else was up. I could hear the rustling of something in the kitchen downstairs, so I went to see what was going on.

I should have known that Mee-maw would be up before anyone else. Her internal clock was insane how well it worked. She could sleep as long as she liked, being retired and all, but she was always the first person up whenever I was around her.

"Rain? Whatcha doing up this hour? It ain't but a few minutes after six. You should be sleeping like the rest of them lazy bones," she said but playfully. At least I think she was playing.

"I passed out early last night and I guess my body had enough," I said back, wiping my face of the sleepers around my eyes.

I saw she was making coffee, and even though I was not

a coffee drinker, something about sitting next to this woman, sipping the coffee she had made before anyone else was up, made me feel important. I would probably not even like it, but it was more about that moment of that experience than it was about the drink.

"Mee-maw, can I join you?" I asked.

She didn't even give me a chance to get it out completely before placing a dark blue mug in front of me and pouring me a cup of black coffee. I thought about asking for milk or sugar, but was too nervous to rattle this moment, so I decided not to.

She sat down, looked around the kitchen, and sipped on her cup. As did I. I followed what she did, but not to mock her none. No, this was more about feeling like I was important to her. Although she was a tough, ornery woman, I still felt a lot of respect for all she had gone through.

Looking at my mom, you would be shocked to think she came from this mountain woman. They had nothing in common, really. They say that people that are polar opposites are as different as night and day, but that didn't adequately define the difference in them. They were more, as Mee-maw had said to me once,

"As different as a bullfrog is to the color five."

That made me laugh growing up because it didn't make a lot of sense to me, which I guess was the point of that. Two things that were so immensely different that they made just no sense at all in anyone's mind.

After a few minutes, I heard her clear her throat and knew she wanted to speak to me. And she did.

"So whatcha planning on doing with that letter? You gonna write him back or let it go?" she asked.

I looked down at my cup, almost nervous to answer her, but then I spoke my mind,

"I think I am going to write him back. I think he deserves that much. Afterall, he did take the time to write me, and it just doesn't seem right to leave a man hanging, no matter who the man is."

Mee-maw sipped her coffee, looked me dead in the eyes, and responded,

"I think you are right, Rain. A man who has nothing left to look forward to but his final day, ought to deserve a little warm side of the sidewalk, even if he brought that final moment on himself."

I felt a little relieved because I had heard how she talked about Tarvis in the past. How she remembered the fear her and the entire community had for those years he was on the run, doing what he was doing. I thought maybe she would judge me for wanting to continue, but maybe she would have judged me more for giving up.

That night I thought hard about what to write to Michael, as I would still call him, and my thoughts went wild. I wanted to ask him so badly about what he had done, but even though I was breaking a rule of the school by simply continuing with the communication, I still wanted to toe the line and not sound any alarms. One slipup and this could end without my, or Michael's say.

"I think I need to keep his hopes up, Mee-maw. At least

give him a distraction from whatever it is he does in there. What do you think he does all day?" I asked her.

"Well, I imagine he counts the days. The ones he spent there, and the ones he has left in him. Must be a hell of a thing to know your death date," she replied.

I had never really thought about it that way before. Maybe because I am so young. But dying is inevitable. The peculiar part of it is that most people, probably over ninety-nine percent of the world, do not know when and how that day will come. But Michael, he knows at least the how. I have no idea if he has an actual date yet, but I imagine he may.

How would I take it if someone said to me,

"Hey Rain, in eleven years and eight months at exactly 4:43 pm, you are going to die."

I cannot even think about that. It's eerie to imagine having a countdown to that day. Would that make the days go faster for someone in that position? I imagine it would. If you think about all the days you have lived already, and look back, it can seem so long ago. But if you knew the exact amount of days left in you, it must play with your mind. As each day passes, your clock ticks down. Each time you wake up, you have one less left.

I guess we all do now, but knowing versus not knowing makes a massive difference in how we would live.

For Michael, that's his reality. He doesn't have a say anymore in when that day comes. I mean unless a freak accident happened while he was behind bars, his days are being counted. There is no hope for a release, and no hope that he will ever see the outside of that prison ever again. Maybe for the right reasons, but still a life of having nothing left has to feel like a waste.

We sat there for an hour drinking the worst hot drink I could imagine. I quickly realized it was not for me, but I did not dare tell her that. I drank it, although slow, and used that time to bounce thoughts off a woman who had seen her share of days.

At one point, I asked her what she really thought of him and the crimes he had committed.

"Well, I remember the fear. Being worried that someone would come on out to the house and tell me someone I cared for had died. That was a tough time. I wasn't so worried for me none. It was more about others. I figured when my time comes, it comes. I may not know the timing of my death, but I know something. It ain't in my control none."

She, despite her hard exterior, was a woman of faith. She believed that God had a plan for everything, and that only he and he alone could take that life he gave you, from you. She wasn't scared of dying, because she, as she would often say, knew there was a plan behind everything that happened. It confused me that she truly felt that but was worried. I guess when you love something, even the right time isn't always easy to accept.

"Listen here Rain. I don't know what writing that monster will do, but ain't nothing happens by chance. God has a purpose for you in writing him. There wasn't no mistake about that. You were meant to write to him, and that's all there is to it. Just do Mee-maw a favor and do this carefully. Don't go getting yourself in too deep, you hear?"

Chapter 12

* * *

Michael,

I am sorry it has taken me longer than I expected to write back. I was with my family for Thanksgiving and life got in the way.

To be totally honest, I wasn't sure if I was going to continue to write back or not. It took a long talk with my Mee-maw to figure that part out, and so here I am.

There are a lot of questions I have, but I am simply afraid to ask. I have to know something, though. Please forgive me for asking, but what does the T stand for in your name?

How was your Thanksgiving? Sorry if that's a dumb question to ask, but I have no idea of what it's like for inmates in jail when the holidays are here. I assume you still know the dates and when it's a special day or not, or am I mistaken?

My family gets together but there is usually a lot of bickering and back and forth over politics, or the football games that are on. No one can have a simple, happy moment in my house. Sometimes it's annoying, but there are times I am glad I have family.

Oh, I don't mean that you don't have family. I have no idea if you do or don't, but I imagine everyone has some family. Even if yours is different now.

I do hope you will write back and that I have not offended you in any way. I honestly am just trying to understand what it is you are going through, and how you deal with it while in prison.

Always,

Olive

I mailed the letter. As soon as I did, I questioned whether I had made a mistake. You know how it is when you do something and you can't take it back? It sort of haunts you. What if he responds and is angry with my questions? Did I cross a line I knew better than to cross?

Whatever I did, it's done. The letter was left in the box and sent off as all of my other ones were. I stopped asking, or caring if anyone else was still writing letters. None of that mattered to me anymore. All that mattered was that I was, and I still had a curiosity about this man, T Michael.

I went back to my schoolwork but the thought of getting a response from Michael was intense. It consumed me most days, and patience was something I was reluctantly practicing. It's nearly impossible for me to wait for something I want like presents under the tree, and here I was being forced to.

Days went by and my family was getting ready for Christmas. Again, I had to wonder what Christmas was like in prison for not only Michael, but all the other inmates. I know the feeling of waking up and coming down to a sea of presents laid out for me. The excitement of Santa had been gone several years ago now, but still that magical feeling was somehow in the air and still something I wish I could have more throughout the year.

But for an inmate? It had to be depressing. I have never seen a photo of someone in jail with a Christmas tree and presents wrapped neatly underneath. It must be just another day for them, and that thought makes me sad. Everyone deserves a little something on a day as important as that.

I had no idea what Michael's faith was, but either way, he had nothing to look forward to and I now wished I could have sent him a gift of some kind just to give him something to open on Christmas morning. Maybe, if my letter hadn't arrived with him yet, it would by then. It seemed as if my small writings were appreciated by him, even if that was all he received.

I called Mee-maw each week leading up to Christmas, as I know she was as anxious as I was to hear what he had to say. It was as if she was living a second life through me, and I loved that. She felt a different kind of excitement, one she had never expressed before. I could tell. I knew her well enough to see that this was genuine and not fake. Nothing about that woman was fake in her entire life.

But as the days turned to weeks, I knew not to get too excited. School was going out on break, and at the very last minute, I checked to see if there was a letter from Michael to Olive. There was not. The start of break was going to be without anything to read, but I told myself at least I was free. For Michael, he was stuck in a cell, away from all the basic comforts of home, alone and probably sad. I tried to comfort myself by thinking that perhaps he was saving the letter for Christmas morning as a way to give himself some normalcy.

We didn't see Mee-maw over break either. Strangely enough, she had fallen ill. That was something I had not seen or heard about her in my life. She was never sick as far as I could remember. If she was, she hid it as well as she did her excitement for things in life. She was the definition of monotone if I ever knew it. So I imagine if she had to tell others she was sick, it was serious.

I still called her though. She reminded me it was just a dumb thing she had picked up somewhere, and nothing to be concerned about. Mee-maw told me,

"Ain't no little cold going to take this woman out for long, that I guarantee ya."

Mom seemed a little more worried. I honestly don't know if she had ever seen her mother ill and struggling. She was ordering food and sending it up to Mee-maws place, and each time she did, Mee-maw would call her and yell at her to stop that nonsense. She said she wasn't sick enough that she couldn't cook for her damn self, but mom didn't listen. She just kept sending it. I almost felt bad for the poor delivery drivers that had to deal with the mad woman cussing them up and down for simply doing their jobs.

The smell of Christmas permeated our home as soon as dad brought home the tree. He had a thing for specific trees, like the ones he had growing up. His tree of choice was the Balsam Fir. Every year he would talk about that tree as if I knew the difference. This was the first year I decided not to go with him. I usually went but I was getting older, and well, I just didn't feel like walking through the cold, searching into the night for the "perfect tree." That was his thing, not mine.

I know he was disappointed and all, but this was my time to express myself and what I liked and did not. I felt an empowerment over the last six months or so, and I was intending to use it as best I could. Afterall, I was almost an adult. Close enough, anyways.

Mom talked about her growing up while we were having dinner one night, a few days before Christmas. She said this would be her first one without her mom since she could remember. It was a big event for her, and I know she truly wanted to have Mee-maw over, but it just wasn't going to happen this year.

She did, though, talk about all the times when she was my age that she would walk deep into the mountains behind their house and chop down a tree with an ax and her bare hands. I don't think it mattered to them what type of tree they had, as much as it did the blessing that they could do so. We had no woods in our yard to search so we had to drive to places that allowed you to go out and search their land on your own. For Mee-maw, all she had to do was to wake up, pick up a sharp ax, and wander around the hills that lined her property until she found the one she desired. You could search for days if you truly wanted to. That's how big the lots were and the trees? They were everywhere. No one cared if you cut a tree down and drug it back home to decorate in your living room. It was part of the territory and everyone who lived there respected each other for it.

But those were also the very same hills and mountains that once scared the death out of people living by or in them. The place where bodies went missing and some, if not most, were never fully recovered from.

For a short time, the woods stayed dead silent. People decided to forgo the trees on a few Christmases, afraid that otherwise they might be next to vanish. Funny, though, that those were the same proud people with little to no fear in their souls. But this? This was different. It was as if whatever was responsible for the disappearances was not of this earth. The rumors always swirled around that the devil himself had come back to this world to claim his souls. So even for those brave mountain men and women, they heeded the warning well. It was better to stay safe from the evil spirits and live another day to tell the tales.

Mom said Mee-maw had sent some gifts for the family, which to be honest, she was always thoughtful like that. The gifts never really made a lot of sense, as usually she sent me a doll dressed in raggedy Ann style clothing or something similar and I haven't played with dolls for years and years, but it was the thought that counted.

This year it was a heavy box, and the box was wrapped

with brown paper with a flannel-type bow that literally looked as if it was cut from a shirt. But it was interesting, and I kind of enjoyed the fact it would look different from all the other gifts.

We usually opened one gift each Christmas eve as a tradition. Mostly it was pjs so we could wear them that night and wake in them, but I opted to open Mee-maws gift if I was allowed to switch it up.

"Well, I don't see a reason you shouldn't be able to but are you sure you don't want to open one I have picked out for you, honey?" mom asked.

"I'm sure. I can wear them another night. I just want to try opening something a little different this year, and well, this is the one," I said back.

There was no more talk on that. I think she understood that over the last year, Mee-maw and I had built a unique relationship that no one saw coming. We had oddly bonded over things we normally would not have, and the pocket watch gift had changed a lot for me. At first I had not a clue as to why she thought I would even want that old thing, but as time went on, it became one of my most valuable, favorite possessions. Dad had said to me that if I wanted to, he could have it looked at to see if they could clean it up and fix it good as new. I told him, it was fine just the way it was, because it still told the time just as it was intended to do.

The present though had some weight to it. I could tell it most likely wasn't a doll this time around. It had to be something much different. Usually the dolls were placed in old shoe boxes that Mee-maw had probably saved each time she bought a new pair. In fact, mom saved them for her as she knew she would want them back over us tossing them away.

I sat down, placed the gift in front of me, but waited. I wasn't ready to open it just yet. I felt as if I was conflicted on if I wanted to open it in front of anyone or whether I wanted to open it by myself. But I could tell this was one battle I would not win. Mom was putting her foot down and making us open that one gift in front of everyone.

I undid the bow that seemed to be tied tighter than any I had opened before, so it took a good minute for me to wrestle it off. Once I did, I opened the remainder of the box and saw something wrapped in some old newspaper. There was a card attached to the front of the paper that spelled out the words,

"Open this first!" across the front of the envelope. And so, I did.

"Rain, this here is something I thought you may appreciate more than I can any longer. But this is for you only. So, open this one when you are alone from prying eyes.

—Mee-maw"

I hesitated at first for obvious reasons but then decided to show mom and dad so they knew, it wasn't me going against the tradition we have shared since I was a young child. It was respecting the woman who had sent me the gift and honoring her wishes.

"Rain, what is it?" mom asked.

I simply slid her the card, and allowed her to read it for herself.

"Well, I don't know why mom would want it this way, but

I suppose it's okay. Maybe you can share it with us all later when she says it's okay," mom replied confused.

Dad looked a bit confused as well, but he never really got in between things like that. Especially when Mee-maw was on the other end. He had a healthy fear of that woman still to this day, and I understood that entirely.

I took the box to my room and placed it on my bed. I wanted to eat something first before I came up to open the gift. Besides, it was Christmas Eve and waiting a few more moments wasn't going to change a thing. I had time.

Chapter 13

* * *

By the time I got to my room, I was feeling tired but excited to see what was in the box that was such a secret. Who knows what that woman could have wrapped and why she felt it was for my eyes only.

I slowly peeled away the layers of newspaper that were neatly wrapped around the object. When I had pulled enough back, I could see that it was a ring binder with papers neatly placed within. As I pulled out the binder, there were words written on the front over a piece of masking tape:

"1983-1986, Falls City Devil"

I had not a clue what the hell that meant, until I opened it up. Then, as a boxer hits his opponent in the ring, it slammed me hard. This was a binder filled with old newspaper articles, clippings, notes and scribblings throughout. It was apparently all about the disappearances that were later tied to one Tarvis Michael Richards.

Mee-maw must have collected these and put them all

together, cutting them out each by hand. Some were stained, a few faded, but overall, they were in decent shape and the headlines were written with bold intent. You could almost feel you were there as the authors of the articles tried desperately to grab your attention from the start.

I flipped through a few of the pages and looked over the photos that had been placed inside the articles. They were of people who had gone missing just as I had seen when I looked them up on my computer, and their names rang out in the air around me as I looked over each one. Shockingly, they all had smiles in each of the photos. I had never pictured them as happy people with lives to live. To me, with all the stories I had heard over the years, they were just people who had died. Nothing more. They didn't even seem real to me, but looking at each of their smiles, it was apparent that they were very much alive and well at one time.

That changed a lot in my mind. For years I had just thought of this as a case of people going missing decades ago, and a man either in jail or put to death for his actions. Up until recently, I had not really thought all that hard about anything pertaining to the case, but now? I felt some pain for those in the photos. What must they have gone through in those final moments before succumbing to death. Just minding their business, maybe thinking about supper or something at work they would need to get back to when they returned the next morning, and then realizing that those final moments of their lives was upon them. It's like when I thought about how Michael knew his days were numbered, but these people?

They more than likely didn't have days to think about. They had minutes, at most, to realize this was the end for them.

It made me wonder what I would think in those final moments if I was faced with that. Would I beg and plead for my life or spend that time thinking back to something I wanted to take with me as a thought, wherever I would be going. I wasn't what I would call a non-believer, but the truth was I had no idea of what to think would come after we died, and faced with death, I would have little time to figure out what I absolutely believed.

As I continued to page through, just to get an idea of what all was in this gift, I saw where the headlines and stories progressively changed. They went from wondering the who or what, to defining a man who was caught, tried and ultimately sentenced for his crimes. The fear in the writings changed to a sense of relief, and where the writers once seemed rattled and confused, they now seemed content with justice as it was being served.

Here it was, all in front of me. The history of one of West Virginias worst serial killers, from the very start to the time he was sentenced and in one place. I had the entire trail of evidence presented, the witnesses who would testify, and the families with stories for each loved one they had lost. The confused tales of how people up and vanished like dust in thin air, with so little to go on, that it's a miracle anyone could be convicted. Yet somehow, they had done just that.

The proud people of the state had wanted justice dealt with their own hands. They did not want a long trial where the potential for an escape from wrong doings often happens. Or some circumstantial evidence that was obtained illegally, to throw off the entire case. I saw where people were interviewed and asked for some "old fashioned mountain justice," to be allowed, but despite the public interest in seeing that, the trial was held in a court of law.

Months of trial transcripts were here, where I would be able to follow along as if I was right there in the courtroom myself. I would be able to almost see Michael, the fear he may have had, or the lack of instead. Was he concerned with what the outcome would be, or because he was a hardened serial killer, would he never fully understand what it was he had done wrong?

It was a strange feeling to have so much of this in one spot, all for me to page through as I wished. Had this been handed to me a year ago, I would have thrown it in a closet and chalked it up to another gift I had no use for. But not now. This gift, although a little eerie and strange, was somehow the perfect present from someone who understood me.

I spent the next few hours forgetting that tomorrow was Christmas morning. As I read about the people lost, I couldn't help but wonder what their families were doing today. Did they still think about them, missing them at dinners and family gatherings around a Christmas tree? Or had time passed them by and sent them into a warped time where they no longer were thought of and they carried on as if those relatives never existed at all?

Life was strange that way. I had never really given thought

to the idea of how long the memory of *us* lived after we died. I mean if you were a famous president or award winning actor, or something along those lines, you would surely live on long after you died. But what if you were just an everyday person, living an insignificant life where no one really thought of you outside of the small circle you created over decades of just living? And would Michael be remembered long after he died, simply because he had made a terrible name for himself by killing those who had a simple will to live? How was that fair that he could carry on and those could not?

I started to wonder if I should even care what happened to this man. Maybe I had wrapped myself in an illusion that somehow, I was making this man's life have a little purpose, just a little meaning, when really the ones he killed deserved it so much more than he did. Not him, for committing the ultimate crime of removing someone's soul from their body without their approval.

Somehow, though, my eyes eventually closed without my say-so. The lids became heavy, and even with me fighting for one more sentence to read, or one more photo of someone to look closely at, I ended up passing out and falling into a deep sleep that lasted all through the night. The binder lying next to me for a while, finally carelessly dropped down to the floor below, but did not startle me awake. I was in a different place in my dreams that would not allow a sound to wake me.

The following morning, I woke and rubbed my eyes roughly with my hands. It was early, and I could faintly hear my little brother downstairs ripping paper off presents and screaming with each one he saw. He loved this morning each year, and although he could be an obnoxious brat most days of the year, I was happy to see him so excited on Christmas morning.

I stretched, and looked frantically around for the binder, only to see it had fallen on the floor next to where I slept. A few papers shifted out, and a photo that was printed was on the bottom of those papers. I picked it up, scanning and studying it from left to right. There were 2 people in the photo, but I did not recognize either. I flipped it around, and saw two names scribbled in pencil across the bottom of the back,

"Hep and Hank-Summer 1964."

I would need to ask Mee-maw who they were because without her telling me, I would have not a clue. They just looked like two older men standing firm next to each other, one with a smile and the other pretending to fight a smile, seemingly on purpose. It was an old photo but still was fun to look at. These men clearly were having a good time at whatever it was they were doing at that particular moment in time.

Just as I was packing the binder back up, I heard someone climbing the stairs. I must have let out that I was awake with me walking around and grabbing the papers that fell from the floor.

"Rain, Merry Christmas honey. You okay? Last night I came in and you were fast asleep. I didn't want to bother you," my mother said.

I placed my things on my desk in the corner of my room and covered them with the old newspapers. I wanted to keep this to myself, at least for now. This was a private gift meant just for me, so I planned to keep it that way. I also planned to call Mee-maw and not only wish her a Merry Christmas, but to thank her for the gift. I don't know if she knew how much this meant to me, and how it got my curiosity flowing.

"I'll be right down, mom. Just need a minute," I said.

Before she walked away, I quickly added,

"Wait! Merry Christmas, mom."

She smiled, as if to thank me without saying a word back. I could tell that meant a lot to her, to hear me wish her Merry Christmas. I'm certain she needed it, and to be honest, I needed her to know I was thankful. Not just for the day, but for her in general. I loved my mom, even if I had a hard time showing it lately.

She winked and walked out of the room and back downstairs to rejoin the others. I made sure that the binder was safe and secure, and grabbed my school sweatshirt, walked out of the room, and down to where my mother and father were seated, watching as my brother opened toy after toy, unaware that I had even entered the room.

"Hey Rainy, hungry?" dad asked.

Chapter 14

* * *

I called Mee-maw after opening the presents my parents had bought for me. She answered the phone, but I could tell she wasn't feeling herself. She sounded drained, and her voice was harsher than her usual scruffy one. I wanted to ask her so many questions but dared not with how she was sounding.

"Rain, I'm glad you enjoyed the gift. It's our secret. I'll talk to you later, okay? I have a few things to tend to. And Rain? Merry Christmas."

It was as if she were a different person altogether. She never got sick. Not that I can ever remember anyway. She was the strongest person I knew, but she sounded horrible, and I hated it. Yet despite how she sounded, she still manages to surprise me with how she wished me a Merry Christmas. In all the times I've spoken to her, she rarely sounded so kind and sincere. That both made me smile but scared me some too.

"Did you get to talk with Mee-maw, honey?" my mother asked.

"Huh? Oh, yea. She said she would call back later. She had things to do. Mom, she's okay, right?" I asked.

My mother never really seemed overly concerned for her. I don't think it was that she didn't care, but more that she knew she was a tough woman, and one who had done things her way for the entirety of her life. Worrying wasn't going to change anything, as Mee-maw would say so many times.

"Yes, Rain. She's just getting older, and as much as she wishes she could still do the things she once did, she can't. I think that just bothers her some," mom replied.

After winter break, I was happy to get back to class. It was a cold winter and I didn't really do a lot at home. I missed my friends that had gone away to visit family, so it was nice seeing everyone again.

On my return, I got back to working on projects, and after a few days, noticed there was a letter. The envelope said "Olive," so it was from Michael. I was a little nervous to open this one, because I had no idea of how my last letter came across. Would he be upset with me for asking about his name? He had to know that I was suspicious about who he was or at least be at some time. That bothered me, but I had to know the truth.

Worse than that, though, was that Mr. Reynolds spoke to the class about the letters. He mentioned that nearly all of the pen pals have stopped writing. "The experiment had run its course," as he said, and while he didn't know quite what to expect when we started this project, he was glad we all participated and was pleased with most of the results.

I felt a little devastated, as if they had no right to stop my writing without at least giving me a chance to argue my case. How could they allow us to get sucked into this, and then without any input from the participants, just shut it down? What if those inmates needed this to get through a brutally lonely day? What then? Seemed counterproductive if you asked me.

I had to figure out something, because this was not going to be the end of this for me. I had so many unanswered questions, and although I knew Michael was a dangerous, horrible human, I still felt that maybe with all the years of sitting in a cell alone, just maybe he had realized his errors in life, and wanted to make a change for whatever time he had left. Not that I was making any excuses for his behavior, but everyone deserves a chance at forgiveness, don't they?

When school was out, I raced inside, threw my backpack on the ground, kicked off my sneakers, and ran straight to my room. I wanted complete privacy as I opened his letter, which could be the last if I did not come up with a plan quickly.

Olive,

I hope you had the most magical Christmas you could ever imagine. What a time to be around family and to enjoy the company of loved ones. One of my favorite moments in my life was when I was just a boy. I was probably five or six years old, and all I wanted for Christmas was this stuffed teddy bear I had seen on one of our outings in town. I saw it and for week told my parents about it. Oh how they searched and searched. They hit the stores and scoured the shelves, looking for this one particular bear, just to give me what I had begged for, if only for once in my life.

As Christmas came closer, I remember my mother telling me not to get too excited, because Santa didn't always give us exactly what we asked for, but I knew better. I told her that I had been especially good that year, and that I was positive he would come through. I hadn't had a thought otherwise.

Well, Christmas morning came, and I had opened the few gifts we received that wintry year. No bear in site. I felt let down, as if all the hard work I had done to be good throughout the year, was for nothing. A complete waste of my time and energy. All I wanted was that one gift, and he couldn't even do that for me.

But then my mother brought over a shoebox that had tape on the outside, but no wrapping paper. I didn't want shoes, so I told her it was okay. I would open it later. But she insisted. My father, who was a hard worker and hardly ever around, sat there with a dark-wooden pipe in his mouth, and a smirk on his face.

As I pulled the tape back, and removed the paper covering what was inside, I saw that within the box were not shoes after all, but the same small bear I had begged for. The only gift I had ever wanted.

Years later, after my father passed away, my mother told me that my dad had gone to store after store searching as best he could, and finally, two nights before Christmas, he had found it. She said it was all he wanted to do. As *much as he was not around for the young time in my life, he apparently had a big heart for the right moments when he was.*

I hope that you found that same joy that has carried me over all these years. Even as I sit here, I realize that they have taken just about everything from me, but they could never take away that little boy's moment. That is mine, for as long as I shall live.

I paused, placing the letter onto my lap, and smiled as I imagined that once, innocent little boy, long before he would become the monster he had, excited to see the gift of Christmas as a real memory and not just a day.

I thought about the innocence of it all, and how, for a short time anyway, this man, this monster as he is known, saw that young boy within himself. That feeling must have been both amazing and troubling. He had to deal with the fact that the loving, carefree child was gone and in his place was a man sitting in a concrete block surrounded by walls as deep as they needed to be, to keep him in his place. His final place while he is waiting for his sentence to end.

But for a brief minute, I felt happy for Michael. Then I pulled the letter back to me, and read on,

There will always be those special moments in your life, Olive. And no matter how hard anyone tries, they will be yours and they will be carried by you throughout your life.

You asked me a question, and I believe you deserve to have your questions answered, and truthfully at that.

My first name is Tarvis. If I had to guess, you or some-one close to you has heard my name before, and that's okay. I am who I am, and if I could ask you for anything, it would be to not judge me based on what you have heard or read written by others, but to reserve that judgement for now.

My Thanksgiving was as nice as it could be for the circumstances for which I am in. They gave us a slice of ham, some powdered mashed potatoes, and steamed broc-coli. I cannot remember the last time I had something that reminded me of home, but this was close.

As Christmas came, I was handed your letter. I thought about waiting until Christmas morning to open it as a gift from you, but I could not wait. I guess sitting here can make a man impatient at times, and besides, I could read it repeat-edly if I wanted to.

I want to thank you for brightening up my day, and for making sure I had something to look forward to. There isn't much here to look forward to, but your letters certainly help. I do get letters on occasion, but they are very different from what you write me. That is a good thing for sure.

I pray you are enjoying your school, and creating hopes and dreams for your own, young life. There is nothing more valuable than the freedom to be who you want, when you want, and how you want. So chase those dreams, and remember to smile through it all, even when the days are harder than you expected. On those, smile even more.

Yours,

Tarvis Michael Richards

He signed the letter with his full name, so there was no denying that this was indeed the man I had read about, and the man Mee-maw knew him to be. But again, instead of fearing this man or hating him for the horrendous things he had done, I felt bad for him. He had been in prison for so many years, and probably had nothing left to live for, but he was being forced to live until *they* decided otherwise. I could never imagine what that must be like.

I tucked the letter neatly back into the envelope, and as I did, it hit me. The address to the prison was written on the reverse side, clearly indicating where it was, and the inmate's number and name. I could not believe that I had not notice this before, but here it was as plain as day, right in front of my eyes. I would not need anyone's permission to continue this writing, as I now had all I needed. But the problem would become, how would I get him to write to me, without him knowing where I lived? The only person I could ask was feeling sick still, and mom said she wasn't getting better as she had hoped.

So, I would need to decide on asking anyway or finally telling my mother and father what I was doing, and hoping they would understand. I didn't have a lot of hope for the second option though. What would I even say? "Mom, dad, I am pen pals with the worst person in the entire state of West Virginia, but don't worry, he's actually a really nice guy trying to give me advice on life while he waits to be shot full of electricity until he is dead? I need to give him our address though, so I just wanted to run that by you." They would think I was out of my freaking mind.

I finally decided I would need to call Mee-maw, even if it meant her getting upset that I was not letting her rest as she desperately needed. I had no other choice and desperate times call for desperate measures.

Chapter 15

* * *

Hearing about the past life of Tarvis Michael was something I didn't expect to have an interest in. Some good children grow up, commit crimes, go to jail and that is who they are always from that point forward. But there was a different man hidden deep away, a boy who once had lofty dreams and small goals, a family that loved him unconditionally, and a past well before he committed terrible human acts, depraving the very existence of 13 human souls.

He most likely had something hidden where most of us never go, as most serial killers do, but somehow people either missed it or brushed it off as a boy being a boy. Even if those signs were minor in comparison to what he eventually committed, I wonder if his family looked back and said things like,

"We should have known," or "how did we not see this and stop this earlier before it got to this point?"

I know when my brother does something stupid, I look at my mom and tell her, "I told you so. How did you not see *that* one coming?"

She usually just looks at me and tells me to mind my own business, but I saw it as my business because honestly, he was predictable in his ways, even at a young age. So, for Tarvis Michael, there had to be signs that were either missed because people didn't look hard enough, or simply ignored because people saw them, but pretended not to or looked the other way.

How was it, then, that someone was born into this way of life? Or did it just happen one day, where he woke up and decided taking someone's life seemed like the right thing to do? I had trouble killing a wolf spider on a windowsill in my bedroom, so I cannot even imagine feeling like hurting another human, and not just hurting them, but killing them, thirteen of them, and how that could make anyone feel sane.

"Mee-maw, it's Rain. How are you feeling?"

I heard her coughing on the other end of the line and started to feel terrible for having even disturbed her. But she didn't hesitate to answer,

"Oh Rain. I'm just as dandy as ever. Not a fly laying on me, that's for certain."

That one I knew. She was saying that she wasn't sitting still long enough for a fly to rest on her for long. My mom said that line over the years, and I always thought it was weird, but it did kind of make sense when you thought about it.

"I'm glad, Mee-maw. I'm worried about you."

She just made an attempt to laugh, but it came out a hoarse coughing fit, and I could hear she was stepping away from the phone in an attempt to hide it from me as best she could.

She was the same strong, stubborn woman as always. It's one of the things I really enjoyed about her, and it could be where I got my own stubbornness from. She did not let anyone get over on her, and lord help anyone who tried. She was sassy, spunky and unforgiving all in one big ball.

"Don't you worry none, there Rain. I ain't going anywhere anytime soon. I would know, don't ya think?" she asked.

Maybe she was right. But I had in my mind that only those who committed crimes and were sentenced to die knew their final moments. Not old people who happened to get sick. They could go on for years like that or fall over at any moment. Neither was predictable, as far as I knew. But this wasn't any ordinary woman. She was born as strong as the great mountains she resided in, and full of rusty nails, as my dad said. A cold wasn't keeping this woman down. That I knew from experience.

"Mee-maw, I wanted to thank you again for the binder. And I had to tell you, he wrote back. Michael. Tarvis. That guy."

There was a pause at the other end of the line, and I was unsure if she was hiding another coughing fit or just trying to figure out what to say back to me. Either way, I sat silently waiting for her to respond.

"Yea, I knew who he was. That's for certain. Tarvis. I'll tell you this much, I bet ain't no one thought of that man, outside of the kin of the folks he's killed, in a long time. You probably brought him back from the dead, that man," she said.

Maybe I had. Could it be that people got on with their lives and just stopped thinking about what had happened

92

those decades ago? Truth be told, I hadn't heard his name in school or with friends or anything like that. It wasn't someone who people sat around and reminisced about. He was convicted and put away and that ended that chapter in the lives of not only him, but the people whose lives he changed forever. But in the end, people must and do move on with their lives. You cannot always live in the past with the what – ifs and the could it had been different talks. It was what it was, and as Mee-maw would say, "and that was that."

"Did ya get far in the papers I sent you, Rain?"

I told her about skimming through and seeing the actual faces of those who went missing over that three year period. I mentioned the photos that dropped out when the binder slipped onto the floor and asked her about Hep and Hank, the two men in the photo who seemed like old friends.

"Well, that's a photo taken long ago. Long ago. Hank was your Pappy, and Hep, well that was his best friend in the entire world. Those two men were inseparable. If you saw one, you knew the other wasn't far behind. Fishing, fixing a thing or two around the house, or just sitting on the front porch shooting the breeze. Ah, Hep. He was a good man. He was good to me and for your Pappy," Mee-maw said.

As I sat there listening, I realized I had never seen a picture of Pappy, and had no clue what he looked like, but now I had a photo to put a name to. That was something interesting to me. When you hear about people, you don't always pay much attention to them being real at one point in time. But seeing his face, as he smirked in that old photo, made him seem real for the very first time in my life. Like I could sit with him and talk about something, and he would respond to me.

"What is the significance of that photo, Mee-maw? Was that included by mistake?" I asked.

"Nothing is ever by mistake, Rain. Nothing. Keep reading. Look over all those dang clippings and put it together like a jigsaw puzzle. Only then will you understand the story better. Yea, I could tell you but sometimes living it for yourself is more valuable than hearing it from some old bat."

She had a point. If I asked five different people about Tarvis, they would all probably say he was a bad human, but they would also all have their theories. Maybe one would think he did it for the pleasure of seeing others struggling and hurt. One could say he was mentally unstable and knew not what he was doing. There could be theories and guesses that made perfect sense from one, and more sense from another. I felt she was right to let me discover what I felt and believed for myself. Besides, no one I knew would have access to the man himself as I did right now. Not that I would ask him direct questions about the crimes, but I could maybe read him well enough to understand more about the man he once was, became, and then learned to become again.

It felt as if there could be three different stories all within one man. A boy who desperately wanted that stuffed bear he saw in a store in town and got it, the one who somewhere along the way lost the innocence of a child and turned a cold-blooded killer, and the man now who seems to have great advice for a total stranger, while coming to terms with the fact he would never see daylight again, as long as he lived.

I would write him back, but I needed to know how to do so without giving away too much of who I was, and where I was located. I knew enough to know that if my parents found out, they would surely contact the school and prison and put a stop to it, so using my address was not an option.

"Mee-maw. I need your advice. And for you to keep this between just you and I. Okay?" I asked her.

She didn't respond, which I took as her way of telling me she understood without having to say it. There were times when no words spoken meant more than the ones you heard. This was one of those moments where I heard her loud and clear.

"I have to find out more. I promise to be careful, but the school is shutting down the entire project. Most people had stopped writing back and forth and there were rumors some idiot in class was mocking one of the inmates and causing issues. I need another way to communicate with Michael. One that will not worry my parents, because you know how they are," I continued.

Chapter 16

* * *

January was particularly cold. The type of cold that even a middle school kid ends up wearing a jacket to class, which tells you that it was brutal outside.

Everything that happened around me made me think of Michael, and how he was living in those conditions. I had no clue on whether he was allowed outside at all, or if he was confined to his cell for twenty-four hours a day. Was it cold inside those concrete walls in the winter, or did it feel the same all year round? Like could he tell just how brutal it was outside those walls, or was it all the same to him, day in and day out?

It was crazy to constantly think about the small things in life that normally would be so insignificant that they would hold as little meaning as dust floating through a breeze. But now, the strangest, smallest moments took on a life of their own, and I found myself both in an excitement for what I did not know, and a strange, suffering feeling for how others had to live out their lives, no longer allowed to make basic decisions of what time they woke up, went to bed, or ate for dinner.

It's a strange feeling to complain about something my mother made for dinner, and have a choice to make something entirely different, but for Michael? He had to eat whatever it was they cooked for him, or he went hungry. I could grab food in the middle of the night if I chose to, but he most likely could not. That didn't sit well with me.

I had to know more, and so I knew in my next letter, I would break the rules some and see how he responded. If he didn't respond well, then so would it be. But I had to try.

Mee-maw came up with a fantastic idea. She told me that I could get a P.O. Box that would not allow anyone to know who I was, and that I could just use that address for any back and forth. The hardest parts would be getting there, knowing when to go, and somehow still keeping that a secret from my parents.

Mee-maw made me promise her one thing. That I would never give more information about me than was absolutely needed. While she wanted me to learn and nurture my curiosity, she also warned me that I needed to be safe as well. She didn't worry that he would escape from prison and come after me or anything like that. She just didn't want me to get hurt is all. I promised her.

The post office was roughly a mile from the house, and despite the frigid cold, I decided to walk there and tell my parents I was heading to see one of my friends. They knew I wasn't a fan of the cold, so it probably made them a little curious and I should have seen that coming.

"I'll drive you, Rain. No need to walk in this weather," dad said.

"No! It's fine. Never mind. I'm going to stay in. Forget it," I snapped back.

I'm sure that it really set off concerns for him, but I didn't stick around. I went to my room and decided to look through more of what Mee-maw sent me, and still, I had to write the next letter that I would send to Michael anyway.

I sat on the edge of my bed and pulled out the binder. As I opened it, I decided to start at the beginning of the papers so that I would not miss anything crucial. It was starting to consume me, and although I should have maybe stepped away for a bit, I could not. The draw was too strong to learn all I could about what happened during those years.

At first, the articles were a bit plain. They talked about a young woman, who was 26 years old, that just up and vanished. More than an article of fear, it was centered around concern. It looked as if the author, and possibly the police, had felt she just took off for some reason and they were asking for her to come home so they knew she was safe. No one felt, at least from what I read, that anything dangerous happened to her. There was no fear of a serial killer on the loose, or anything like that. It was a small article, just a paragraph long, asking her to contact authorities to let them know she was safe. That was it. Nothing too much.

Her name was Joyce Adamson, a brunette haired, fair skinned woman who had little family and worked short term jobs until she lost them due to her lack of showing up most times. That was one of the main reasons no one seemed to be concerned with her going missing. She would go for days without contacting her employers, so this just seemed like a normal occurrence.

The police believed it was a case of Joyce having a new boyfriend, as she often did, and running off, as she had done on a few occasions in the past. She would come back when things didn't work out, they figured, but to look like they were on the case and taking it seriously, they did what they felt they were supposed to do. The truth was, they had done little to nothing. In their defense, who would they put a lot of resources into something that had happened so many times before, and would again for certainty?

There was a follow up article that was just as much a waste of time as the first, asking if anyone had seen her. This time, though, they added her photo. I looked at it, black and white as it was, but felt as if I could feel her pain. Her eyes looked as if they were staring off into nothing. She wasn't what I would call pretty, but she wasn't what I would think as ugly either. She was more unassuming but still, she had a sadness to her eyes that caught my attention.

I looked at her photo and wondered what she must have lived like back then, having so little family and structure to her days. She was from the same side of town as Mee-maw was, but a few miles up the road.

When I pressed on, I noticed that a second article, written a few months later, sounded eerily similar to the ones written about Joyce. Turns out that an elderly man was missing, only no one had reported it up until now. He was known in the area for all his life, and had spent weeks alone in the mountains just fishing, hunting and doing as he pleased. So even though he had not been heard of for some time, it was not that unusual.

That man's name was Hep Wilson. My heart stopped as I saw the name within that first paragraph. It wasn't a long, alarming letter, just as Joyce's wasn't, but it was clear that the police had a little more concern for this man. They mentioned that Hep was known to drift off into the woods for weeks on end, but that he was meant to return over a week ago, and therefore people should be on the lookout if they spotted anything suspicious.

Hep was Pappy's longtime friend, and he would be part of the thirteen. That is why his photo was included in the binder, and that is why Mee-maw probably had such a fascination with this entire case, other than that it took place so close to home. This was almost as close to home as it could get for her.

But they had stopped asking about Joyce, at least from what I could see. She wasn't born here, and although she had spent many years in West Virginia more recently, she was new blood to the area compared to an old man like Hep, who grew up in the same house he lived in his entire life. That seemed to have made a difference to the locals. Joyce was a lost soul to begin with, while Hep was a staple of the town, and loved by pretty much everyone that knew him.

I felt for Joyce, though, because she was just as important as this man, yet until he went missing, it seemed as if no one really bothered to care much. Maybe Hep going missing would somehow bring light to her as well. It was sad to have to be that way, but it is what it is.

As I read on, you could see that a true concern for those missing was building. Once a third person was reported as gone in a short period of time, a man in his thirties named Edward James, the tone of the articles took a shift.

One missing person, you could rule out foul play if you wanted to and maybe you would be right. A second person missing who was known to go away in the woods for weeks at a time, and maybe you put a flyer up out of concern once he was not heard from for a longer amount of time. But when a third went missing, one who was home with his siblings, who were all in the thirties and early forties, you had to shift your reasoning to the what ifs. People did not simply vanish from the face of the earth, yet for these three, you had to wonder how they could.

I read on through the writings and those tattered newspapers and saw panic, read doubt, and could almost smell the fear in the air. If this were today, it would be all over the internet. There would be claims of sightings, conspiracy theories about where they really were, and blame on politicians for causing this.

But back then, there was none of that. Maybe a conspiracy theory or two, but no one wrote about them in the paragraphs that spelled out the concerns for the missing. It was more about the "how do we find them and stop this?" versus placing blame on one person or party.

That is, until it continued.

"Rain? Are you okay?" my dad called from just outside my door.

I could tell he had his head up against the wooden frame, listening to see if he could hear anything from within my room. He was concerned, I'm sure, for about how I got up and left after telling them I wanted to walk alone to a friend's house over getting a ride, which would have made much more sense. I had to do something.

"I'm fine. Sorry I snapped earlier. I'm just having a rough day, dad," I replied, hoping to convince him enough that he would simply walk away and that would be the end of it.

But he did not go. He asked if he could come in, and to avoid making this bigger than it was, I told him I needed a minute. I quickly put all the papers I now had spread out on my bed back into the binder, slid it under a pillow and sat back against it.

"Come in," I said.

My dad sat on the edge of my bed, and without looking at me, asked me if everything was okay. He mentioned something about a child meeting up with who they thought was a boy, and it turns out it was an older man who had lured that kid out of their home, attacked them, and nearly killed them.

"Oh God, dad. No! Nothing like that. I was not going to meet a boy or a man. No. I just wanted to get some air and visit with a friend. It was not that big of a deal. Honestly, don't you trust me enough to know I have a better sense of right and wrong by now?" I asked.

Throwing my parents off was always my defense mechanism. I learned a year or so ago that the more I questioned how they saw me, the less they pushed back. It was as if they were afraid to let me down and make me look as if I had no clue on how life worked. Trust me, there were times when I did not have all the answers, but I had enough of them by now to know what I was doing.

"Rain, we just want you to know we love you and if you ever feel the need to tell us something, anything, we are here to listen without judgement, okay?"

Oh that was not true, but I knew what he was trying to say. They so would judge me if they knew I was writing a serial killer in prison and growing a bit obsessed with the story of how and why it all happened. That much I knew. And honestly, I could understand that, which is why I was not telling them anything about what all was going on. Mee-maw knew, so it wasn't as if I was doing this blindly. I asked her for advice, and she gave that to me. I didn't need more opinions clouding that up for me.

He sat there for a second, awkwardly patted me on my head, and turned and walked away. As he closed the door behind him, I felt a sense of relief. I wanted to let everyone know what I was doing, as I found it absolutely fascinating, but I knew better. At least for now, it was best to keep it to myself.

And then I decided to write Michael back and step up my game just a little. I figured by this time, there was nothing to lose.

Chapter 17

* * *

"Rain? Can you come down here please?" Mom said Saturday morning.

The sound in her voice made me slightly concerned, as I could tell from the tone she used that something was wrong and troubling her. Had she found out what I was doing? What the hell would I say to her and hopefully she didn't know my intentions to write him from a PO Box, although I don't know how she would know that as only one other person knew, and she wasn't going to tattle on me. That was not in her DNA to go against her word.

"We need to head out for a little. I need you to watch your brother until we can get back. Can you do that for me?" she said.

"Why, what's wrong? Is everything okay?" I asked.

Dad was getting his jacket on and warming the car up. It was early. Far too early for me to be up, so I knew it wasn't something silly. They knew better than to wake a teenager up on a weekend before ten.

"Mee-maw took a spill. She was trying to carry some wood in from outside and stumbled on the ice. She's been sick and should not be doing things like that, but you know how she is. Thank God your uncle was there to call the ambulance. I'm sure she's alright but we have to go and make sure, okay?" Mom continued.

I wanted to go. She was my family, too, but mom and dad said I needed to watch Hudson as he could not be left alone, and nor could he go to the hospital and stay still for longer than thirty seconds. This sucked, but I got it.

"Yea but call me. Let me know how she is, okay? Please mom," I asked.

My mom smiled at me. I could tell she was proud of the relationship that Mee-maw and I had developed over the last several months or so. It was unexplainable as she didn't bond with anyone really, so she knew it was genuine and filled with purpose that maybe only Mee-maw knew. But I wasn't worried about why we had figured this out. I was just happy she and I had found that familiar bond. I felt as if I could trust her with anything and she would always have my back, keeping what was meant to be between us, between us.

They left once mom got her coat on. Hudson was in the living room watching television, so I didn't bother to say anything. He was a hand full, so giving him time to relax was exactly what he and I needed.

Those minutes felt like hours. I knew the hospital was a drive, so I should not have been so anxious, but still, I was. I thought about calling the hospital and asking for her room but thought better of it. What if she was struggling and just needed a rest? I didn't want to be selfish until I knew she was okay.

I made lunch for Hudson and I, cut up some carrots and sat down at the dining room table to eat. I wasn't all that hungry, probably because I was worried about Mee-maw.

Then, just after 1:30 in the early afternoon, my phone buzzed. I looked down and saw it was dad and answered it, trying not to sound anxious, but I'm not sure it didn't come across that way regardless.

"Hey kiddo," my father said.

He usually only called me kiddo when there was something bad to tell me. He always called me Rain, or sometimes Rainy day just to sound funny, or on special occasions, Rainbow, but kiddo was reserved for those moments where he genuinely wanted me to feel good or safe from what was to come.

"Mee-maw took a terrible fall. She's alive, but she's not well right now. She's going to need a lot of rest, and more than that, a lot of prayers. Mom is sitting in her room and probably going to stay here for a few nights. I'll be back as soon as I can to help out. You and Hudson doing okay?" he said.

I felt like I was in a daze. What did he mean she was not well? As in she may die, or just that she was bruised up and would need surgery and then to sleep there until she could get back on her feet? Those were two very different scenarios. Just saying she was not well told me nothing.

"So, she's going to be okay though, right? She's fine, right dad?" I asked.

He paused, and then said,

"She's a tough woman, Rain. You know that. Let's just give her time to get well and go from there. If anyone can pull through this, it's her," he said.

He got off the phone, and I went back to Hudson. He was oblivious to what was going on, which was good. I don't even know that he cared mom and dad were gone. He had his shows on, and snacks as much as he could handle. What did I care? I just fed him as he asked and did my thing to pass the time.

Later that night, I saw headlights pulling in the driveway, heard the garage door open and knew dad was home. I also knew mom would not be with him, so that wasn't a surprise to me at all.

He had a Hawaiian pizza in his hands, dropped it onto the kitchen counter, and smiled at us. You could tell he was cold and tired from a long day and the drive back home. I felt bad for him, so I told him to sit down and I would get the plates and drinks together. He did as I said.

Hudson came in and jumped on his lap, asking where mom was for the first time.

"Hey buddy. Mom's with Mee-maw helping her out for a few days, so I am going to take a few days off work and keep an eye on you. How's that sound?" he asked.

Hudson just shook his head up and down with his tongue hanging out his mouth like a looney toon. He was a bit goofy at times, but that was just how his personality was. It was normal to see him overly excited about not much at all.

After dinner, I cleaned up and dad said he was going to rest. I got Hudson into his pjs and told him to watch something before it was time to go to bed. He said he wasn't tired, but he was rubbing his eyes as if he was. I don't ever remember that kid saying he was tired, though. He fought sleep like it was a battlefield and his life depended on never falling asleep.

I went to my room, took out a few sheets of lined paper, and decided it was time to write my letter. I will figure out the post office mess next week after school. I had a good plan for that. I would take the bus to a friend's house that was within walking distance to the post office and get what it was I needed. Then I could call dad and ask him to come pick me up at my friends, which would not set off any suspicion, and that would be that.

Dear Michael

Thank you for letting me know your true name. I'm not suggesting that you hid that or anything, but it's nice to know exactly who you are when I write to you.

I'm a bit confused by how the letters even got to you, as honestly, we were supposed to get letters to those that had committed petty crimes and had two-to-four-year sentences tops, and the ones you are in there for are far from petty. At least the ones you were convicted of, anyway.

I'm going to be honest, I have a lot of questions I am not supposed to be asking you but am going to anyway. I just feel this overwhelming need to learn more, if that is alright with you.

For starters, the school has decided to stop the pen-pal

program. I guess some students or inmates had made some issue with it and they thought it was better to just put a complete stop to it. Not to worry, though. I found a way around that. I'm pretty resourceful when I need to be.

I'm going to include a P. O. Box address that you can continue to write to. This way I will still get your letters, and the school will be cut out. I know that may seem wrong, but I still wish to write and learn. I don't think it's fair for them to begin something they did not intend to finish and I intend to.

So, I was wondering if you would tell me some more about you. I enjoyed hearing the story of your childhood, and what made you smile on Christmas morning. What was it like growing up for you? Was your family always close to you?

I was hesitant to ask too many questions, though. I was careful not to cross the line in my letter, because if I did, he could get upset and simply stop responding whenever he wished. Why would he want to talk about the events that put him in that awful place to begin with and relive those horrible times he put away as best he could? I imagine he would rather forget those crimes and focus on the better things in his life, so that was where I kept my focus for now. So I continued,

Anyway, whatever you wish to share, I am happy to read. And please don't feel bad if you would rather not answer anything. I understand completely.

I'm going to go now. My mee-maw is in the hospital

and I want to check in on her. She took a hard fall, but she's one tough lady so hopefully she pulls through. I will keep you posted on that.

   Olive

The following Wednesday I was finally able to convince one of my friends to let me take the bus to her house. I told her I had something I needed to do, and then I would come back and have my dad pick me up. I don't think she understood but that didn't matter as she shrugged her shoulders as to say, whatever, and agreed.

I ordered the box, got the key and asked them how it worked. The only issue was that I would not know if there was a letter there or not, so I would have to stop in when I could to retrieve any mail left for me. That was going to be a giant pain in the butt, but the alternative was my home address and that was not going to fly.

I included the address in the letter to Michael and sent the letter off. Now I would need to wait for a reply and hope that when I checked, the letter would be there and it would not be a wasted trip.

On the ride home, my dad told me that mom was coming back home. She said Mee-maw would be there for some time, but there was nothing her sitting there was going to fix. She felt that she would come home for some time, and if anything changed, she could head back over and be there within an hour or so. Plus, I bet anything she needed a break from Mee-maw probably yelling that she was ready to get up out of there, every five minutes or so.

I was happy that she was coming home, but sad to learn Mee-maw was in a coma that the hospital placed her under. Dad said it was because she had some swelling in her brain and they wanted to keep an eye on things.

It scared me to think that she was sleeping and unable to hear or see what was going on around her. She was never one to sit still long, and not being in control of things was not on her bingo card. She hated anyone doing things for her, and I am sure this was no different.

I was home and continued to read everything she sent me. I was up to the point where the authorities realized something was terribly wrong, and instead of the short paragraphs that made their way to the middle of a newspaper, the ones after were now front page for all to see.

"Something is not right in the great state of West Virginia," was the headline I saw next.

Chapter 18

**

Mom's phone went off and I could hear her quietly speaking in the next room as she responded, "Yes thank you. No, I understand. I'll be there just as soon as I can, thank you. Goodbye."

I went in to see if everything was okay, and she looked at me and said,

"Mee-maw is awake. She's throwing a fit and cussing at the doctors and nurses and telling them to let her out of that dang place," and she smiled as she told me as if some sense of relief had come over her that her mom was back to mostly herself.

It seems whatever the issue was, Mee-maw was getting back to her normal, bullish behavior. I cannot imagine having to deal with her when she was hot as a red ghost pepper. I loved her but when she was on her warpath, she could be brutal to be around. I was just thankful that as I got older, she found something in me she liked, because that woman scared the hell out of me growing up.

"Can I go, mom? Please? Can I come with you?" I asked impatiently.

Mom knew I was not going to sit back this time and take no for an answer. Besides, I was good with the old woman so the chances were good that having me there would make her feel a little better about what was happening all around her and possibly keep her mouth from spitting fire. That was my hope, anyway. You never knew. Hopefully she didn't bump her head so bad that she totally forgot she liked me. That would suck like nothing else, but I had to believe she was the same woman, with just a few more bumps and bruises.

The ride to the hospital went by fast. I was messing around on my phone most of the trip, texting friends from school to let them know what I was doing, and mom was trying to have conversations in between my responses to pass the time for her as well. I wasn't trying to ignore her, but I didn't feel like talking much either.

When we arrived, I walked in behind my mom and followed her to the front desk to let them know we were here for her. They told mom the room number, and we went to the elevator and stepped in, pressing the button for the 5th floor.

I felt a little nervous but had a bit of excitement that I would be able to see her in just a few minutes. As I stepped off the elevator and we turned left, I could swear I heard her complaining to high hell from the end of the hall. As I got closer, I was right. It's exactly what we heard. She was cussing and telling them to leave her the hell alone. She could take care of herself just fine without all these dang idiots poking and telling her what she could eat and not eat. Safe to say, she seemed back to her old self.

"Rain, tell these damn fools to leave me the hell alone. I ain't gonna do no more of this, so they are wasting their time. Damn inbreed sons of bitches," she hollered back.

I had to smile, because it was music to my ears hearing her scream like that. The things that came from her mouth to my ears were a small victory, as just a few days ago, she was silenced completely. But thankfully she had found her voice and as mom said, her moxie again.

She wasn't coming home today, but soon they assured us. I think if they could have ethically sent her home today, she was heading out the door faster than a roadrunner. The one nurse told her when she demanded her release,

"Soon, Lord willing and the creek don't rise."

Again, I had not a clue what she meant but Mee-maw must've. She glared at the nurse, unsure if she should be thankful or take offense to her remark, and just responded,

"From your mouth to the Lord's ears, missy."

I don't even know if there was a creek nearby, which by the way was weird because everyone here in my town called it the crick, and it happened to be the dead of winter, so I highly doubt there would be any flooding, But if I had to guess, this was one of those West Virginia sayings that meant something long ago, that most people today had never heard of.

Mom wanted to grab something to eat quickly, so I told her I would sit with Mee-maw and keep her company. As soon as mom left, Mee-maw started,

"Rain, whatcha say we break out of here, you pull the car up and Mee-maw will drive off. I'm fixin' to get going. Sound like a good idea?"

I knew she was kidding, but if I had the guts to actually help her, I believe that woman would attempt it without a second thought. I suppose we all hit a point in our lives where we earn the right to not care much about what happens and live on our terms. Mom said often that Mee-maw certainly earned herself the ability to not care as much as others had to. She lived her life as she saw fit and now? Who would blame her for doing something others told her not to. What would they do, put her in jail for skipping out of a hospital?

She started to speak again but was cut off by another coughing fit. I started to stand up, not knowing what to do and she just waived me off as if to say sit back down, I'm fine.

"Listen, Rain. Your momma will be back up soon. When I get back home, I'll tell you more about what I remember about Tarvis and all those missing folks from back then. There's an entire story that I don't believe was ever told, or if it were, it ain't reached the papers or the courts for that matter," she said.

Just then, mom walked back into the room and handed me a brown paper bag. She had picked me up a turkey sandwich and chips with a bottle of water to hold me over. I wasn't really hungry, but it was a nice gesture that she thought of me when she ate.

"Thanks mom," I said.

We sat there and just talked. There were no important

conversations back and forth, and no talk of when she would get home. Mom kept things light I think on purpose. She was glad her mother was awake and safe, but I think she always was aware that she was getting older, and a time would come when there would be no more visits. No more phone calls or demands coming from Mee-maw. No more of her crazy phrases. Those phrases that would eventually be lost with a generation who tried to keep them alive, sharing what their parents had shared, despite no one caring if those sayings died or not.

When we had sat there long enough, Mee-maw said she was going to get some rest. She was getting tired and the meds she was on were beating up her stomach something awful. It was nice to see her but hard to watch her struggle, so we said our goodbyes and told her we would be back in a day or two, hopefully when we were taking her back home to the mountains where she belonged.

I kissed her on the top of her forehead, and she reached out to touch my hand,

"Now you be good Rain. We have a lot of catching up to do when I get out of here. Keep reading and writing. You hear?"

And with that, we finished up and walked back out of the hospital. Mom was tired. This had been a lot on her, and I know as much as Mee-maw was tough on her, she was her mother and she loved her. She always said she would not be the person she was today if it weren't for her. I asked my dad once what the biggest lesson mom learned from her own mother, and he jokingly said,

"How not to live."

But the truth was, she lived on her terms, unafraid of life, not worried about what others saw in her or thought they knew of her, and she was respected, or feared perhaps, by so many. What was not to love about that way of living? She took no nonsense from anyone, and always learned to do for herself, or to do without if it was how it would go. She was as plain as plain could be, but she did not care about that. It wasn't about the materialistic things others saw value in. It was about surviving and living off what she had, not what she did not have. The true gold was in living and not wanting.

I was happy to have some time on the way home to think. I wanted to get back and page through the binder some more to see what all I may have been missing. There was a lot to go through still, and I had plenty of time before Michael would send his next letter.

It was hard only having only one person to share what I was doing with, and any number of people could put an immediate stop to it if they knew. I wasn't ready for that yet. There was an entire story to learn and I planned to see it through.

"Rain, it's good to see you and Mee-maw talking. I can tell she enjoys that time with you. It's funny how people can surprise you, even when you've known them your entire life," mom said on the ride home.

As she said that, I remembered the pocket watch she gave to me. How the man in the photo, Pappy, had that kept in his pocket for years and years. I had to assume that it was in his pants pocket in the photo, but that would only be an educated guess.

It was interesting to think about how Mee-maw explained to me the value of something old and a bit different than it what it once resembled. How something could be worn down, dirt underneath it's complex mechanical parts, and full of years and years of tiny scratches and dust that would never come clean again. Maybe she was also talking about the people in our lives. I know at one time she was a young woman herself, and probably like Michael, had thoughts that brought her some joy when she was a child. Even if she didn't talk about those times, they were hidden there for her to find whenever she needed them for herself.

I wondered what thoughts would hit me when I was her age and make me smile about a time that was once here and then was far gone without a hope of reliving it. Would I think about the Barbie house my mom got me when I was eight? Or the hot chocolate we would drink as we walked the neighborhood we lived in, looking at the Christmas lights our friends had put up? Maybe it would be the binder my Mee-maw had sent to me that kept my interest like nothing else I could remember. Or, maybe, just maybe, it would be the time I got to spend with her, without the gifts or the need for much, other than the gift of her words she placed so roughly, yet purposefully onto me.

Whatever it would be would need to wait for many years though. I was still so new to the journey that she was starting to see the finish line of. Although I knew she had years left in her, I was not sure if that was two or ten. And would her mind eventually go like dad's mom had? She could barely remember who he was most times, and I knew that hurt him. If Mee-maw started to lose her grip on reality, it would crush me for sure.

We had just pulled into the driveway when mom's phone went off again.

"Yes this is she," she said.

Chapter 19

* * *

It was frigid out. The kind of cold air that screams at you angrily and beats you down, as if you have no option other than to stand there and take it. The air seemed to pause whenever I breathed out, suspended in midair inches from my frozen cheeks, taunting me, almost daring me to stand longer.

But I stood there in defiance and promised myself that it was going to be alright. But I don't know that it was.

As the cold wind slowed for a moment, just long enough for me to understand what this really all meant, I found myself crying. Afraid my warm tears would freeze to my face; I wiped them away and tried like heck to stop. She would not want me crying here and now. I doubt she ever cried a day in her life, so if I was going to be tough like her, I had to control my emotions.

Dad walked over closer to where I was standing and placed his arms around me, pulling me in close as he whispered,

"Rain, you made that woman happy at the end. That meant more to her than you know."

I hoped that was true. All I can remember up until she took a strange liking to me was this angry, bullish woman who never smiled and never seemed to care much about anything. But then she let her guard down just enough, allowing me a tiny glimpse into the person behind that rough exterior.

I had so many questions for her still, and she promised me she would answer them all. But she left before she had the chance, and although I wanted to be angry with her, I could not. She was my Mee-maw, and the world without her was going to be strange for me. I had learned to trust her more than anyone, and she gave me a sense of purpose that I had never experienced.

How could she leave without saying goodbye?

When the ceremony was over, everyone started back for their cars. Except I was not ready to go yet. I walked over to her casket, knelt down, and talked to her, as the wind tried desperately with all its might to push me back.

"I wasn't ready for you to leave, but I had no control over that. I just want to let you know that I appreciated you more than you could know. I have a lot of reading to do, and more letters to write. I promise to do so with you in mind with each word I say. I don't know why you were so fascinated with that time in life, but I hope in the end I understand more."

I paused, looked at my parents who were standing next to the car, and knew it was time to let her go.

"Thanks Mee-maw. I have to go now. I'm sorry."

And with that, an era, an entire generation and a way of living that will never be repeated, ended.

The coming weeks were busy. We made several trips to her house in the hills, and went through decades of loose papers, through things she had saved for fear of not having when she needed it and made piles out of other stuff to donate because we could no longer use them. I took my time whenever I tagged along, hoping to find anything to help me understand who she really was deep down where she would not allow anyone to go.

Mostly, though, things would have to be donated. While she was a simple woman who did not care much for the comforts of life outside of what she basically needed to survive, she had most likely not thrown anything away in her entire life. What she had, she kept close by. Just like that pocket watch she had given to me. Nothing was useless to her, and she lived her life knowing that to be true.

Because of everything happening around me, I had forgotten to check for a letter at the post office. Enough time had passed that there was a good chance one was waiting for me when I opened the box. I also had to go through more of the binder and see if there was anything else to look over that would give me more of an understanding on how Michael had killed those people, seemingly without a care in the world.

Yet, I felt the inherent need to sit with myself and let my emotions run for a little longer. I hadn't known a lot of people that have died, so this was still all new territory to me. My mind felt confused, and at times scared of dying. I woke up in the middle of the night and thought I would hear Meemaw calling out to me. I could not make out what she was saying, but I felt her presence, saw her hands reaching out towards me asking for help and then swore I saw a shadow outside my door. I closed my eyes tightly and screamed for her to just go away.

Mom walked down the hall and came into my room, scaring the hell out of me. She turned the lights on and asked me what I was screaming about.

I just told her I had a bad dream. I did not want her to think I was hallucinating or anything crazy like that, but I still swear, it was her letting me know she had more to tell me before she followed the light or whatever we need to do when we go. I just could not handle her like that though, and I believe she understood that I was afraid, and left. I don't know. Maybe I was a bit crazy.

It was starting to warm up just a little outside considering how cold it had been, and I needed the fresh air to clear my head and offer a distraction from life. So I decided to take that walk I had been meaning to take, as the ground around me thawed just a little below my feet. I headed to the post office, and when I arrived, I was strangely reluctant to open the box. I think a part of me was worried that I had no one to help me navigate the letters anymore, but still, I made a promise to Mee-maw and I was going to keep it. I just needed to stop worrying so much, was all.

I slowly put the key in, opened the box, and pulled out a handful of items. I was caught off guard as no one but Michael had this box address. Well, him and Mee-maw because she knew everything that I was doing and had promised to keep that our secret. But as I went through the papers, I saw mostly junk mail addressed to "resident". I most certainly did not live here, but I guess they just send this junk to anyone.

But then I saw two envelopes leaning to the side of the opening. One was clearly from the prison, so I knew that would be my letter from Michael, and another from Meemaw, which was odd to me because she could just have sent it to my house. I didn't know what to do with it, so I placed it in my backpack I had with me, along with Michael's letter, closed the box and headed back for home.

The walk home was refreshing. The sun was out, and the air smelled of the start of spring, although it was still a little ways aways. I loved that distinct smell. It was a clean, earthly smell that reminded me of growth and change. Just as the flowers bloomed out of nowhere, so did a new version of me. I didn't play with dolls anymore. I loved my parents but now felt more to myself than ever. I even had a style of what I wore, where once my parents could buy me anything pink or purple, and I would have gladly worn it without a care for how I looked at all.

But as I grew in age, so did my personality and my resistance to what others thought I should be. It was an awakening of sorts, and the weather outside agreed with me as it, too, grew up.

I arrived home, said hi to my dad who was sitting with Hudson helping him with his letters, and headed up to my room. I kicked off my shoes, threw my backpack on my bed and unzipped it. Inside, the letters sat next to one another. I wanted to open them both so badly, but something held me back from opening the one from Mee-maw. It would be the very last message she would ever send me, and I was not ready to hear what she wrote. I just needed some time to come to terms with it first, and then when I was ready, I would.

But with Michaels letter, I knew it was time. The postmark said it was delivered just over a week ago, and so I was anxious to read what he had to say. Besides, I now had to write him back to let him know the changes in my life. Maybe he would not care at all, being that he was a stone-cold killer and had his own troubles in life. Perhaps death, to him, was as easy as waking up in the morning and pouring a hot cup of coffee around a kitchen table. Anyone that could take a life not once, not even twice, but a total of thirteen times, had to have an ice-cold heart and blood of liquid steel.

Olive,

I hope this letter finds you well.

So first, thank you for continuing to write to me. I find myself looking forward to your letters as they are far different from the other ones I receive. Usually people ask for me to send a letter back with my signature, or the occasional one where people tell me they are going to ensure I get what I have coming to me, and then, well, there are the odd marriage proposals from those I have never set eyes on. I've had three of those just in the last month or so.

People are a bit strange, but I guess one could say the same about me as well.

I asked a guard who works here if there was anyone

else that had the same last name as I in here. He checked and told me there was indeed a Michael Richards who was here on a petty theft charge, his second conviction in a year. Apparently, he was caught, clearly intoxicated and ended up fighting with the arresting officer, which landed him a two plus year sentence. So that would solve the mystery of the how and why your letter got to me. It was sent to the wrong inmate, but I have to tell you how happy I am for that mistake.

So you wish to learn more about me. Well, there isn't a whole lot to tell. I was a normal child, who grew up in a family that always seemed to just get by. The strange thing, though, was that I never knew how close we actually were to living on the streets. My parents were both proud people and kept that hidden quite well. For that, I am always grateful.

My father passed away many years ago when I was just a teenager. Probably not much older than you are at this very moment. He was a tough old man but had his moments where I truly treasured the man he had to be.

After he passed away, things became difficult for my mom. She remarried again, more out of necessity than love, and that man was not as sturdy a husband as my father was. He had a fierce temper, drank more than a man should ever drink, and when he didn't come home at night, I wonder if my mother was more frustrated, or relieved.

I tried to be there as best I could, working odd jobs after school, until there was little choice in life. I dropped out and started working full time just to ensure my mother could get by without the struggles she was accustomed to because life can be cruel and unfair.

I don't have regrets about that, though. Sometimes in life, we have to "man-up," as the saying goes, and that can involve drastic changes during the course of your life. It certainly did for me.

After I turned eighteen, I walked into an army recruiting station, signed some papers, and went off to basic training. I had not a clue of what to expect, but the fact was, it was exactly what I needed. I had lost those years of learning to be a man when my father died, and this was making up for that.

I was basic infantry, which just means I was labeled a grunt. When I got home on leave, my mother had told me how much she had truly missed me being around the house, but that she was happy I was away from the chaos at home. She was worn-down looking and had a scar on her cheek I had never seen before. Her husband was a bastard more than not, and apparently one night came home feeling as if she owed him the world and was not providing that.

A long story short, I ended up putting him in the hospital, and I had to spend the night in the county jail. That was still nothing like the life I am living in now. What a world of difference those two places are.

My army career was over before it got off the ground, but I still learned enough to be the present man my mother needed. Her husband got out and ended up leaving for somewhere down south with a cousin or something. I can't remember exactly, but it doesn't matter much, and it didn't matter then either. We never heard from him again, which was a blessing in my eyes.

Anyway, I don't want to bore you with a lot of things you may not care about. If there is something in particular you are after, I want you to feel free to ask. You are not going to hurt my feelings, Olive.

By the way, I am sorry to hear about your Mee-maw. I hope she is healing well and back to herself in no time. She sounds like a strong figure in your life, and those are important.

Take care, Olive, and I will look forward to your next letter.

All the best,

Michael

Chapter 20

The fourth person to go missing was visiting family in the area. He wasn't from West Virgina, but came from the nearby state of Ohio, right along the Western Pennsylvania boarder. He was twenty-two years old and had just finished his senior year of college.

He wasn't gone but a day when his family feared the worse. Not one to wander off on his own, it was shocking that he was home in the middle of the night, but by morning he had simply vanished into the dew-filled morning. Nothing about him leaving the home that early made any sense.

By this time, the news of what was going on in and around Falls City had grown in attention and captured more papers that would have otherwise never mentioned this small out of the way town. But now, it was put on the map for all the wrong reasons and people were paying attention.

His name was William, and because his family was prominent back where he came from, there would need to be more done to satisfy them that they were in fact doing all they could.

Everyone knew time was not on their side, so they had to act swiftly and find something.

A team was assembled, consisting of local law enforcement, many adults from the town itself, and even neighboring men and women who feared it could spread further out at any time if something wasn't done now. They searched the hills and valleys. They searched higher up into the deep wooded mountains where families who did not subscribe to the government's way of life, called home.

It was hard searching, as the dense forest made it nearly impossible to find any clues. Even those men and women who knew the trails like the back of their hands struggled to find anything that resembled what they were after. No one even knew what they were looking for, outside of the body.

The search went on all day and into the night, until it got too dark to see your hand in front of your face. They resumed it the next day and then the day after that but could not find anything that would help lead them to William or the other people that had gone missing. Nothing made any sense to anyone, as they figured something would point them in the direction of hope. But there were so many places to hide something, one had to feel as if they were searching for a needle in a mountain of haystacks.

After a few weeks, and nothing new to go on, people eventually stopped looking and focused on what was in their control. They could be more aware of their surroundings when coming and going. People who never locked their doors, or had no locks on their homes at all, began to change that. Routines were adjusted to throw off anyone who may be stalking in the darkness, looking for patterns to take advantage of.

An entire town and a growing part of the state was feeling helpless against whatever or whomever was responsible for the disappearances. It made no sense as the people that ended up vanishing seemed to have no ties to each other. It wasn't as if they were all from the same family or worked at the same local factory or anything like that. There was no rhyme or reason to the lack of connection, which made it nearly impossible to come up with a plan of where the person responsible might strike next.

The truth was, people still had no idea if these people were tied up in an abandoned trailer somewhere, or if they were indeed deceased. That gave the families some hope, but very little. As more time passed by, the people whose loved ones were missing were demanding more from their local police force and the government that they expected to solve this and end the torment for the town.

Back at home, I was starting to accept having lost Meemaw. Life was getting back to normal, even if it was with one less person in it. I knew that eventually she would die as everyone does, but I think seeing her at the hospital and then finding out she died just hours later, shocked me some.

I wondered if we had stayed longer would she have put up a better fight to continue on longer. Maybe she just gave up, knowing that she was alone there and still not ready to go home. I know she hated spending any time in the hospital. Mom said she could not remember a single time that

Mee-maw ever saw a doctor, although she was sure as a child she had at least once or twice.

I would let Michael know about Mee-maw, and see how he reacted. That would tell me a lot about the man on the other side of these letters. And to be fair, he did say I could ask whatever it was I wanted. I'm not sure if he is prepared for that or not, but I aim to test that out a little at first, and if all goes well? I will have stronger, more to the point questions to ask. Besides, maybe he knew he had nothing to hide after spending decades away, with no hope of ever getting out. What would be the harm in coming clean?

Mom started to get a little more suspicious of my time alone in my room. I promised her I was just being a normal teenager, but I guess I was spending more time than I should in there, paging through piles of papers both from the binder, and from the stack I took from Mee-maw's home. I also took a photo album she had in her bedroom closet home with me. No one seemed to mind, so I figured it was better left in my hands, as I had a strange feeling that it would mean a little more to me than it would anyone else.

The photos were of people I had never met, as far as I knew anyway. Old black and white mostly, with a few slightly dull colored ones mixed in. I had them out on my bed, when my mom came up and knocked.

I didn't hide them though, because she knew I had these with me, unlike the binder that I hid anytime someone wanted to come in. Perhaps mom would be able to help identify some of the people in the photos, which would be helpful to understanding why they were kept in her closet.

"Hey, mom. Just looking through the photo album. The one I brought back from Mee-maw's," I said.

Mom sat down and cocked her head sideways at the photos I had pulled out. She immediately recognized a few of them and smiled.

"Oh Rain, I haven't seen these in many years. You know who this is?" as she held up a photo of a little girl in what looked like an old-style confirmation dress, or something at least you would wear to a wedding if you had to have something that looked halfway decent a hundred years ago.

I did not have a clue, but I looked at it just to see if there was a reason I should know.

"It's Mee-maw when she was probably three or four years old. Her parents borrowed the dress from someone so that they could get a decent picture of her. Her mom and dad had no money, so they would never have been able to afford anything like this. Look how small and innocent she was here," mom said.

I could not believe this was that same woman who easily tossed around firewood like a lumberjack and cussed at anyone who had no business getting in hers. Here she was, smiling, although looking a little lost in that smile, as if she was happy at that moment but wasn't sure what to do.

I remember thinking about what Michael said, where he remembered the gift of the bear that made a permanent memory for him that not even prison walls could disrupt. This may have been one of those memories for her. I wondered if throughout her life, she ever went back to this time in her own mind, just to steal a piece of innocence that she no longer held as an adult. Maybe she did but never let anyone else know. It's one question I regret not asking her, and now I couldn't.

"Mom, was Mee-maw ever happy?" I asked.

"Oh, sure she was. I know her exterior was rough, but deep down, she had her moments. She loved Pappy, but when he passed away, so did a part of my mother. She relied on him for certain tasks, and when he was gone, she had to pick that up. I knew she would never marry again. Her husband, even after he died, was still her husband to her. She never wanted another man in her life," she replied.

That had to be something. To love someone so much that even after they had left this earth, you knew you were still meant for no one else. When I think about it that way, I see a romantic side to it, and who knows. Maybe Mee-maw was a big softie on the inside.

"What was life like for her?" I asked.

Mom smiled, as if she was more than happy to share this time with me. We didn't have a lot of time to just sit and talk. Mostly because I had pushed her away over the last year or so, but this was a good moment for us, and I was unusually enjoying the time we had here.

"Well, she grew up dirt poor. When they say things like people are so poor they didn't even have a pot to piss in? That was Mee-maw growing up. She worked hard from an early age, and even after she met Pappy, she kept that same work ethic close to her. One thing about her that I always admired was the fact that she never complained about not having things. She was more focused on the things she had."

I sat there looking around at all the things I had. My parents had basically spoiled us, and despite that, I still complained, wanting more. I don't know if there would ever be a point where I was satisfied with what I had, as things were constantly changing and improving. Even phones were getting better each year, and I just felt like I had to have the newest and greatest the second anyone else did.

And then I look back at these photos. The house with the roof that looked as if it could cave in at any time. An old out-house that wasn't for show, but a way of life for so many people back then. I saw a photo of Mee-maws dad, looking twenty years older than he was, faced covered in dark coal, and his clothes worn down to tattered rags. The life they lived was rough, hard and scary. I honestly don't know how anyone could even call that a life, but that was their fate. They knew no different.

I felt sad for Mee-maw, that she never had the same comforts that we take for granted. But maybe that wasn't how she wanted to live her life. Maybe she enjoyed some of the harsher memories of what made her the woman she was. Without those lessons, she may have never been the same, strong, determined and independent woman. And maybe, just maybe, that's the way she preferred it.

She always told me that anyone who didn't agree with how she lived was about as worthless as tits on a boar hog. Again, it was something I never understood, but it was just how she talked and she was probably right.

As we glanced through the photos, now and again mom would point out a great aunt or a second uncle, maybe a friend of Pappy's, and even both of Mee-maw and Pappy's parents, who even when they were young, looked old. It was interesting to see the lineage of people it took to get through those rough times to where I was here today. I would have never guessed that those were the ones responsible for creating the line in my life, even if it were only because of the children they produced.

I felt a small sense of pride, knowing they had overcome so much with so little, and never gave up. I doubt most people living today, if any, could go through the merciless struggles my ancestors had, and survived. The winters must have been brutal for them, yet somehow they found a way to survive and not only that, but a will to carve out a piece of happiness for what it was worth.

Yes, I was going to grow a little bolder with my questions to Michael. I wanted answers and felt as if Mee-maw would have agreed with that. Who knows, maybe she would have liked to know more about the why of all that happened. I was only a quarter of the way through the binder, so I am unsure of what ended up happening and why Michael was finally arrested. I'm sure if he doesn't want to tell me, it'll be in that stack of papers eventually. It was like putting a puzzle together, and I found myself feeling almost like a detective would, looking for evidence and coming up with scenarios and reasoning with the bad guy to see if they could find that missing last piece and complete the picture before sitting back in awe.

Chapter 21

* * *

My work started to suffer at school some, and the guidance counselor pulled me in to see if there was any help they could offer to get me back on track in order to stop my grades from slipping. They had known about the passing of my Mee-maw, and thought maybe I just needed a little extra time to grieve my loss. But that wasn't it. I was becoming obsessed with Michael's story and all the research I was doing to explain why a man would go from a small child with a future to a man on death row, waiting for the executioner to finish him off.

With each letter I received, I questioned how this man who seemed perfectly normal and content, could be such a coldblooded killer behind the scenes without anyone seeing the signs. I wondered if he had never gotten caught, how many more there would be, or if he would have just stopped altogether one day without explanation as if he was simply bored.

That day when I got home I decided it was time to write

Michael another letter, but I also wanted to read more of what was given to me first.

In October of 1983, the fifth and sixth people to vanish hit the papers. They were both men, one who owned a local repair shop and a part time employee of his. Neither had returned home after work, causing the wife of the owner and the mother of the part-time worker to file missing persons reports. But they knew before calling the police. They knew that this was not going to end well, just as the last four had not.

The police immediately closed off the area, scoured the surroundings for a sign of anything that didn't fit in, and even closed off the road coming in and going out of the service station. The newspaper said it looked as if the police were putting on a show to ensure everyone that they were going to find the person responsible come hell or highwater, but that no one had much faith in their ability to do so, or they would have found something by now.

With each prior lead, they had hit a dead end like a ton of bricks. It was as if the victims had vanished into thin air and away from the entire town without anything solid to follow.

People headed into the woods with rifles in their hands, feeling as if enough was enough and they intended to show whoever was responsible a little West Virgina vigilante. Even when the police warned them to let them do their job the lawful way, folks ignored them completely.

"Shoot, if ya'll can't catch those responsible for all the disappearances, then we'll just have to find the man responsible for ourselves," one old man was reported to say.

But what were they looking for? Not a single sign of a body had been found anywhere near or away from the vanishings. There were no bloodstains left, and nothing showing a forced entry or signs of a struggle. It made no sense at all, but people were fed up and ready for this to stop.

The chief of police, a mister Hick Walton, or Chief Hick as he was affectionately known as, had spent almost a lifetime in law enforcement of one fashion or another, covering the same county and towns for nearly five decades. He had seen his fair share of deaths, mostly hunting accidents, or the occasional drunken fight that ended in some idiot shooting a friend over a girl that really should have meant nothing to no one. He was even there for the suicide of a man who could no longer go on raising a son who was becoming more trouble than he could handle.

He was in over his head, but apparently seemed reluctant to agree. Instead, he spent long hours climbing on the paths around town, occasionally walking off the beaten path to see if there was something they were missing up in the hills.

He was convinced it had to be a mountain man: unhinged, intimately familiar with the mountains, and capable of hiding six souls without a single trace of evidence. There were caves and areas of overgrown brush that no man would visit without a deep struggle. But people thought he was reaching. They suspected an out-of-towner, because who on God's green earth could do this to their neighbors? It had to be someone who could slip in, do the crime, and slip out, taking his prey and any evidence along with him before anyone noticed a thing.

They saw this as a calculated crime, where they knew when people were relaxed enough to let their guards down just enough to make it dangerous. Eventually they thought this person would climb in through a window of the wrong house or business and find themselves on the other end of a sawed off shot gun, which would quickly end the saga.

People in this town were proud, gun-owning, hard-working men and women, who would not think twice about killing someone who tried to harm them or the ones they loved, then go to church in town on Sunday and not ask for forgiveness—believing instead that what they had done was not only lawful, but just, even in the eyes of God.

My dad was not one to carry a gun, and I don't think he would ever be one to hurt anyone and feel it was okay. Mom, the same, but I can tell you that Mee-maw would shoot raccoons in her back yard every time they caused a disturbance in her trash pile before she burned it. She told me "Killing 'coons ain't no sin in Gods eyes, Rain. He leaves them here for target practice in case we ever need to shoot something that really matters."

I never bought that, but she sure did. At least I think she did. Maybe some of the things she said were just passed down by an older generation and she never learned to figure out any different for herself. I don't know, but I can tell you I heard her shoot that rifle of hers on more than one occasion when we visited.

I pulled my pen and paper out from my backpack, sat back down, and wrote.

Michael,

I have some bad news. Well, it's not bad news for you, but it is for me.

Mee-maw died. We went to visit with her in the hospital, and she was fine . But later that night, without any warning, she just died.

I found this letter to be the hardest one I'd written. Even harder than the first one where I literally had no idea of what to say. This one brought tears to my eyes, and I had to take a moment before continuing.

It was a hard few weeks, but I'm starting to get back to life without her. I wasn't always close to her, but over the last few years, I don't know. We just seemed to develop a bond I did not see coming. She was a good person, but only if you took the time to get to know her. You know what I mean?

So you told me I could ask questions if I wanted to, so that is what I wish to do.

I was wondering if you could tell me more about why you are where you are. I mean, you don't need to tell me the details and all, but I guess I'm curious. Are you sorry for what you did? Do you think about it often and have regrets or do you just accept fate for what it is?

I could never imagine being away from my family like that. It would hurt me terribly, so I can imagine it hurts you. Maybe a day or so, but after a while, I would cry all day.

Before Mee-maw died, she left me a binder with articles

and photos of things that happened when you were out of jail. I've been reading through things, and the truth is, I'm confused. Maybe I'll learn more, but for now, I feel as if I am reading a detective book and trying to piece it all together, waiting for the ending.

I guess you know how it all ends, but I am still learning. To be honest, I want to hate you for all those missing people, but I can't. Mom says hate it such a terrible word and you should never use it. I don't know if I agree, but for now, I still don't hate you.

Anyway, I would be happy if the next time you write to me, you give me some more of the story. Whatever you wish to share, I would be happy to read.

I hope things are going okay for you there, and that you have things to occupy the time so you aren't feeling lost.

Olive

I don't expect much from him. Even if he could tell me everything that happened, and why it happened, would he really want to write that in a letter to someone that could easily turn it over to authorities as a confession of sorts? Who knows. Maybe he took full accountability for his actions and accepted that his fate was in their hands now. Maybe he fought the charges vigorously and claimed his innocence until this very day. I did not know that part of the tale yet, but I would eventually. That would also tell me a lot about the man, Tarvis Michael.

The letter went out, and I decided to take the weekend

to do some assignments that needed to be completed like a week ago. I knew I had some extra time, but the quicker I did those, the quicker I would get them behind me.

Dad always told me that. He said that the hardest thing he had to do in a day, he would do first, without any hesitation. His thinking was that if he got that out of the way, nothing else could ruin his day any further. It made sense, really. Why stress all day knowing you have to make that call, when you could get it done and know, for good or bad, it was finished and no longer needed to be made.

The weather outside was breaking nicely, and mom said she was taking another trip down to Mee-maws place to finish clearing it out. I wasn't sure if they were going to sell it or if someone in the family was going to take it over. It wasn't exactly the type of home a family would move into easily, as it was old and rundown, and sat on the side of a hill with literally nothing around for what seemed like miles.

I told her I would go with her if that was alright. She thought it was a good idea, and because this was possibly the last time we would ever see the home we once hated but somehow grew to appreciate, I thought this was my chance to feel close to her one last time.

Chapter 22

* * *

I decided to head out for a short walk on the trail that ran through the rear of her property, and up into the thicker forest a short ways above where I began. Mom reminded me to be careful and not to venture to far off where I could easily get disoriented, but I had been up here before when visiting and having nothing else to do. It wasn't going to be my first time.

The thinly homemade trail was full of green growth, as the preceding rain had allowed everything that died off over the winter, to come back to life once again. That part of nature fascinated me. When things died off, it left huge voids in the views that were once blocked, and all the green would turn to crisp browns, wilt away, and die, showing off the miles of lost scenery.

I could see birds flying above, and those sitting in the trees singing as if they knew exactly how to get the attention of all those around them. It was peaceful, and without anyone nearby, all I could think about was the feeling Mee-maw must've had wandering these woods anytime she needed a little getaway of her own. I knew she walked these trails for many years, creating them with her very own footprints, but seldom did I ever ask her why. It made more sense now that I was alone here and doing exactly what she had done.

The air had a damp feel to it, but it was not overpowering or cold in any way. The recent rain had allowed me to feel its effects just by passing the tree's new growth leaves that were starting their life cycle following months of dormancy in a brutally cold winter.

I paused a few times to listen to the sounds of nature, trying to figure out what each noise was and where it was coming from. A deer ran in the short distance, and then a fawn, struggling to find its balance, not far behind. It was beautiful here, and I regretted not walking this path more often the times I had been here. I felt as if I missed out by not doing so, but no one would tell me the value in the simple moments.

Then there was a strange sound. One I had never heard before in all my time in the woods, as if a small animal was injured and crying out for help. I pushed my body through the thick branches, wondering if I could find this poor creature and see if there was anything I could do to help it out without putting myself in any trouble.

The closer I carefully pressed forward, the farther it seemed to move from where I thought it was. But then, I heard it again. A sound that made no sense being here, especially not when I was up in the thick alone. It sounded as if someone was crying to me, but not in pain. More a cry for attention, and I crouched down as low as I could to hide from whoever it was, afraid to move a muscle.

I began to feel a warm nervousness throughout my body and no longer wished to find out what this noise was and why it was here where I was. I slowly shifted my body around and walked as quietly and as slowly as I could back to where the trail was. The sound seemed to follow me with each tiny step I took, and I began to have a panic attack. I stood up, no longer willing to go as slow as I was and raced back, unable to find my way because of the confusion I was feeling. I let out a harsh scream that was loud enough to wake the dead, hoping to scare away the person who was messing around with me.

Somehow, I managed to find the trail I came up on and hurriedly walked back down away from where I had just heard whatever the hell that was.

I swore I heard someone beg for me to stay with them, and that was all I needed to know, I was not staying anywhere with anyone. I ran. Because the ground was still wet, I slipped on the descent, skinned my knee pretty bad, and cried. I was scared out of my mind and begging for this person to just leave me alone! I'm just a kid!!

And then, I covered my ears, pulled my bloodied knees up to my chest, and rocked myself back and forth, for what reason, I don't know. But it was the only comfort I had at that moment and a reaction I was not going to question.

When I eventually pulled myself together, I removed my hands from my ears and listened. Nothing. Not even the birds that had a song on their beaks before were doing anything. It was the quietest I had heard the trail since I first came onto it.

Feeling as if I must've scared away the person who was

messing with my mind, I stood up slowly, got my bearings on where I was and where I needed to be, and started walking once again. The cuts on my leg would simply need to wait until I was safe. I could not be bothered by them for now, as this felt like a life-or-death situation.

As I got closer to the house, I felt the panic start all over again. Maybe because I felt like I was so close to my mom, but I've seen enough horror movies to know you are never completely safe from harm, especially when you think you are.

I burst into the door, screaming for my mother, and she ran towards me asking what was wrong with me.

I had trouble telling her at first, sobbing as I was. She took my red face in her hands and said,

"Rain, what happened? Are you okay? Your knee, it's bleeding. Come here, let me look at it closer."

Those simple words were the most comforting words I can remember ever hearing from her. I felt safe at that moment. As if my mother's job was to protect me, and that is what she would do, no matter what the cost. Plus, I felt as if Mee-maw was somehow there looking over me, and even in her death, she would whoop on anyone that dared tried to mess with her grandbaby.

After calming my nerves just enough that I could open my mouth, I told mom I had thought I heard someone in the trees up the mountain, but it was hard to tell for certain. She asked what they had said to me, and I told her it was more of a cry than anything.

She told me it was better that I stayed there, and that

Uncle Rusty would be by at any moment and she would have him go off and make sure no one was hurt or anything. Although she said she couldn't imagine anyone was out in those trees, as no one lived close by and it wasn't a path that anyone would naturally follow for any good reason, other than to get themselves lost.

Uncle Rusty was one of mom's brothers. He was awkward at best, and didn't come around much, but he was going to pick a few things up from the house so he figured it was as good a time as any to get those and visit with my mom.

When he got there and mom told him what happened, he just said,

"Alright, alright I hear you. Stay inside. I'll take a look up there and see what is going on. Just hang tight here."

He had no sense of urgency and no worry or tone in his words. He simply walked back out the door he came in, turned towards the yard and started on up the trail. He didn't seem to believe that he would find anything, so I think he probably thought it was a big waste of his time. But I would feel much better if he figured out what it was. But returned okay. That part was important to me too.

Mom went back to grabbing and packing a few things but kept close by to me. I don't think she was as concerned, knowing Uncle Rusty was there. He was also mountain tough, so whatever it was, he would know how to handle it.

I watched my mom's face as she looked around at the almost empty home, and smiled ever so slightly at something she found a memory in.

"Lot of memories here. Lots. Oh the stories I remember. It's hard to believe it's over, Rain. Time is starting to speed up and I have no control over that," she said.

She was smiling but she was hurting deep down inside for sure. I could tell as she looked all around without placing her eyes on to mine. She was clearly in a memory from a time gone, and she was feeling it as if she was back in that moment. I didn't wish to disturb her, though. This was her time that she needed to heal, and I could feel she needed it.

I've been hard on my mother for several years now, and honestly, I don't have a clue as to why I am. I just get upset and angry easily, and it comes out as if I don't appreciate anything she does for me. But I know she cares for me and has a lot of advice she wishes to pass down to my brother and I that she learned along her own path.

After about another twenty minutes or so, my uncle returned to the house. He scared me initially as I had forgotten he went off to check on things, but as soon as he walked in I felt some nerves come over me once again.

"Okay, everything checks out. No one is up in the woods. At least not now. I checked back and forth and called out to see if anyone was there, and not a single reply. If I had to guess, Rainy, you just heard a hungry fawn waiting on its momma, that's all," he said.

I knew it wasn't a fawn, but maybe I had made it up in my head. I knew I would sound crazy if I asked him to check again, so I just let it go. Besides, even if it was someone playing a trick on me, my uncle was here and although he was slow to speak, he was a large man in presence so I felt perfectly safe in his care. I did make him promise not to leave until we were finished, and he nodded without saying a word.

My mom had finished doing all she had left to do, and said they were waiting for the REALTOR to get the photos done, and would put the house on the market in the next week or so. I could see her and Uncle Rusty taking in whatever last minute memories they could, as this place was in the family for a very long time, and would now belong to someone else entirely.

When mom asked me to place a few bags and a box in the car, I did as I was told. But outside, I found myself listening hard and intentionally around to see if I could hear those cries again, but I did not. Only the birdsong could be heard, and so I shook it off and forgot about it.

It was time to head back home and get back to normal. I felt a pull to the binder again, so I would open that back up and give it another look to see what else Mee-maw had left for me.

And I had almost forgotten the letter she mailed. It was tucked inside the binder waiting for me, but for some reason the pull to open that wasn't as strong. I don't know why, but I figured I could not write her back, so waiting a little longer would change nothing for me. I would open that when I felt it was time, and for now, it was not.

Chapter 23

$* * *$

December 24th, 1983. Christmas Eve in West Virginia, and families were tucking kids into bed, placing gifts under the trees they had cut down a few weeks prior, or those without children or who had grown children now out of the house, were having a few drinks with neighbors and reminiscing about the days they played Santa for their own.

Things were mostly simple in those parts of West Virginia, and despite the missing six that still produced no leads whatsoever, people had to get back to living, and so living is what they intended to do. But things once again would shock a community that was simply trying to survive whatever had caused them fear to begin with.

An elder at the Baptist church in the center of town, on the main strip that most people passed by when leaving or entering the town, had some small things he wanted to do while the night was still fairly young. He told his wife that he would return as soon as possible so he could help tuck the kids in and read them a story about the night before

Christmas, but as time went on and dinner came and went, his wife began to worry.

The roads were slightly covered with black ice, but nothing he had not driven on before through all the winters he had spent in the area. She thought about loading the small children into her car and driving over to the church to see what was keeping him but thought better of it. She called a neighbor who said he would happily drive downtown and check on things so she could stay with the young kids and get them ready for Santa. "I'm sure everything is fine," he would tell her.

Roughly about nine at night, a knock came to the door of the Jenkins house. It was one of the parishioners they knew well, who happened to also be a part-time police officer in town. Wilbur Jenkins Sr. was nowhere to be found. His car was still in the church's parking lot, and the back door he used to enter was wide open. When they walked in to check on Wilbur, they heard only Christmas music playing in his office. There were no signs of struggle anywhere, and everything looked as if it was placed where it would be on any given day.

The officer explained that it didn't mean the worst, but that he would be patrolling into the night and promised he would check every nook and cranny he could think of to see where he may have wandered off to.

But for the pastor's wife, she feared that he was now becoming one of the missing people that had all vanished without a trace over the last year. Her stomach was in knots as she had no idea what she should be doing. She wanted to run out and search for herself, but where would she start?

The officer, Raymond, told her it was best she stay put. No sense in anyone else having trouble if it could be helped. But he cautioned her to lock the doors and not to let anyone in unless she absolutely knew who it was.

Raymond was baffled by the fact that there were no signs of trauma in the church, no blood stains to follow out the door and into the parking lot, and no witnesses who could come forward with any helpful information. It was just as the others had disappeared. No one saw or heard a thing, and there was no body anywhere to examine, dead or alive.

"Number Seven," was all the headline read. Unlucky, if you asked me, and the people of town knew it was time. The people had enough and demanded that the mayor do something, anything, or they would ensure he never got re-elected again. His hands were tied locally as there was nothing more he could order the chief of police to do, so he went higher.

On December 26th, 1983, he phoned the Governor's office and demanded that they get him a message even if he was sitting safe at home with his family. Because his town was not safe at all, and if the Governor didn't step up and assist, they feared the entire town would be gone without someone cracking the case.

The Governor returned the call within the hour, and asked what it was the mayor would like for him to do. Never one to mince words, the mayor replied,

"Whatever it takes to keep an entire town from disappearing before the end of the year, that's what I am asking you to do. We've had seven vanish into thin air, and it ain't slowing down out here. I'm asking you to do your job."

The Governor had obviously heard what was going on, but up until now, had done nothing. Not even a phone call to the mayor to see if there was a problem they were having trouble solving. But the more that went missing, the more news traveled across the state, and beyond.

His state was looking as if they were back in the olden days when things happened and you just accepted it. He was not willing to let the great state of West Virginia get called out as useless to the rest of the country. They could and would find the person or persons responsible for all this nonsense. If that meant sending in troops, then that's what it meant.

For now, though, he decided he would send in some of the state troopers to see if they could get a handle on things. They were better trained and had more modern technology at their disposal than the local guys did. They could afford what the police could not, and although they didn't know the town as well, there were a few troopers who had come from the surrounding areas, and so he would ensure those were the ones called first.

He promised by the start of the year, he would have some more help for certain, but that he better pull his weight too and figure this mess out. He was not going to be the laughing stock of the Virginias, if it killed him.

At this time, Tarvis was working odd and end jobs both down low in town and higher up overlooking it, helping anyone who needed something minor done. He was going to school at night, trying to get a better education that had eluded him years ago. He had made a pretty good name for himself as a young handyman, and people seemed to trust him with the things they could not easily do.

He even volunteered on some of the searches up in the hills when the towns people had searched for a few days. He knew the area well and had gone off several times on his own as a child, searching for adventure wherever he could find it to escape life for as long as he could.

But there were no leads. Tarvis was liked, worked hard, kept to himself mostly, and was in school trying to better himself. There was nothing that led anyone to believe he was involved in anything, certainly nothing of this magnitude. It was not likely that the person responsible was a decent person, they figured. So their efforts were placed mainly on the troubled men of the town. If it were anyone that knew something, it would be those that had no love for a civilized society.

Seven people in one town, over the span of twelve months, all gone without the hint of a clue, or the promise of an end. The names were becoming more household as families prayed for their return, or at least for closure of some sort. They knew that if they were in the shoes of the families begging for answers, they too would want them. Even if it was not the news they were hoping for. It was about the finality of it, and knowing that either they were safe, or moved on to be with their Lord, no longer in fear or pain.

The stories were gaining more attention. Mee-maw must have had relatives from all over the country saving newspaper articles for her to collect, because I read one as far away as Texas all about the mysteriousness of Falls City, WV and the loss of trust in a small town.

The photo of the pastor was hard to look at. It had his wife and two small children, all smiling as if there wasn't a care in the world. They looked genuinely happy, full of life and real. That photo hit me harder than any of the others. This poor family just wanted to enjoy Christmas and open presents as a family, throwing wrapping paper all over the living room floor while their parents drank coffee and tried to wake up a little more.

But they didn't. That family went to bed that night, one short. I doubt his wife had a single hour of sleep, and somehow, had to handle the young children waking up, and wondering if she would tell them what happened, or allow them to have that Christmas as their dad would have wanted. The articles never mentioned that part, but whatever she decided, it could not have been easy.

This was the first time I felt anger towards Michael. In fact, when I felt angry, I wanted to refer to him as Tarvis and not Michael. He didn't deserve the name that once made me excited to hear from. I hated not feeling good about this, but I could not change. He took the life of a man who had a family waiting at home for him. On Christmas Eve no less. What type of monster would do that? Only the devil could be capable of something so terrible on a holiday meant to rejoice in a child-king, and then act as if they were good and nothing happened.

It got to the point that I didn't even care if he wrote to me again. If I didn't hear the rest of the story from his mouth, then so be it. It was all here in black and white and he was not going to change that for anyone, which was why he was behind those miserable walls.

I wish Mee-maw was here to talk to me about this. I felt like I needed her to tell me, "Rain, there is good in everyone if you look hard enough. Look deeper, Rain. You just aren't trying hard enough."

Or maybe she wouldn't. What if she was just being nice because she thought it was what I wanted? Maybe she had felt that he was a brutal demon that had no right to walk the face of the earth, even if he was locked up in a prison with no chance of getting out.

I needed a break. I closed the binder, slid it under my bed, and swore that I would take time away until I was ready to look at it again, if I ever was. At this point, I didn't know what good would come from opening that damn thing up again. I will not be going to the post office anytime soon either. That much I was sure of. How could I even feel like this guy had good in him when people died? And where were they? Did they ever find them or did the state just rule them as dead because they found no signs of anyone ever?

The next week, I did exactly what I said I would do. I spent more time with my girlfriends. I even started to like a boy at school, who oddly ended up liking me back. He was not my typical type, if I even had a type, but he was nice and honestly, the first boy to give me attention in a romantic way.

His name was Hunter, and he lived not far from the post

office, and my friend Alexa, who I would visit on occasion when I was grabbing letters from my box.

My time was spent in a positive way, and I needed this. Life was a little crazy for a few months, so slowing things down and getting back to being who I was, was important to me. I felt new, and fresh, and on top of that, I felt like I was actually falling in love with someone for the first time.

Chapter 24

* * *

Tarvis was awaiting some news that had been long overdue. His attorney appointed by the court had requested that the governor of the great state of West Virginia, commute his sentence to life in prison for the good behavior he had exhibited, and pull him off death row after having spent years there already. The attorney felt he had a good a chance as any, since they were not asking for a release. Tarvis, however, seemed uninterested in the outcome either way.

He had spent almost forty years behind bars, and through legal loopholes, and appeal after appeal, they had kept that man moving along with a faint bit of hope that his execution would somehow be changed to allow him to live out his life until his time was determined not by man, but by God.

Time had taken its toll on his body, spirit, and mind, and at this point, he no longer cared what anyone decided for his fate. He, in his mind, had decided that if man served his final sentence onto him, it was the way it was meant to be. For his part, he never really fought the charges, but he also never took full responsibility for the crimes he was accused of committing. He was mostly silent and felt that fighting the inevitable made little to no sense, as he was going to die at some point regardless.

He was called into a small room that was light blue in color, had a table in the exact middle of the room, with two steel chairs on each side of the desk. Seated as he walked in, was a thin balding man, who wore a suit of gray, with a red tie that most would call a tad flashy for a prison. He had one simple folder on the desk, with just a few papers inside and a pen laying perfectly parallel next to that.

"Tarvis, nice to see you again," the man started.

Tarvis faked a smile, and sat down, his hands secured by the guard's cuffs in front of him. There was a prison guard just outside the room, who walked slightly back and forth, giving them their privacy, but also there just in case he was needed.

The lawyer who was sent there to speak to Tarvis did not seem afraid, but rather wishful that this man would understand the words he was going to say.

"I had the chance to speak to the Governor's office this morning," he said, clearing his throat.

"They told me that they had a long talk with the Governor late last night, and that he had come to a decision first thing in the morning. I'm sorry, Tarvis," he said.

Tarvis' demeaner never changed once. He didn't look down, or confused, or even surprised at the conversation. He simply said thank you, and sat back in his chair, fidgeting gently with the cuffs on his wrist.

"Tarvis, I did all I could. I really thought there was a shot at this, but the lack of presenting anything new to help them change their opinion, well, it didn't help. I looked as hard as any men would. I went through the files repeatedly, and even though I am not convinced they gave you a full, fair trial at the start, I don't get to make that decision unfortunately."

And with that, the attorney shook Tarvis' hand, wished him well, and told him he would keep him on his mind.

What Rain did not know, what she had never been told, was that Tarvis Michael had his final date set in stone prior to the first letter to him. There would be no changing the date or the time, or the way he would be put to death. As she had talked about before, it would be strange to know the day and time you were going to leave this earth, and for Tarvis, well, he had that.

He had not written back to Olive, the name he knew her by, yet. His mind was on other things, and truthfully he struggled with how much to tell this young child, and worried that she may not be able to understand completely what was to come. Even though he did not know her well at all, he felt that she could get confused or even feel some sadness as he no longer had a say in the rest of his life, and that could impact a child for many years of her young life.

They had taken that decision from him, and having no control, it made it hard to express his feelings properly, as even he didn't know exactly how he felt. He had realized long ago that seeing the outside of the prison was never going to happen in this lifetime. The warm sun he once felt on his face while working on a neighbor's home with a sense of complete freedom, or the dirt trails he had walked a hundred times both up and down, listening to the birds speak and the trees waving gently in the wind, were all just fading memoires for him now. He thought often about those moments so he would not forget what they sounded like entirely, or the way they smelled, or how things felt in his hands and at the bottom of his feet.

Forty years though, takes the life out of just about anything. The leaves have blossomed, and then dried out, falling to the ground a total of forty different times. People have had their own children, and their children have had children that were now grown up, in that same span of time. Criminals had come into the jail, served a few years sentence, were released and corrected their lives, building families and ensuring they never came back, although some did return. Guards had started careers at this very prison and retired after a lifetime of service, also in the time Tarvis was here.

Rain's own mother was just a small child when Tarvis was convicted, well before she had any thoughts of a family of her own. Then she went through school, attended college not far away, found love and married, and had children that she raised for years, all while Tarvis was serving his sentence.

He would need to think hard about what to do, but little did he know that Rain was having the same struggles and thoughts about not writing him again, ever. But how could he know that about her? The two of them seemed to be in precarious spots, with neither of them knowing what was right and wrong in the heart of the other.

Back at Rain's home, she had not opened the binder since last reading about the pastor and his loving family. It had struck a nerve deep within her that she did not expect, but it had without her permission. She blocked everything she could from her mind, as teenagers often do well. The thought of that night was haunting, and if she dared to read on, she was afraid that her frustration would catch on even more, and she didn't want to live like that. She wanted to be happy and not have hate in her heart.

And so time passed and the season ended with a new one beginning. The school year finished, and for Rain, her life was changed. Her boyfriend was someone her family liked well, and he came from a good line of people that were well respected. This was exactly what she needed in her life, she told herself.

She was so distracted that she forgot all about Michael and the box at the post office. She even put thoughts of her Mee-maw behind her, as her new life seemed to be such a good distraction, and the past could stay where it was. It wasn't that she didn't care any longer, it was just a changing of the guard type of situation for her. Whatever was weighing her down before was now lost in time and her new world was her only desire.

But Tarvis Michael was realizing that he had little time left for which to make things right before he was executed, and even though he was willing to accept his fate, he was wondering if there was enough time to do just by people. So he sat down one May night, after having finished his dinner that had no business being served to any man anywhere, and wrote a letter to Olive.

His mind became a bit clearer in what he wanted to say, and what he should say. At this point he felt it important to not mince words, but to give whatever guidance and advice one could give to another. If anything good was able to come from his death, it would be the lessons he left behind with those who were still on their own journey. And people would praise his death with little thought about the inhumanity or finalization of it all, but that, too, he understood well enough. Why anyone would feel bad for him at this point, he didn't know.

Chapter 25

* * *

By the end of the summer, as Rain was preparing for her sophomore year in school, life once again took a turn in a direction she did not want to travel. Her first boyfriend, the one she had credited with pulling her from the loss and distractions that she felt had held her back, was moving away to a different state. Not just a different state, but on the completely opposite side of the country, to Seattle, where his father had applied for a promotion.

She felt betrayed and frustrated that no one had even considered what she and he felt. You should never interfere with love and emotions that others had, and to do so seemed selfish in her heart. But no matter how she felt, and no matter what she tried to change, life was happening as it was.

She closed off to her parents again, not because she blamed them, but because she just wanted to be left alone to deal with her emotions for herself. No one would understand how she felt, she assured herself, so why bother? They would just say stupid things like, "It'll get better," or "Oh Rain there are hundreds of boys at your school. You will forget about him soon enough."

But what did they know? They didn't feel like I did. This was terrible for me and the last thing I needed was to hear about all the damn fish in the sea.

I spent the next few days alone in my room, which was something I had not done for a while. It was a bit depressing as just sitting there with no clue of what I needed, didn't make me feel warm and fuzzy. I would have preferred to be happy, back to where I was just a few weeks ago, but that apparently was too much to ask for.

I stared at the ceiling, as tears rolled down my cheeks and onto my comforter. This wasn't going to be easy at all, and that sucked the air out of me.

Then, for whatever reason, I thought of my time with Mee-maw. She had not entered my mind much at all over the summer, but now, with my eyes swelling up from tears, I imagined she was sitting in my room telling me to pull my damn self together and get on with things. "There ain't no boy on God's green-earth worth dropping those raindrops from your eyes," she would most likely say.

She'd be right, of course, but only because she had lived a lifetime like no one else I knew. She had lost the only love she had ever known, and yet she managed to live for decades without that love. I'm sure she hurt, but she didn't show it at all. I wanted to be as tough as she was, with just a little more refinedness about me.

I decided to continue with the binder. It was Mee-maw

who saw the importance of that for me, and I had let it slip away after learning about the pastor disappearing. I felt it was time to see what else was going on at that time, and just how they came to find Tarvis Michael as the man, the devil, behind the sad stories the country was talking about.

Winnie May. The story of Winnie sparked outrage more than most of the missing, because they knew she had died for certain, and the manner in which she had was apparent. She had fought back, evident from her broken fingernails and items in the home that were clearly a mess. Unlike the others, she seemed to have known something wasn't right. But what did she see that the other seven had missed?

And was there an absolute way to tie her death with the other seven, or was this more of a random one-off, or worse, someone trying to mimic the one responsible for the others? That was a real fear, a copycat causing more harm and trying to make a name for themselves at the expense of an entire community already on edge.

By this time, people had to wonder why no leads had been found, and why and how they had no suspects, and worse than that, only one of eight bodies. Sure the town was tossed in between mountains and hills, with miles of trees on all four sides where one could go weeks without ever being found. But with all the people keeping their eyes open, and all the hunters who used those hills to fill their freezers, something felt terribly wrong.

I read on, as now with a body, more eyes were on the crimes and experts were brought in to determine if there was blood that could be used, perhaps a hair sample lying around somewhere, or fingerprints that seemed out of the ordinary.

Winne was laid to rest, and nearly the entire town showed up to show their support and frustration for what was going on. They held a meeting the very night of her funeral to voice their anger with the lack of a suspect, or suspects, depending on who you asked.

People slammed their hands on the podiums in an attempt to show just how frustratingly tired of this they were growing. A single mother was brought to tears, fearing that at any moment, she could be face to face with a killer no one would see coming, and then who would raise her young children? Did they have an answer for her?

The mayor tried his best to calm their fears, but he knew that was only going to push these people more. This was an old town, filled with generations of mountain folks that preferred simple over fancy, and calmness over fear of the unknown. They wanted to get up in the early morning, put their boots on and head to work for a long day, return home for a few hours of family life, and rinse and repeat. It wasn't just a way of life for them; it was the only way of life.

As the weeks passed, nothing changed, at least from the eyes of those watching for a sign of something that would make them feel as if work was being done to find an answer. The paper wrote about Winnie for a few weeks, and then other news took over as more important. I guess it made some sense, as what would they write? With no new leads or news to report on her death, and the disappearance of the others, life was moving on and there were other stories to be printed and published.

And then, over the next several months in 1984, two more people were unaccounted for. It became so bad that you would need a spreadsheet to keep track of all the missing people, where they were located when they disappeared, and what tied them together, if anything. They were dropping like flies, as my father would always say whenever people died, but they were real people, with stories for each that families, for most of them anyway, missed deeply.

It was time to head back to the post office and see if there was anything waiting for me. I had to believe Michael was writing and now wondering if I had given up. I had, but something told me it was time to see where things stood. Now with more information, I had questions, no, demands, for him to address. If he didn't like it? So be it. He may not need to answer them, but I had every right to ask what I wished.

There were three letters, which may not have been a total surprise given the time I had not written back to him, but it made me curious as to what he was thinking with each one. I'm sure being behind bars and having nothing to do but wake up, eat and sleep, was not the life he enjoyed nor wanted anymore, but he earned that. The letters were a distraction for him, but I wasn't sure if he deserved a distraction or not. Not one of his victims was able to smile, or enjoy a good meal with loved ones. They were not able to write letters and wait for replies or find peace in the way the sun danced on their faces.

They were all postmarked, so I could easily see the order

in which they were sent, which was how I wished to read them. Otherwise, they would make little sense to me.

The first, really threw me off. Michael was clearly not himself. The person I had gotten to know over the first few letters he wrote was more forthcoming and upbeat with his words. His mind seemed consumed by something he would not write about, but you could feel the pain in the words he placed so neatly on the paper. At first, I was angry that he got to have any emotions at all, because who the hell was he to have that right? But then, I read on and knew, whatever was going on in his circle, his life had turned completely around for him, and he was desperately trying to balance letting me understand that, without actually putting it down. But why?

On my nightstand sat the pocket watch Mee-maw left to me. I remember how she asked me to describe it and tell her what I saw. The broken face, and the hands that still went around, but looked like they were frail and on their last trip in a complete circle, if the hands even made it that far. The dirt that covered the back, making it almost impossible to see the inscription. What I saw as useless, still to this day had purpose beyond what I thought it had. And so that is what I tried to give to Michael. A chance at some sort of purpose, and a usefulness that went beyond what I or anyone else could see in him.

He seemed to want to say more than he did but stopped himself short. Maybe that was just how I was seeing it, but I swear I could almost hear him pause in just the ink he used to talk with me. It was as if he stopped, thought for a moment to himself, and then continued on, not knowing I could tell, but I could.

But after I finished reading his first letter, I felt as if I knew nothing more. It was short and filled with what my teacher for English called "filler words," that were meant to make a paragraph look more useful than it really was. Words added for extra volume or to fill a void in a story, but without really saying anything of great importance. That was what I saw in his first letter, and I wasn't sure why.

I placed it down on the bed, pausing for a few moments before deciding to open the next. Before I did, I remembered that I still had a letter from Mee-maw that I needed to open, but now was not the time. I wanted to open that one when I felt it calling to me. It was not, but Michael's was.

Olive,

I have not heard back from you in some time, and I fear I may have upset you with something that I did not mean to.

One thing I value in the life I have left to live is total and complete honesty. So if I said or did something, I would like you to know it's okay to let me know. I will not judge you at all, as that is not my job to judge. As people, we deal with judges more often than we should, but even their rulings cannot go over the ultimate, and only true judge.

Many years ago, there was a period of time that life was very different in these parts. Families went from the joys of a simple way of life and focusing on what they could pass down to future generations, to total and complete chaos, filled with fear, anger and confusion. They had every right to worry and panic, and the fact that I am sitting here where I am, is justice served for many reasons, even as I have questioned them.

I have regrets in life that will follow me until my last breath, but not as others may wish for me to have. When my time comes, and that final hour is upon me, I will let those regrets go, for there will be no reason to spend that last hour wishing for change. I would hope I could spend it with the memories from a life before the awful change in circumstances, focusing on the best memories one could have.

Remember, Olive, that what others see in you is not necessarily what is within you. Only you will know the truth in your heart, despite what anyone else says. They can judge you, sentence you, and control you, but what they can not to is break your spirit unless you allow them to.

I hope you are doing well and are okay with me writing you these letters still, even if you do not reply. It's one of the simple pleasures I still have, and, I would like to keep that alive.

My best,

T. Michael Richards

Chapter 26

* * *

As the year 1985 came, things settled down throughout Falls Creek. The winter arrived as it should and left with not so much of anything to write about. Even spring, which changed the landscape from a brown and gray backdrop, shifting to lush greens and canary yellows, with hints of other tiny colored flowers spurting out as if they were in a painting, had not much else to say.

People began to think that maybe things were turning, and that whatever had happened to the people of the town, while sad and senseless, was finally over.

The country began to back off from reporting anything about the mountain town, and looked for new, fresh stories to share with their readers, that would attract greater attention than yesterday's news was going to.

It's not known if this infuriated the person, or persons responsible for the disappearances, but whatever it was, it woke that hellion back from the depths of complete darkness, as within just days of each other, two more members of the

JAMES J. HILL III

community had not returned from their shifts at work, and
without a second guess, the good folks of Falls City knew it
meant their nightmares had been simply on hold and now
back once again.

Both men were in their late fifties, and had worked together
in the same lumber mill for many years. They often could be
seen stopping off at Bristol's pub for a quick drink or three
after work, but once they left there, they were home within
minutes and sitting with their families for the evening. Both
men were responsible, decent men with no criminal history,
and no enemies that anyone could point out.

Everyone seemed to be a suspect, and people wondered
if the person responsible was resting just under their noses.
It could be a neighbor that lived alone and normally kept to
themselves. There were plenty of those in Falls City. Maybe
it was someone who had recently lost a marriage, and had
spiraled helplessly out of control, unable to see that those they
were removing from town had nothing to do with their bad
luck. People looked at others up and down while walking in
town as if they were measuring them up for a sign of anything.

Men stayed in groups and marched back up into the
woods, thinking that if this amount of people had vanished,
they had to be where it was hardest to find them. They held
their rifles close to their chests and listened for sounds of
anything that didn't make sense, while pushing the tall grass
and overgrown brush aside, hoping they would not find what
they felt was going to be the outcome regardless.

Not many had faith that they would be found alive. Not

after this amount of time had passed by. To keep all those people alive and a secret from the rest of the world would fall just short of a miracle. And miracles did not happen in these parts, so the consensus was that they were looking for bodies, not survivors.

I read through the reports Mee-maw left, and saw that there was a map folded on the next page, neatly tucked into a plastic sheet. When I pulled it out, there were red stars handwritten throughout the town. As I looked closer, I saw there was a legend to the side that stated the names of each of the missing. Each star had a number next to it, denoting the order in which the victims had either disappeared, or in Winnie's case, died and had been found.

But there were 13 stars placed around the map, and not 12 as I had read to this point. That could only mean there was another to come. That next one, if you believed in numbers having meaning, would be unlucky 13.

I didn't feel the same sad impact with the eleventh and twelfth people, but maybe that was because I was becoming numb to what had happened. They were gone, and a man was convicted and behind bars. I was maturing and learning more about myself, so I felt that I could handle this a little better than I had previously.

Without warning, my mother opened my door, as she had never done before without first knocking and seeking permission. I was flustered, and had papers and a map, plus Michaels letters scattered all over my bed. There was no way to hide them this time, and so I panicked.

"Mom! What are you doing, I'm in the middle of something," I screamed at her.

She looked at me with eyes that told me she knew more about this than I expected her to. As she walked over, she pulled my chair out from the desk and sat down.

"Rain, where did you get this all? Honey, what is this all about? Why are you reading about that awful man and all he did?"

I think she was worried I was enjoying this reading more than I was, or that I was happily fascinated by the behavior of what this man did to all those people. It was neither of those, but more a curiosity into something I did not mean to stumble upon, but when I was placed in this mess, I had to see it through.

I thought for a moment about what I wanted to say. At first, I thought maybe yelling would get her off my back, but the fact she sat down without asking showed me that she was going to stay stern and not going to allow me to bully my way out of this one. She wanted to know what was going on, and I knew I had to give her something.

"It's a long story, mom. But it's not what you think. I will tell you, but you have to promise me that you will listen and understand before judging me. And please, don't get upset with me. I honestly had nothing to do with this, and I need you to know that. Promise?" I asked.

She didn't immediately say anything, sitting there with her arms crossed, trying to get herself comfortable for what the truth was going to be, and probably figuring she would need to be strict in whatever she said, even if it meant I was going to be upset with her for years to come. She knew I was a good kid, but she also knew she needed to be a parent, despite what I said, felt I needed or wanted.

"Rain, let's start with one thing at a time. Where did you get the binder? Did you take that from Mee-maws house?" she asked.

"No! Mom, I didn't take it. She gave it to me. Remember when I told you she gave me a gift, but I never told you and dad what it was? Well, this is what it was," I responded.

Now she would wonder why the hell her mother thought it right to give a teen girl a binder filled with stories about a serial killer who sat on death row, and rightfully so as far as they were concerned. It would be a fair question, but I wasn't exactly sure how I was going to answer that one. I would need to divulge that I was writing that same man, and I could not for a second find a decent way to do so. Not yet anyway. Mom would call the school, and probably the prison where he was being held, and put an end to that, when I wasn't ready for that yet. A few weeks ago, when I had no feelings for what happened to Tarvis Michael? Sure. But not now. I needed to do more, even if I remained unsure what more that was.

"But why? Was this something you had talked about with her? I don't understand," she asked confused.

It was clear that dad didn't tell mom, because he was on that ride home with Mee-maw and I when she was forbidden to drive because of her failing vision. He knew exactly who the man was, even before I had, but I was unsure why he decided to keep that from her and for me. I can only assume he was put in a bad spot and was either going to have his teenage daughter love him for the decision he made, and or hate him for one he could have made.

I just sat there in silence, afraid to tell her more than I needed to, but also keenly aware that she was going to wait for answers that at least would put her mind at ease. Otherwise, she would have me committed for being crazy, which I was most certainly not. Maybe a bit difficult and moody, but definitely not crazy by any means.

"Mom, it's not that big a deal. I had asked Mee-maw about Pappy, and then we just got going down a road of stories. She mentioned his friend, Hep, and started to tell me how he vanished years ago. It really just was conversation and curiosity. Haven't you ever been curious before?" I asked, trying to turn this on her.

"Of course, Rain, but not over a serial killer. What that man did was terrible, and to this day, people miss their family. I just don't want you getting all caught up in that as if he's some type of celebrity is all," she responded.

I didn't see him as a celebrity. In fact, I had not a clue what he looked like, sounded like or how tall or short he was. I simply knew his name, and that he seemed educated by the way he wrote his letters. I hadn't once thought that he was someone to hold high but instead struggled excessively with my back and forth feeling of wanting to be there for him, as an olive branch is, and wanting to know he has left this world, unable to hurt or impact anyone ever again.

There were days I hated him, and hate is such a terrible word that I try to never use. But there were also days I saw him as a pocket watch, who just needed to be seen for what worth it had left.

"Just trust me, mom. Please. You know me better than that. I am only reading to learn more about that terrible mess, and to educate myself some. I do not believe he was good or right at all for what he did. I promise. Okay?"

I also wondered how much she knew. What if she did know about the letters, as she most likely peaked through my room to see why I had been spending all my time there. If she did, she did not give me any clues about just how much she knew.

Then, she stood up, walked over to me, looked at me with that slight smile that said without words, I want to believe you and I am trying, and kissed my head. I hated that. I wasn't a child anymore, but I resisted saying anything to her, other than "Thanks mom."

There was still another letter to open, and I wondered if this was him giving up. I had not responded to two letters in a row now, and for him to write a third seemed odd, even if this was all he had to do in there. It bordered desperate, as my friend Angela had that guy messaging her nonstop and she was so put off by him. The rule was you message some-one twice. If they do not respond, that's your answer. But he didn't know the rule apparently. Being locked away for decades probably changed a lot of what he knew and didn't know.

The letter began with a familiar greeting.

"Olive."

Chapter 27

* * *

I had read about the number thirteen and the reason it was considered to be unlucky to others, and at least from a Christian standpoint, it meant this; When Jesus was having the last supper, there were twelve disciples with him. So when you added those twelve with him, you got thirteen. The unlucky part of that was that Judas ended up being the thirteenth guest, and for Jesus, that turned out to be the unlucky one.

I don't know how much of that I believe; a number being considered unlucky and all, but for one young man, it turned out to be his unlucky number.

He was born to Ralph and Rosemary Blemings and was their one and only child. He was born in the spring of 1965, just south of Falls Creek, in a time where life moved differently. His family was excited to bring in their first child into this world, but when he was born, it was discovered he had an intellectual disability. But back in the sixties, it was more commonly known as being born retarded, a word that seems more removed from civilized talk now.

They had a name picked out, believing their first son should be named for his father, Ralph, but when he came out and they saw what they were faced with, his mother asked for them to wait before officially naming him. Ralph was devastated, knowing that not only did his son have a hard life in front of him, but that he and Rosemary would surely struggle as they tried to raise a young boy with such clear limitations.

He did not fight Rosemary on the name, thinking that he could save that for the next, healthier child to carry on the legacy. But unbeknownst to him at the time, this would be his first, and last child he and his wife would bring into this world.

Rosemary was confused as to why her God would give her such burden in life, when she had gone to church every Sunday, volunteered wherever she could, and had been a decent and good follower of Christ most days of the week. Yet here she was at a moment that should have been the best blessing in her short life, confused and scared for what was to come.

West Virginia, as well as most of the country at that time, did not treat all children the same unfortunately. Children with severe disabilities were often looked at as less than half a human, and many wondered why anyone would spend their lives raising someone who, in their mind, would be a burden on an entire society. Let them go to a home where people that get paid to take care of them could. No one would fault you for doing as you did, because they all knew that you had a right to a good chance in life, free of struggles that you did not need to take on if you did not have to.

But for Rosemary, she knew better. Although she struggled with the reason why, she never fought with the fact he was her son, and it was her responsibility to do all she could to give him a life worth looking back on with admiration.

After a few days of careful reflection, she asked Ralph to sit next to her as she had come up with a name. His name would be Shawn, which Rosemary discovered with her Irish origin, meant, "God is gracious."

She figured that if he were born to her, it was a blessing for the two of them, and not a curse as others would view it from their limited perspectives. She leaned hard on her faith, knowing that for every difficult day in life, there was a plan and a reason that you may learn in this lifetime, but if not, you would most certainly in the next. That was her strong faith coming through, and although Ralph had a decent amount of faith as well, it was not the same as his wife's.

They took Shawn home and did what any good parents would do. They raised him as they would any other child, careful to understand that there would come a time when he would experience the harsh realities of life. For the first few years, Shawn laughed as babies did, cried when he struggled, and for her part, Rosemary sucked it all in. She loved her son and promised him that no matter what the world saw in him, she knew he was destined for good things.

Ralph worked hard but seemed to fall into a depression over the years. He loved his son, but felt that he failed him somehow, even if he didn't understand just how he did. His drink a night routine turned into much more as the years went by. Rosemary tried talking to him a few times about it, but the more she did, the deeper he began to sink. He now not only felt he failed his son but was failing his wife as well.

In 1974, just a month before Shawn would have his ninth birthday, Ralph took his life. The burden of being what he thought was a failed husband and father became too much for him to handle, so he sat down, poured himself one drink after the other while Rosemary and Shawn were in town doing some shopping for the week, and ended his life.

It was never mentioned just how he had done it, but the rumor was that Shawn ran up the steps and into the house to fetch his father and found him. Shawn, not knowing what had taken place, sat there with his father with his legs crossed in front of him on the floor, asking him over and over, "why you not hearing me?"

Life was already hard as any could be for Rosemary, and now she would have to dig much deeper into her faith to find a reason that made any type of sense for the why of this new tragedy. She would not find any answers, and her faith would slowly diminish as time went on for her.

Shawn, from what she could tell, understood very little about the incident, but she did notice a change in how he acted going forward. His happiness that seemed to come from simple things like finding a bullfrog down by the river's edge or chasing a lightening bug to place in a jar so that he had "night lights," in his room, left.

Rosemary wondered if it was time to put Shawn in a place where he could get the help he needed, that she would no longer be able to provide. Her small but supportive family in the area told her that no one would dare question her decision, especially after what had happened to Ralph. It left her little choice, and for a struggling, single mom, maybe this was the best for everyone involved.

She decided that Shawn, although showing signs of struggle, would lose much more if she just dropped him off at a strange place and only visited him, rather than being the support she had been for almost a decade, and the support he would need for the next however many both she and he would live.

When Shawn vanished in 1985, Rosemary knew in her heart that he was gone. She did not need to wait around for others to say they had looked everywhere and anywhere, and that they could find no signs of anything, just like the others that went missing over the last few years. Shawn, her child that she had tried so hard to give a better life to, one that she shared all of herself with, was now no longer struggling to fit in.

If she had any faith left within her, it was that she somehow accepted her son was back with his father, looking down on her and laughing, as if to say, "ah, that's why things were as they are, and the struggles needed to happen in the order they did. It all makes perfect sense now!"

But with Shawn's vanishing, something finally surfaced for authorities to grab, giving them a clue as to who may have been the last person to see Shawn while he was still alive. A simple, plain business card was left where Shawn was last known to be. The card read,

"Handyman for hire," and had a number and name typed out just below.

That name, was Tarvis Michael Richards.

In 1985, after a baker's dozen had left the streets of Fall Creek, West Virginia, a suspect was finally apprehended and brought in for questioning. Tarvis put up no fight, instead remaining inexplicably calm when questioned about the disappearances.

They asked him why one of his business cards had been left at an address that he was not known to have done any work at, and what relationship he had with Shawn, or his mother Rosemary. Wanting to appear as though they knew more than they had, they even told Tarvis that they had finally discovered more evidence that they kept from the general public, so coming clean would be his only option, and could at least save him from a death row sentence if he cooperated.

They were not sure, though, what, if any role Tarvis Michael had in the vanishings. Maybe Shawn had found his card somewhere in town and picked it up for unknown reasons. Perhaps Tarvis was in the area and dropped a card that had randomly caught a head of wind, floating through the air like a paper airplane, and landed at Shawn's home.

Tarvis remained quiet, stating that he wished to have a lawyer present before answering any further questions. He knew he had rights, and although the police had little else to go on, the fact he requested an attorney as calmly as he had and used this calmness and time over one of looking confused and scared over something he had not done, was alarming.

He was placed in a cell, told he would have one phone call

when they had time to grant that to him, and then left there for the night.

Tarvis sat in that cell, alone and there with only his thoughts to him. Other than the clothes he had on his back, everything was stripped away from him, including his dignity, as the police that were there to guard him, taunted him and swore "we will watch you hang for what you did, that's a guarantee."

By morning, news somehow had circulated to a few locals that there was someone possibly in custody, but no one knew much else. As that news traveled from neighbor to neighbor, from the small town below, up to the mountains high above, people grew both curious and relieved.

Maybe this would be the end of all this nonsense, and they would have answers that have eluded them for years now. They may be able to rest their heads down, without wondering about each sound they heard in the night. People were on edge for several years, when they once had not a fear in their lives other than were they living a decent enough life.

As the days passed, Tarvis was moved to the more stable county prison, where he would remain until his trial. There would be no bail, and because Tarvis had little to his name, a lawyer was appointed to him, but that lawyer had never tried a murder case in his short career.

Things seemed bleak for him, but he remained as calm and quiet as he had from the start. Even when his attorney pressed him for details that could help protect his client, Tarvis would just sit there, nod occasionally, but say nothing that would help, or even hurt his defense. It was as if he refused to cooperate with the investigation, even if it meant he would hurt his case going forward. The attorney and the state's attorney did not understand what he was doing, but they had no other choice but to continue with their work.

After months had passed, the town that had once made headlines for all the wrong reasons was finally making them for a better one. A man had been captured and as far as the police were concerned, the killer was off the streets and would be for good.

Even though no one could state that the missing were all deceased, having no sign or contact from them over the years, it would eventually be left up to a judge to determine if they could legally be marked as dead. The only chance of knowing if they were in fact alive or dead, was sitting in a cell, just miles from the town that feared so much over the last few years but said little. If they were going to get answers, it would be from more evidence they could find, and not what he would speak about. So they obtained warrants, searched where he lived and the car he owned, for anything that would connect him to just one of the missing, or to the death of Winnie.

Chapter 28

* * *

I had seemingly convinced my mother enough to back off, and so once again, I felt the draw to find out more. There was still one more letter to read, and despite wanting to message Michael, I decided it best to read all of what he had sent first, in case there was anything that needed addressing before I eventually did reply.

In the third letter, Michael went back to his original ways like when he wrote me those first few times. He gave me advice, reminding me that the journey through life would be filled with choices on the road, and that it would be up to me and me alone to figure out which path I should take. He cautioned that sometimes the calling was too strong to go one way, but that if I just looked deeper, there could be a better reason to go on the other path, against what your heart was pulled towards.

He said his own struggles with walking along the path of life by himself were defining. That even when he felt he was doing the right thing at times, and almost every bone in his body agreed with him, there were also moments when he knew if he had more time to decide, his decisions would be very different, and he begged for a second time around.

I wondered if he was referring to the murders, and if he was saying that he regretted committing them but didn't at the time they had taken place. That maybe he had justified in his own mind what he did, and that years behind thick iron bars on death row had allowed him to come to terms with the fact he had made terrible, life changes choices, for him and for the victims and their families.

He could never go back and change them, but there was a feeling in his writings that he had wished he had the ability to do so. I could feel his pain and sorrow coming through, but I didn't know how to react. When I read about what he did, I wanted to hate him and not care for what happened next, or for the years he had to sit there knowing it was his last home until the day he died. But then there was the side of me that questioned more than I could read. That his heart had understood the severity of the past, and begged for forgiveness, even if only from one soul.

I had no clue if anyone had ever granted him that. Had the trials produced anyone that took the stand with a slight hint of that forgiveness or was it all about him burning in hell for the rest of eternity?

Then I began to wrestle with that. My faith had taught me that if we seek forgiveness, we are granted it. I don't recall a lot about the level of the sin impacting that, and if it had, was there a cutoff as to what was forgiven and what wasn't?

Did time play a factor in the decision, meaning that because he had spent so many decades away, and if he truly was sorry for all that he had done, was he somehow forgiven because he had served enough time here on earth?

Michael reminded me to smile through life, even when faced with the certainty that it would change over time, often without your input. But smiling in the face of defeat was something he felt was important; standing your ground and showing courage.

"Olive, when you have a choice between right and wrong, you must first decide whose definition of right and wrong you are using. For one decision you make could impact one, while another could impact many others. That is something I beg of you to understand," Michael wrote.

But I had no idea what he meant. I knew if Mee-maw were alive, she would probably know better, although her explanation would be filled with analogies about the mountain breeze in the early afternoon, laying down a path of justice on the screaming frogs in a pail while the 'coons ate a full meal, or something crazy like that. I would pretend to understand but would not.

I felt that it was time to write back to Michael, before continuing with my binder reading. I wanted to use what I felt in the moment rather than what I expected to feel later. My thinking was that this was the path I was on at the moment, and the fork, as Michael said, was immediately in front of me. I would probably make back and forth decisions as I learned more, and that would be okay. But this was about the now.

Michael

First, I apologize for my delay in getting back to you. I don't really know what to say, other than to let you know that I've been struggling some.

I've been reading about the missing people that you are sitting there for, and it honestly hurts at times. I see their faces, read their stories and strangely enough, I feel as if I can hear their voices.

Why? What made you do those terrible, horrible things? Did you feel regret because you genuinely understood what you did, or because you were caught doing what you did?

I just cannot understand how anyone could take another life and find it justifiable. So that was the reason for my delay. I struggled with letting this letter writing go and finding the words to write you back.

I don't know how much you are willing to tell me about those lost years, but I feel as if I have earned some expla-nation. Don't you?

Please let me know. I don't know how much longer I can do this, but for now, I will try my best to get through this all and continue with responding.

Olive

The next morning, I got up early and noticed my mother had been up, going through a few of Mee-maws final belong-ings, as she placed them neatly in two piles. One seemed to be items she decided she no longer needed, and the other one was clearly what she knew she was not ready to let go of yet.

"Morning," I said.

"Oh, hey Rainbow. Good morning. I'm just going through a few things, trying to figure out what I intend to keep and what it's time to let go of," she replied.

I know this wasn't easy for her, as a lifetime of having someone is incredibly hard to let go of. You have them whenever you want to talk with them, or ask them a question, or just hear their voice, and then all of a sudden, that is all removed. Usually without notice, and when you are not prepared. Words you meant to say, never get heard. Questions you always meant ask and those answers you never got are lost for the rest of eternity.

I know I had my own questions I wish I had asked Mee-maw, but I did not. So, getting those answers was just going to be impossible. If I could just hear her tell me a story about that pocket watch once more, or to listen to her talk about Pappy, which I rarely gave an ear for, and to learn about what made them fall in love and last as long as they did. And why had she decided to never marry again after her husband had passed?

It made me think back to Michael, and helped me to understand that my asking the questions was okay, because there would be a day I could no longer and then what? The truth would die when he took his final breath.

Dad told me that sometimes finding the answer to a question turns out to be the exact opposite of what we had hoped to hear, so not to worry so much about getting all my questions answered. Maybe he was right. I wasn't going to tell him that, but maybe he was.

"Mom, can I ask you something?" I asked.

She stopped what she was doing and nodded.

"Do you believe it's possible to be forgiven for everything, if you truly want that forgiveness? Or do you believe that there are sins that just can never be completely forgiven?" I asked.

She sat there for a moment and then went back to looking at the items in front of her. She picked up a photo of Mee-maw and her when she was about two or three. Mee-maw was seated in an old brown colored couch with wood paneling behind her, and mom was standing next to her, straight as an arrow.

"I love this picture," she said.

She tilted it slightly so I could see it better.

"I sometimes wonder how I got to where I am from where I was. There were many years I feared my mother, but I now wonder if it was more fear of her being angry, or fear of disappointing her," mom said.

I wondered why she had not answered my question, but I knew she had heard me. Maybe this was one of those moments dad was talking about, not needing to know the answers sometimes.

But she did continue after placing the photo in the pile of absolute keeps.

"It's a hard question to answer, Rain. I wish I knew for certain, but I think if people knew that answer, they would find it easier to live terrible lives with no rules, knowing they could simply ask for forgiveness at any point before they died, and have it granted."

I hadn't thought about it like that before, but it did make a great deal of sense. If I knew everything would be fine, I could steal whatever it was I wanted from a store, and not fear God being upset with me. As long as I was sorry, it wouldn't matter. Of course there was the part where getting arrested was probably not a great feeling, but when you talk about murdering someone, I don't know. I was genuinely confused but didn't want to alarm my mom with a direct question like that one.

Hearing her answer, I decided not to press the issue. Realistically, no one would know for sure. My friend's dad always said, "Unless you have died and come back, none of us know what to really expect."

When I got back to the binder, there were more articles on the arrest of Tarvis Michael. I was finally able to see what the man I had been writing, looked like. I realized I could have just googled it, but I found it more fascinating to learn through the letters, binder and photos I was sent.

I noticed that I had the unopened letter from Mee-maw still sitting neatly on my dresser, and I smiled. She thought enough of me to write a letter, but I knew I was not ready. I hoped that I would eventually get an overwhelming feeling to open it, but I had to wait longer for that. Today was simply not the day.

Tarvis Michael was lean but had a good upper body. His face at that time was a young-looking chiseled type, and his hair looked as if it could wave in the photo. He had a nice look to him, but he did look scared. Surrounding him in the photo were either police or FBI men. I could not tell, but I knew they were important men in uniform, ensuring he went nowhere.

The writer stated that although not much was known about him, he had still not offered a defense, or an alibi. It was as if he had sealed his fate and was resolved to the fact he was caught and going away for a long, long time.

I don't know how he felt in that moment, but scared was probably the least of it. Whatever they had on him, it wasn't known outside of the business card that somehow ended up by the thirteenth, but I assumed they had more by then. Fingerprints, blood samples, something. Maybe a few hair strands that belonged to him, placed him at the scene of all the missing and, of course, Winnie's home.

I would need to wait, though. Either for something else to come up in what papers remained in the binder, or for Michael himself to let me know more. He did say I was free to ask questions, but I would have to learn if that was what he really meant when he offered that statement.

And then as I waited for Michael to respond, I began to experience a strange sensation anytime I opened the binder. I had never had any feeling one way or the other, other than to feel incredibly sad or angry about those that vanished, but this was different from that. This almost reminded me of how the short hairs on my lower arm stood straight up that night I was up in the mountains and swore I heard the sounds of someone or something crying for help in the dense green brush.

It wasn't a feeling of panic, though, but more a feeling of something, or someone, trying to get my attention. Thinking about it later, I should have feared it more as a young girl, but for some strange reason I felt I had to listen to what it was that it wanted from me. And so I sat there in perfect silence, free of any outside noises or interference, and listened as best I could.

Chapter 29

* * *

Silence is an interesting state to be in when you are so used to being around the noises that life constantly throws at you. Alarms first thing in the morning to wake you from your resting state, or the sound of the school bus that you hear sometimes a minute or two before you even set eyes on it coming into view. There are constant moments of noise, but seldom can you hear your own heart beating in your chest, because nothing else can get past your ears for that short period of time.

Tarvis Michael was silent. He spoke so few words when questioned, that they started to wonder if he was mentally off, or just scared out of his mind. One article called him "The Silent Devil," because he refused to say much, but the more they looked, the more they felt they had their man, and that man was an absolute demon on earth.

Something was changing, though, in the stories I was reading. They centered on the possibility that Tarvis knew some of the victims, specifically Shawn. That seemed odd to me as Shawn had severe issues that limited not only his communication but caused him to have angry outbursts. I would learn this as time went on, but I would assume so many involved in the case had to have known if they were piecing together the link between them.

I waited for Michael's letter, as typically they took several weeks to arrive. I wasn't sure if that was due to the guards taking their sweet time getting them to Michael, or maybe because of where he was, everything needed to be reviewed first.

But I somehow doubted the letters were read, because if they had been noticed, someone would have undoubtedly put an end to them.

Then, after a few trips to the post office and seeing nothing, there was a letter from the prison, and it was from Michael. I raced home to open it, and this time, sat on our back porch to allow the sun to act as a good backdrop over me. Plus, no one was home to bother me, so what difference did it make where I opened the envelope?

Dearest Olive,

I sense a lot of tension coming from you in this last letter, and I cannot blame you for feeling as you do. I guess if the shoe was on the other foot, well, how would I feel? Very much the same, I would have to imagine.

The first thing I want to remind you of though, is to smile. I fear when you are looking deeper into my story, you are forgetting that whatever happened, happened long ago. While I don't expect you to smile exactly when learning more about that terrible time, I do expect when you are finished, to let that all go away like a feather in the wind and to find something good in your day to replace it with.

Smile when the day is good, but also when the day is bad. You sometimes have to trick the day into believing it cannot change how you are going to approach the rest of it despite the direction it seems to blow you in.

I don't know how far along you are into your research of my life, but I ask that before you continue to judge the man you read about, you take a moment to understand that not everything will always be as others have written it to be. Writers have broad leeway in how they romanticize everything they put to paper.

I know it seems terrible, and that it truly was. All those different lives lost and believe me, not a day goes by that I don't think about each and every one of them. There are times I wake in the middle of the night or first thing in the early morning, praying for that split second that I am outside these walls, back at home and working on some-one's home in town, or that this entire situation never took place. For that fraction of a moment, I am free once again. And let me tell you what a feeling of joy that single short moment brings to me.

I can't fake it, though. It has to be in a moment of confusion that for some reason, I am somehow granted a temporary time of grace I may or may not deserve. Who really knows.

I will try to find the right words to give you in time but understand I may need to think of what you will be able to handle, and what you will not.

I also have some news, but unfortunately, it's not the good type that one would choose to hear. That news will need to wait just a little longer as well. I am unwilling, or unable to write that down at the moment. I've tried, but some things a pen cannot transfer without complete acceptance and a willingness to let that out.

I will share this with you, though. Your letters have allowed me to feel a slight bit human for a change, when I felt anything but. There was a time when my life was full of beautiful hope and a crushing desire to create a much different future for myself, and that was lost entirely. But with your letters, I have some hope again.

Olive, if there is anything that you should be striving for, it would be the hope for a beautiful, full life of freedom and happiness that each human deserves. A life where the bad days cannot rule over the good ones, and where no matter how tired you feel when you return home at the end of the night, you breathe in, smile, look at that warm bed and loving family awaiting you with smiles and accept that the end of this day and the very next day are a gift.

My very best, your friend,
Michael

I sat there looking over the letter, wondering if I had missed anything while reading it quickly. I was slightly confused by what he wanted to share and could not, but I guess if time was what he needed, what was I to do? All that man had was his time. He had no work schedule or clients to tend to, and no shopping that had to be done before the storms rolled in so he could prepare a meal for his family before they starved.

But the end of the letter, how he signed this one with the "your friend," was odd. Was he my friend? I quickly shook my head, confirming he absolutely was NOT my friend. He was someone I had to learn about, and nothing more than that. I swore to that. Can you imagine becoming a friend with a serial killer who could sound so majestic that you would question, could he really do it? That was what people called psychopathic behavior, where they try to justify their gross actions or change your perception of who they were, as if they were incapable of doing what everyone else knew they did.

Shawn, as others would testify to, was an often-troubled young man, who could be extremely helpful on one day, and impossible to control on the next. He had unexplained anger issues, and that caused some to steer away from both him and his mother whenever they were around. It got to the point that Rosemary kept him inside as much as she could, but even for her, times were sometimes more than she could bare and she would spend days on end breaking down.

But there was a little help and relief, particularly from the church Rosemary and Shawn belonged to, and the pastor with whom Shawn seemed to have a strong bond with. Not having a father in his life was unacceptable to pastor Jenkins, and so he offered a few hours a week of his time to sit with Shawn and go over anything he could to help the boy out.

After Pastor Jenkins had vanished, Shawn lost a support system that he desperately needed, and for Rosemary, life was throwing another punch in her direction where she felt her hands were tied tightly behind her back.

Shawn was strong, and so there were a few contractors in the area that tried to use him for the simplest of tasks to give the kid something to do, like carrying lumber up a long driveway to a room that was being framed out, or holding a wall in place, while the more capable men nailed them to the flooring. And there were times it worked, but more often, those jobs ended the same way. With Shawn, having a bad day was much worse than you or I having a tough afternoon. He would shut down almost completely, and either you would need to get Rosemary there to coax him out, or worse, Shawn would lash out towards anyone within shouting distance of him, and storm out of the job, screaming and throwing his hands in all directions, as he spoke words that made no sense.

It was just too much for people to handle, and rightfully so, everyone felt. Even Rosemary, who prayed that this would work and give Shawn a sense of purpose around other men, had to abandon all hope.

There was a handwritten note placed between two articles, folded and yellowed from years of being flattened out and tucked away. I opened the fold, so that it was lying flat for possibly the first time in decades, and read what was written neatly in cursive on the page.

"Loss is one of those things that you have to accept in life. We all must say goodbye, most often when we are least ready to do so. But I have come to accept that my life, for reasons I may never know, is meant to be lived alone, without love or understanding, without a hand extended to offer relief, and without all that I have accepted without question. And that, is my great loss."

I did not know who wrote the letter or why it was placed where it was. Perhaps it was a letter Rosemary wrote to someone, or even herself, as a way to let go of all she had endured. Without a signature, I would suspect that only Mee-maw would have known. But I felt in my heart that it had to have been Shawn's mother, who seemingly lost more than most would have been able to manage. It made me wonder where she may be now, or if she had died and finally was able to let go of that feeling of hopelessness.

I made a note to myself to look her up if I did not find out more about her with what was left to read. If she was still in the area, I wonder if she had found love again, or if she had taken the same path as my Mee-maw and stopped at the one love she had as being her only love in this life.

The trial for Tarvis Michael was a national event. People from all over the country converged on our little town, hoping to snap a photo of the man they felt was responsible, and if they were lucky enough, to hear him give a reason for why he had carried out these brutal crimes.

The articles started to focus more on Tarvis than they did on the deceased from that point. They talked about his family, or lack of, and the fact that he had fooled so many into believing he was good when he was anything but. Newsmen and women interviewed neighbors he had lived near, and family members of the ones he had taken the life from.

Some felt a little relief, but others knew their pain was still very raw and until they found where their loved ones had gone or what had happened to them, there would be no way they could find any closure to get them moving forward. But would they ever get their answers? That would be the ultimate question.

Chapter 30

* * *

As the Summer of '85 came to an end, and no one else seemed to disappear in or around Falls City, the sentiment grew that they had their man, whether he decided to talk or not. He was sitting in a cell, not much bigger than my brother's small bedroom, and rotting away the hours of his life.

In the early winter months, a detective named Hoffman was sent from Wheeling, West Virginia to see what it was he could learn from Tarvis. He was trained in psychopathic behavior and had spent nearly three decades in law enforcement in many different capacities that gave him an edge over local authorities. The thought was that with his unique training, maybe he would be the one to break Tarvis down enough to have him slip up and talk openly about where he placed the missing bodies, and maybe even why he had so that there would be closure for so many residents and families.

Hoffman sat for several hours over the next few weeks, trying to convince Tarvis that he was only trying to help him out of his grave situation. He mentioned that he had a strong rapport with the judge who would be overseeing his trial, and that with any cooperation on his part, he swore he would put in a good word and try to save Tarvis at least a little of his life that had so many years left in it.

Tarvis remained quiet, answering only the basic questions that the detective already knew the answers to, but patience was the one thing this seasoned detective had. He knew the games played by these types of psychotic criminals, and instead of growing frustrated, he continued to assure Tarvis he was only interested in helping him out.

I wrote back to Michael, figuring that at the very least, I could do my good deed for the day and give a man who had nothing left, a simple letter to get him through a night.

Michael,

Thank you for your letter.

Of course I am curious as to what your updated news is, but I understand if you are not quite ready to let others know. Maybe in time, you will be ready to share.

I've learned a lot about you from my readings, and the more I read, the more confused I seem to get.

I cannot understand why someone like you, with the way you are able to speak and share your thoughts so clearly and easily, would throw that all away and have nothing to show for it. It doesn't make sense to me, but I guess at my age, I would not ever grasp how you did what you did.

Tell me, was there a time when you were taking these

people, that you stopped and questioned what it was you were about to do? Did you ever feel any regret or doubt before you were caught or was it all an afterthought once they had put you in jail?

I want to believe there is something good left in you, but I am having a lot of trouble finding that. Can you help me understand the good left in you?

I felt as if I was pushing at this man, but honestly, I had gotten to a point where I was just about to demand answers. Not that he had to listen to me and my demands, but what did he have to lose? When we die, do the secrets we take with us make it any better in the afterlife, or does the reputation we leave behind make any difference, or as my mom said, a hill of beans, once we left this world?

I believe in God for certain. I mean if you thought about it, how could all of this we see, and all the sounds that lay on our ears, be for nothing? There had to be more to this entire world than to live and die. But would the God I believe in forgive Michael for the terrible things he had done if he had asked, or even, if he had not? That I was still struggling with.

I asked Michael a few more questions, but nothing I would really need answers for. What mattered was why?

In the articles posted in between the trial of Tarvis Michael, I found a strange clipping that was clearly not from any of the newspapers of the time. It was a shiny paper, more out of a magazine than a black and white newspaper. The article was titled, "The single footprint of the devil."

Basically some man had wandered up into the hills during the trial, and burst into the courtroom once it had started, explaining that he had proof of the lost souls and their where-abouts. The judge immediately ordered him outside of the room, as he tried to keep order for this trial that already had so many moving parts and a tremendous number of emotions.

The deputies walked over to the man who protested again that he knew where they were, and that he had taken a photo of the devil's footprint himself, just north of where I had been behind Mee-maws house. The chills filled my body like a cold breeze had penetrated my skin and decided to stay.

He was known as a man with many issues, and the fact that he claimed he had information did very little for anyone there. In fact, he was told by the prosecution for the case to let the professionals handle what they had to do. Even though they had only one body, and they still had no answer for the remaining missing twelve, they had no intention of speaking with him about what he claimed he saw.

When the writer for the magazine decided to speak with him, probably more for ratings and a juicy tale than anything else, he was a bit taken back. This man that others felt was off his rocker, eerily explained that those lost had begged to be found. As he walked along the trail with a large stick to help him manage the terrain, he could not only feel the presence of others, but he heard them with his own ears.

When pressed for more on what they said, he tightened up, almost as if he had seen a ghost. The first fear he had was what if they thought he was the one responsible? He quickly gave alibis for proof he could not have done a single thing to those poor people. Then he continued that he was haunted by the cries in the hills and swore he could never go back to share the area he had once heard them so clear.

The writer placed a map in front of the man, and said that he completely understood, but if he would just point with his finger to where he heard the exact location of those cries, he promised the man he would not have to return. In fact, he would himself travel into those woods and up that hill to see if there were any words he could hear for himself.

He honestly did not believe there were any sounds. His thinking was that if this crazy man had seen anything, maybe it would be something he could find once again, and crack open the case with hard, solid evidence that those missing twelve were still high in the hills.

The crazed man seemed to reluctantly point to an area of green, just to the rear of where my mother had grown up, and where I had too, heard the cries for help. I began to wonder if maybe I was crazy as well, or if, truthfully, I had heard what this man had heard long ago, and those cries were from the lost, still haunting the same area, until they were found and returned to their families.

I had to shake my head and stop for a moment. This was crazy. Even I had come to terms with what I had thought I heard that day, believing that it was some type of animal calling its mother, letting her know that it was ready to eat, and needed her back now. That would be the only logical explanation for something so strange, and yet so real.

But the man that wrote the article explained that he went into the area, walked around for over an hour and a half, and although he did say he felt the hair on his arms stand up more than once, he heard nothing out of the ordinary. The crazed man was probably just that. Out of his mind.

As the trial went on, there were testimonies from the families of those missing. It was an emotional time, as the pastor's wife spoke about how her life had changed at one of the most celebrated times of the calendar year. William's family, the one missing from Ohio, also spoke about their son who had such a bright future in front of him, and then to have it pulled away for nothing…just made no sense at all. They begged Tarvis Michael right in that court room to give them their child back, or that he would surely burn in hell for keeping what was theirs and not his to keep.

Through it all, Tarvis Michael sat there, emotionless, and without a word in his defense. He had not taken the stand as of yet, and instead of apologizing to any of the members in the courtroom, or attempting to explain why it couldn't be him, he just let the trial go on as it was going to anyway.

As it headed into the next year, only the local papers kept track of each of the hearings. There was not much to report, though. Tarvis never took the stand in his defense. He sat silently through the entire length of the trial, day after day, and week after week, as if he were not even there. But he was there, and he heard all the pain in the voices of those present, the loss of the community that just needed to know why, and the hope from some of the families that he might eventually tell them where the dead now rested.

It was clear, though, that it would not be as they hoped. In fact, several years later, all of the twelve would be declared deceased by a judge despite no bodies having been found, allowing for whatever closure someone could get to happen.

Funerals were held, but there would be no remains. Only photographs of those missing, some personal items that others remembered them by, and for Hep, my Pappy's dearest friend, a set of rosary beads that had been passed down in his family and placed neatly in the coffin, along with his favorite pipe and a pouch of tobacco.

There was nothing else to do. That would need to be the end for all. Tarvis Michael, with limited evidence, only one body, and a strange defense of not speaking a word to claim his innocence, was convicted and sentence to death. No one expected death to be life, but he still, to this day, sat in the very jail he was remanded to years and years ago.

I still, though, felt as if the story did not end there. Something about a man so well spoken, and so able to share his thoughts and words like serving apple pie for a group of friends, was wrong. Very wrong.

Chapter 31

* * *

The strangest thought crossed my mind, and as much as I tried to talk myself out of it, there would be none of that. I decided to reach out to Rosemary, but first, I had to figure out where she was at, and if she was even still alive.

I typed her name into Google and began to look at the different links that appeared. At first, there were stories about the trial, and the disappearance of her son, Shawn. I scrolled further down and sifted through the nonsense links that asked you to pay and in return, they would disclose the exact address, phone number and email for her. But I didn't trust any of those.

But then, I saw one that seemed promising. Her name was placed in the text, and when I clicked on it, I saw it was an obituary for her sister who had passed just a year and a half ago. It was her for sure, as it mentioned her sister, Grace, having a nephew Shawn who had sadly passed many years back.

I looked through it, reading about the small family they had, and saw that Rosemary, at least when this obituary was written, was still very much alive. She was living in an assisted living home roughly forty-five or so minutes away. But how would I contact her and what would I say if and when she answered the phone? Hello, I am looking to speak to you about the disappearance of your son? She would think I was an idiot, opening old hurtful wounds that had probably long since healed and expecting her to relive that time she had allowed to die?

Not knowing what to do, I decided to sleep on it. I knew that I had to do something, but what and why, I did not know. Maybe I felt there was a story not being told, or missing information that somehow, needed to rise to the surface for my closure. But how selfish would that sound, that I, a young teen woman who had not been a thought in my mother's young mind when all that took place, and who was "befriended" by the serial killer responsible for the loss of her only child, wanted closure. I had no idea if she had accepted her own closure or if she, despite all the hours and years that were placed in between the day it happened and the moment I would speak to her, had found peace.

That night I fell into a deep sleep. One where I should have forgotten any dreams I had throughout the night, but at some point, early in the morning, just before the sun would rise, I woke up in a panic. I heard it again, and even when I wanted to chase it away as just a nonsense dream, I could not. The cries had come back and although it was incredibly hard to hear what they were saying, I swear I heard a begging to come home.

I was clearly going crazy, and not only that, but I was

also scared. My mind raced, and my heart pounded as if I was having a panic attack. But because it was still early in the morning, and the darkness was still a blanket all around, I shut my eyes, pulled the blanket over my face and prayed. I prayed the voices would just stop asking me for anything. I was a kid and was unable to help any of them get home, and besides it had been so long ago that they had vanished. What good would it be now?

Maybe I needed to stop this. If my mental state was suffering the more I investigated things, was it worth the answers I was chasing? All I wanted to do was to complete my school project, get a decent grade, and enjoy myself. This was absolutely not part of the deal, yet here I was, smack in the middle of some weird spirits that wanted help, and a serial killer that wanted to be my friend.

I felt as if I was so deep into this now, that if I didn't at least make an attempt to find out more about the story, I would also suffer from lack of my own closure. It was inevitable that I would move forward and contact Rosemary, and at least see if she was open to talking with me or not.

When a man on the other end of the call answered, I asked to speak with her. He sounded confused and questioned who I was.

I was afraid of that. I hadn't really thought it through enough to answer that question, and really, it would obviously be the one question they would most likely ask at first. But dumb me, stuttered as if I was a twelve-year-old child worried I would get in trouble if I gave the wrong name.

"My name is Rain, and I was hoping to speak with

Rosemay for a moment, if that would be okay," I replied sounding as confident as I could.

"Are you a relative of hers?" the man continued.

"No, not a relative, but I'm someone who knows who she is and would just like a few minutes of her time," I said.

I could tell the man was apprehensive about putting me through, and clearly he was good at his job, which usually was a good thing but for me, it sucked. He was going to be tough to get around, and I needed to think fast.

"I have a package for her, and I was told I was not to mail it, but had to give it to her in person, but only after speaking to her and confirming it was indeed the same Rosemary."

I thought that sounded brilliant until I realized I had no package, and if he pressed on with any more questions, I was going to give up the fact that I did not know her personally at all, had nothing to give her, and that would be the end of that. So, I did the only thing I could think of, the last resort fade away Hail Mary end zone shot....

"Mr., listen. My name is Rain. I am hoping we can start over. I was simply wondering if I could speak with Rosemary and just talk with her. I was doing a project in school, and through that process, her name came up and the story of her life was brought back. I swear to you, I mean no harm to her at all. I wanted to ask her about her past, and if she was willing to discuss that, I would be very grateful." I finally said.

This is the moment where I wonder to myself, am I doing the right thing or am I just causing more heartache and pain for not only her, but me as well. I could not begin to understand what it's like losing a child, and if someone were to ask me about that loss, I may tell them off. But maybe she had kept things to herself for so many years that sharing a fond memory before all the hard ones came would be useful in her older age.

But I had to get there. I thought about taking the bus that went not too far from the home, but I had never done that before. I couldn't ask my mother, because she had already worried so much about the binder, that to worry her more was not going to be in my best interest. Only one of my friends had their driver's license, but they were not allowed to drive anything over a twenty minute drive and I didn't want them to push the issue on my behalf and lose that.

The only other option that I could think of, and I wasn't even sure it was an actual option, would be my father. He had been pretty busy as of late but still found time to check in on us to make sure we were good. His traveling lately was a bit more than my mother liked, so he was working closer to home over the next few weeks to keep his marriage going.

I had to ask him, but I also had to swear him to secrecy. Just as Mee-maw had done on the drive back when we first discovered who my pen pal was. I trusted my dad, but at the same time, he was a parent and would never want to overstep my mother and what she had done to raise us while he was mostly away.

Thankfully, and a bit reluctantly I would believe, he agreed to take me, asking very few questions before answering. I told him this was part of a school project, which if you think about it, it kind of was. I had never agreed to stop writing Michael, and so I felt it was simply a continuation of what they started, not me.

Dad was I think more excited about spending an afternoon with me, just him and I, which is something we had not done in quite a while. I think that drive down to Falls Creek to get "that lovely mother-in-law of mine," as he called her, was the last time we had spent more than five minutes together without distractions and interruptions. I was a little nervous that he may begin to talk about what this woman had to do with school, or maybe start a conversation about my attitude with my mother lately, but it was a price I was willing to pay to get to the assisted home and to meet this Rosemany, whom I had known only what the papers decided I should know about her.

It was raining the day we headed out in the late morning, and my dad always made a dumb dad joke any time it rained, because of my name naturally. He found it funny, but I just found it more annoying the more he said it.

The ride was a bit scenic, as much of this part of the state was at any time of the year. But we were off and the conversations were basic for the most part as we talked about school, or a place he had traveled to for work recently, and then as we were getting closer, he shifted the conversation entirely, catching me completely off guard.

"Rain, I want you to be careful talking to that woman. I know you mean well, and I believe you are doing what you feel in your heart is something you must do, but I still need for you to understand that people have left a lot in the past for good reason, so proceed cautiously and read the room," he said.

That was something he said often. "Read the room." I heard it for years as a kid, but one time he explained it to me. He meant that, in this instance, if Rosemary seemed to be frustrated, for me to back off. If she was willing to continue, then do so, but keep an eye on how she responded, even if not with her words. Her words would not always match her intentions and feelings.

Somehow, he knew exactly what I was doing there. I'm not certain he knew that it was *the* Rosemary, but he knew this had to do with Tarvis Michael, and it gave me a warm feeling inside as if I had thought I somehow got over on him, and got caught with my hand in the jar.

"Dad, I know what I am doing. Trust me on this, Okay?" I replied.

At the entrance was a set of double doors leading into the older building, and a main area where two men were seated for any guest that came in.

"Can I help you young lady?" one of the men asked.

I straightened myself up and spoke clearly as I could.

"I'm here to see Rosemary. I called a week ago and spoke to someone," I said firmly.

The other man raised his head and looked in my direction. He was the one I had originally spoken to when I called, and he spoke up.

"Yes, Rosemary. Listen, kid. She doesn't talk all that much. So, I will walk you over, introduce you to her, but from there, it's up to her on how well she is feeling and how much she wishes to say. That's the best I can do, okay?" he said.

We walked down the hall, and to the rear of the building. There, I could see a set of doors, one after the other, packed tightly together. He knocked on one, called out her name, and said that he had someone here to see her. There was no reply at first, so he knocked once more, and gently pushed the door open, just enough that he could peak in and ensure she was either up, or possibly even still alive.

A faint voice could be heard on the other side of the door, and the man who had walked me down the hall nodded in my direction, and pushed the door open enough that I could see a frail woman who was covered in a multicolored blanket at the waist, seated in a chair with the tv on.

I slowly walked over to the doorway and entered the room just a few feet from where she was seated. I had no idea how to introduce myself, so I just stood there like an idiot for a few moments.

She looked up at me and motioned for me to come in closer. I did. She looked at my face, with an expressionless look on hers, and then patted a seat that was next to her, motioning for me to take a seat.

This was it. The mother of Shawn, the last of the missing victims, seated right next to me in the same room. I was speechless knowing that this could provide the answers to some of my questions, or open myself up to many more I had never thought about.

Chapter 32

* * *

There are thousands of stories that die every hour of every day, across the country and across the entire world for that matter. Stories that should be passed down by an older generation that may be on the verge of leaving this place, to newer ones that really have no stories of their own yet to tell.

I know that I will eventually share the story of the importance of a pocket watch to my children someday, and possibly lend a phrase or two that I had only ever heard my Mee-maw say. I didn't know it at the time, but her experiences from her humble life were the simple tales I missed hearing about the most. When she was alive, I didn't care all that much, but now that she's passed, I wonder if I had just sat down with her a few more times and instead of asking her questions, just listened in silence with more patience. What stories would she have shared with me? What times in her life were the most memorable ones she had? Would there be stories hidden deep away that she hadn't thought of for years upon years, but somehow in that moment of sharing, they resurfaced?

As I sat down with Rosemary, I wasn't sure if I should lead or sit there patiently for her to ask questions about why I was there. But it was almost like a game of who would break first, as she sat there looking at her TV as if I wasn't even in the room.

At first, I felt slightly intimidated, but then I sat back and just watched her as she looked blankly forward in her chair. Maybe she wasn't right in the head after having experienced the life she had, and this entire trip would be a big waste of not only my time, but hers as well.

After several moments of sitting in absolute quiet, outside of the noise coming from the show she had on, she broke the silence first.

"What is it you want from me?" she asked.

What I wanted was to know about her son, and how he vanished. What she was feeling the months that came and went without a single word that would lead to the where-abouts of his body. I wanted to know what she felt towards Tarvis Michael Richards, and if she had at any point forgiven him for what he did. There was a lot I wanted to know, but what was appropriate to ask and what wasn't? It was about balance, and as my parents say all the time, "learn when to speak and when to listen." I was reading the room.

"Ma'am, I wanted to spend a little time with you, and learn about your life, whatever you would be willing to share. That's all," I managed to say.

She watched a few more moments of her TV and then turned the volume all the way down without turning it completely off. Maybe just having the scenes play out in front of her was a comfort that she needed. Who knows.

"But why? What about my life interests you, and why on earth would you need to know anything about me?" she asked.

It made sense for her to question my motives. Honestly, I was beginning to question those myself. What right did I have to ask her about the most painful times in a parent's life? I was feeling incredibly selfish and hesitated to answer her because I had no idea what to say. I thought about getting up and running out of the room, but I felt frozen in my chair, like when you have those dreams where your legs don't work and you cannot run fast enough, or even run at all.

Coming clean would be my only option, and if she got upset, then she did and I would be on my way. It was this or sit here and lie to this woman who had earned the right to the truth for all she had experienced. She had at least earned that respect from anyone if nothing else.

I told her about the school I went to, and the project that was handed to us for grading. I mentioned that I somehow was given the wrong inmate because of a similar name, but that I honestly had no idea who he was until much later and it was too late. Then I said that although the teacher had decided we were done with all that, I had no choice but to continue it for a reason I did not fully understand myself.

Rosemary was now looking at me, possibly trying to read the level of my sincerity, or the level of my insanity. I was fifteen years old, and instead of chasing boys or going to the Saturday night football games with my girlfriends, I was learning all I could about an insane serial killer who had nothing left to give to this world but his final breath.

She looked out towards the window in her room, the only window she had, as if she was looking into a past that only she could see. I looked where she was but saw nothing other than the trees that lined the back of her room, offering mostly shade, with a little sun sneaking through.

"Do you hear them?" she asked.

"Hear what?" I replied confused.

"Them. They cry at times, and I can hear them, but I can't help them. I wish I could because it gets so loud sometimes and I feel like going mad, but all I can do is listen to them and allow them to get it out of their systems," she said.

I instantly felt chills go up my back and wondered if she was talking about the screams I had heard on the trail, the same ones that crazy man had heard and told the reporter and the people of the courtroom that declined to listen. Had she the same ability to hear them begging for help? For them to be found and brought home for the closure that maybe they even needed in death?

"I can't hear them now, but I have heard them," I replied.

She turned her head and looked towards me and smiled. It was the first time I had seen any emotions in this woman's face. Her eyes locked on mine, and she could tell I wasn't just saying that to make her feel good or to open up. She knew for sure; I had heard exactly the sounds she was referring to. And I knew that she wasn't out of her mind, because when you heard them, you had no way of forgetting the painful cries, even if you tried to reason with yourself that they could not be real. They were very real.

She leaned in, and whispered,

"They need everyone to be brought home, young lady. They need their rest."

I have no idea what she wanted from me, though. How could I bring them home and would Michael admit guilt to me? Something he had never done in all his life and all his time away from his outside world? I could not see why he would ever disclose such a thing to a girl he had never even met.

"They do," is all I could think of to reply.

Rosemary finally opened up, and she sat there and told me the stories I had been there for. How her husband, Ralph, had died many years ago because he was hurt and feeling useless when he was not. Her words were full of loss and regret, but she allowed them to flow out of her heart as she continued.

When she spoke of Shawn, she reminded me of the origin of his name. She mentioned believing that God would never give her more than she could handle but feeling as if he had failed her on several days. Things were hard, she said, and although she was a proud, strong woman and mother, there were more days she wanted to give up than not, and she always felt more alone on those days.

Shawn, he was not easy for her and at times, she felt the best thing would have been to put him in that home they had heard about from others, and she regretted not doing so. Perhaps Ralph would still be here by her side in the years that mattered most, and she would not be a shell of the woman she was meant to be.

She didn't blame Shawn for her life, because as she said, Lord knows it was not his fault, but she did blame God and she said that if that meant she could not enter into heaven, and all that she had suffered through was not enough to gain an entry into whatever came after this life, then that was just how it needed to be, and she was okay with that.

She tried desperately to provide for him, nurture him, and forgive him for things he had never asked for forgiveness for. Shawn was strong and had hurt his mother many times with violent outburst that she still showed signs of today. He wasn't the gentle, loving boy she had wanted, but instead seemed to never grasp that this woman who brought him into this world, who had made incredibly hard decisions no mother should ever need to make, had done all she could for him out of love.

He was dead, and for that she was terribly heartbroken, but she felt that she never would have survived a lifetime of continuing to raise him. He would need constant care and she would never have made it this far in her mind, especially as she aged and her bones grew weak.

I sat there and listened, not worrying about any notetaking as this was more a time to listen, feel and understand. She was spilling her soul here to me, and I was a sound board she may have needed for a great deal of time. If was what I needed to be for her, and I understood that well.

Why was Shawn chosen as the thirteenth victim? Maybe he had rubbed Tarvis the wrong way as he did with so many people he encountered. People tried to give him grace over the years, maybe more out of respect for Rosemary, but she had known that behind the scenes, people had wished she would have just let him go when she had the chance.

After about an hour or so, I realized my dad was still sitting in the parking lot and I quickly jumped up. I did not want him to be pissed off at me, and we never really talked about how long I expected to sit with her, so I asked her to excuse me while I sent him a text.

He replied with a simple,

"I'm in no rush, Rain. This is your thing."

He was being so understanding and that meant an incredible amount to me. I was grateful for his patience and his understanding, and thankful I had asked him over anyone else to drive me here.

Rosemary asked me if she had given me the information I was after from the stories that still remained in her old, failing mind. I think she felt more lost and useless than she was, but at her age, and after struggling through a lifetime of guilt and grief, where she not only questioned her decisions, but also the person she believed created all of this, I got it. This woman had earned her frustrations and I was only glad to have had the chance to hear what she knew and remembered from a time that would someday be entirely forgotten.

"Ma'am, can I ask you something more personal?" I asked.

She knew. I didn't need to ask her anything because this woman could tell exactly what it was I wanted to ask and that took a lot off me.

"You want to know if I have forgiven Tarvis? It's a fair question," she replied.

But she did not answer me, and that, too, was okay.

As I got up to thank her and leave, I remembered I had that folded note with me that was left in the binder. I quickly pulled it out and handed it to her, asking if she had written this or perhaps known who did.

She looked it over, reading it from the beginning to the end, and closed it gently, handing it back to me for safekeeping. She then patted my hand and smiled.

"Those hard, long days are gone now. I am focused on what tomorrow brings to me, and not what yesterday took," she said.

Chapter 33

* * *

Forgiveness is not always about giving others what they need. Sometimes it's more about letting go of something you never thought you could, just so you could get on with your own life and not let that drag behind you like an iron ball and chain, weighing you down as you try to move forward and keeping you from smiling again when you needed it most.

I know that there are times when I want to forgive my friends for stupid things they've done, and it's hard. But I also noticed that when I cannot, I constantly go back to whatever it was, and I give my energy to something I would rather not give it to.

Rosemary told me something before I left that will stick with me all my days. She said in order to forgive Tarvis Michael, she didn't need his permission. She needed her son Shawn's. He had yet to give her that permission, and so she was still waiting, but she knew he would eventually.

But she also mentioned that although she blamed Tarvis

for certain things, there was something that always bothered her. She never felt right about the trial. She knew there was more to the story, but she could or would not explain how she knew. It was a feeling she had felt several times during the trial, and she struggled greatly with it. For every day she wanted Tarvis to rot in that prison cell, she also felt as if maybe, just maybe, there was something massive missing that no one could see.

Because Tarvis decided to keep whatever he knew to himself, the secrets would eventually die with him, unless he somehow decided to speak up as to what happened, and where the lost were. But in the years that he had been placed away from the rest of the world, he had never spoken another word about the trauma and grief and the chances of ever finding out, diminished more. Instead of speaking out, he studied law and earned two degrees while in prison. He would never use those on the outside, of course, but it wasn't about obtaining them to use. It was about feeling as if he had some worth left in him, even if no one else would see it. He was telling himself he wasn't giving up on what he had left just yet.

I gave Michael worth with my letters, somehow, and when he got to write me back, he felt he was giving me a piece of him. I had to respect that and admire that this man who had seemingly nothing left in this world, still decided he did and that no one got to take that from him.

Worth is often associated with wealth, education or career accomplishments, but it is rarely seen as what you recognize in yourself. We expect others to determine our true worth at the end of the day, but for Tarvis Michael, he was the only one that got to determine his worth.

On the way home the day I met Rosemary, my father and I had a great talk about life. He knew he had not always been there for me because his travels for work got in the way more often than not, but he swore that the time we did share, he appreciated more than he could tell me.

The simple car rides, even when I was staring at my phone and giving him one word responses and clearly not listening to what he was saying, were strong moments for him. He said that in his entire life, outside of his wedding day and the birth of his two children, the car rides with me were his favorite memories.

That made me smile, and instead of being my typical self and trying to hide it, I gave him that one. He deserved it for letting me know I was one of his favorite memories.

I had learned a good deal from my time sitting with Rosemary, and although I knew I would most likely not be going back to see her, I felt that she and I connected with that one visit. What truly shocked me was that we both had heard the screams. If she told anyone else, they would think she was crazier than a three-dollar bill. If I had told a single person, they would surely think the same about me. But telling someone who had experienced exactly the same sensations, and heard the very same faint cries for help, made it truly believable. We had that bond, and that was something I both hated and loved at the same time.

The hard part was that the more I learned, the harder my

dreams were on me. I heard the cries in my sleep on more than one occasion over the following week. I wasn't as afraid, but still, it had me thinking that what if they were trying to be found, and here I was, the only person who could possibly get through to Tarvis Michael and figure out where their remains were hiding. Why it mattered, I had no idea.

When someone dies, that's it. Even if there is a heaven, the body we have while here on earth dies and eventually turns into fine dust. Our spirit does not. So why would a spirit care about something useless for the rest of eternity? I was struggling with the idea of ghosts as it was and starting to feel as if there was something else going on with me. It scared me, but I would tell no one. I wanted to deal with this myself.

Then, a few days later, I got a call from the postmaster. By this time, I had convinced him to let me know when a letter was waiting for me. He had seen me in his post office on several occasions and offered a warm smile and wave each of those times. The last time I asked him if it was unconventional to have him let me know when a letter, not junk mail, had been there for me. I explained it was a hassle to get there each day, and that if I could get there when I knew I had what I needed, life would be that much easier. He said he would see what he could do and offered no promises. But he had.

Olive,

As always, thank you for your letter. They each mean a great deal to me, and I cherish each of them.

I owe you an explanation, and although I am not ready

for that, I must remind myself that there are others that deserve what it is I may not be prepared for.

We all have an expiration date in life. Yours will hopefully be a long, long time from now. The hope is that you get to live out your dreams, while creating new ones even greater than the ones you have now. That you get to explore life in ways only a few do. For me? Having a date is more of a reality. Most will never know theirs, but I now have mine, so I guess one could call me special.

I wanted to tell you because Olive? We have a deadline for our writings to each other. By the end of this year, November 13th to be precise, I will wake up as I always have, get dressed and brush my teeth. I will look at the letters you have written to me, sitting neatly on my desk and will smile for a moment or two. I will have my breakfast and finish my juice they send to me. Then as I complete my morning routine, the same one I have completed for more years than I can count, I will meet with a chaplain from the prison and speak about life, and what he believes comes after. The clock on the wall will tick without pause, and I will keep one eye on it, and the other on the few things I have left in this world.

I get to pick a dinner that night, which will be nice. I have to decide what exactly I wish to have, but I will without much fuss. Then after I'm finished, it will finally be time.

Maybe not telling you would be the best thing, I thought, but eventually you will hear about it somehow. And how fair would it be for you to hear about it from someone who wasn't your friend?

I want you to know, though, I am fine. I've known for many years that this day would come, and although I had always felt I had more time than I actually do, I have to come to terms with the fact I am finishing out my sentence.

In life, we have tasks to perform, and situations to figure out. Each has meaning, either for us, or for someone else. This is my task. It will be for the families of those lost, and it's about time they got what they ultimately needed in their minds.

But promise me that whatever judgements others hold, you will first consider your own. Don't let anyone impose their beliefs on you—develop your own instead.

I promise you I will answer the questions you have to the best of my abilities but know that there will be those that simply must go unanswered. It's not out of fear, or concern for myself. That has long since passed. But it will be out of respect for the truth, and what it is I carry within.

Until I can tell you more, be safe my friend.

Always,

T. Michael Richards

The letter was powerful, yet explained little other than the fact, he was going to die. I had known people that have died before, like when I visited with my Mee-maw and just a few hours later, she was gone. But no one told me when I left the hospital that very day,

"Hey kid, say your final goodbye because this is it for her once you leave."

I knew the exact day Michael was leaving. I knew that there would be one final letter to him and from him, and that whatever I would forget to ask, would go unanswered forever. I found that completely unfair. Even if he had done all those terrible things, why could he not just sit in his cell until God decided enough was enough? How did a group of humans get to pick a date and time to decide another's fate? It felt as bad as what Michael had done, truthfully.

I hated this. It didn't seem fair at all, yet he seemed to be very acceptant of an unfair decision that would end his life. How he remained so calm, was a complete mystery to me, but it could be that he was just putting on a front and was scared shitless. I would be as if someone had told me November 13th of this year, that's it for you. I would spend the entire night before bawling my eyes out. And how could one sleep the night before when waking up would mean it was your final day? I would want to stay awake all night to prolong the hours I had left in me. Sleeping could be done for the rest of eternity, so who could possibly sleep at all?

I knew I had to prepare for what was to come, but a part of me wanted to comfort this now aging man just a little. He was alone and had no one who cared an ounce for his life. God would decide his true fate, so as long as he had breath in his lungs, I could offer the branch I agreed to in the beginning.

Right or wrong, I saw no life as more valuable over another one, and killing a man who had killed so many others, seemed more like ego than it did justice.

There were months left, not years, so I had to think about

what I wished to know and offer what I could for him. He constantly reminded me to smile and live my life on my terms. He never seemed to judge me, even when I seemed angry and upset with him. He took each letter in stride, as if he expected them to be written the exact way they were. He could sense emotion from the way I wrote, and allow it to sting without judgement, offering his understanding and grace in return.

It made me wish that he had lived a much different life. That he had built a business out of his work and met a woman who he could not live without. That his children would have laughed in his arms when he tickled them, and that he would have watched them grow as children do. He would probably be retired by now, and enjoying the later years in life with his loving wife, as they welcomed grandchildren into their modest home.

I pulled out my phone and looked at November 13th. It wasn't far to scroll at all, and that pained me. I marked it as "Michael's day," because I did not know what else to call it. I refused to call it his last day, so just his day was enough for me.

I went through the binder with more purpose and noticed that the end of that was also coming quicker than I was ready for. That meant that at some point, no one cared enough to write about him or those missing. It was an old tale that no longer carried any meaning, and for those that had lived it, it was over. As over as it could be, I guessed. But for people like Rosemary, there wasn't ever enough closure. Never enough time in between when it happened, and the now. Years would not close all the wounds so many had felt, and there would be times those wounds would open back up for sometimes no reason at all.

When I talked with Rosemary about Shawn, I wondered what Michael knew about him. I realized he was never going to tell me what lead him to kill all those people, but maybe he could connect some dots for me which would allow me to understand what I seemed to be missing about Shawn, because clearly there was more to that part of the story.

It was something I would ask him, and because he had so little time left, so did I. I could not wait for the right time, or the right questions. I had to be bold and forward, while maintaining that I truly felt remorse for Michael and his day to come. But that balance was breaking me down and causing my mind to wander not only in my dreams, but as I lay awake as well.

Chapter 34

* * *

September 15th. A little less than two months away, which I figured gave me roughly four letters of back and forth between Michael and I. Usually each letter took about a two-week period to arrive at both my place and his. This was not how quickly I expected this to go, but as Michael said before, the clock doesn't pause because you want it to.

I decided to beat the system some and write more than I had previously. I would write letters while he was answering others, just to give him something to look forward to more often. Maybe that would keep his mind off his date that was rapidly approaching, but seriously, could anything do that?

The first letter, I focused on what he had written to me. He mentioned his final day and time, and I told him that I was sorry to hear about that and asked if there was anything I could do to help, which now seems stupid of me. I mean really, what could I do to help a man who was facing certain death? It wasn't like I had any high connections to the Governor and could pull some strings to ask for a favor or a pardon.

But it seemed like what people would say in a situation like this. People always said things like, "if you need anything, don't hesitate to ask," when something was difficult but I wonder if anyone ever called them out on that to see if they truly meant it. Probably more often than not, they didn't.

I mentioned to him that if he needed to say anything, he could trust me completely with whatever he had. Partially, I was selfishly hoping he would give me a look inside of his mind, to find out what I could not readily see with my own eyes, but truthfully another part of me felt like he may want to say things in the hope of getting them off his mind. Things he could never tell anyone else, I assured him, he could open up to me and I would keep them as if they were never said.

The letter was a little different from the others, as I had more purpose with this one, and if I had to guess, he could sense a change in my thoughts and my concerns. I did not want to scare him more by acting as if this was a tragedy for me as well, but it was hard to hide that.

I've written this man for over a year now, and in that time, I have never once felt like he wanted anything from me, but for me to experience a life of happiness, purpose and to just simply smile through all the hard moments I would undoubt-edly face at different times in my life. He knew enough about life to understand I would face more than my fair share, as he had over the hardened path of his own life. The fact he seemed to accept that so easily made me think perhaps he had it all figured out. Or maybe that he knew that what was to come after he died, had to be better than what he had lived here.

I think he felt this was his penance of sorts. That once he left, and the air left his lungs for the final time, he had done what was required of him. If he died and still had more to serve, maybe what was coming for all of us was not as good as we have always been told. So I asked him what he thought would come, and was he scared.

As he sat in his cell, the only home he had known for some time now, he smiled as he read my letter. It gave him a moment of calmness and he knew he had enough purpose for me but not enough time to show it. That was his simple regret in life. Not that he was where he was, or that he wished he could go back and make any changes to how he had lived, or how he had been arrested, tried and convicted. His regret was now, when he could feel the time slipping away like tiny grains of sand in an hour glass and finally, for the first time in decades, he felt useful. Not having any control over the present was painful for him to accept, more now than ever.

He quickly wrote down his response, fearful that the longer it took the letters to get to me, the less he would be able to share.

He thought about fear, and while it would be perfectly understandable for him to have it, he just didn't. Not yet, and not even after he was told that his final appeals had been denied, signifying an impending ending. He calmly accepted his fate, as if he had been waiting for this day longer than the families of the victims had been.

Dearest Olive,

I hope this letter finds you well.

I need you to know something, and I hope that in your heart, you will feel this. I am not afraid of what is coming, as I have accepted this day long ago when I was a much younger, different version of the man I am now.

Fear should be reserved for what we don't know, and not what we do. I know I am dying soon, and to be afraid of that makes no sense to me. There are plenty of things to be afraid of, but this for me is not one. So I don't wish for you to concern yourself with that day more than you need to. It will just be another day, for which you will have so many more after. I must use the remaining time to live and live I will.

I know you have so many questions and if I can answer them, I will. But there will be ones I can never answer, but not out of fear. Some questions are not meant to be answered, no matter how hard we look and beg and plead.

Know that I am forever grateful for the simple mistakes in life. Had there not been another inmate with a similar name as mine, this ending for me would be very different. Had another student received my name and not you, well, I would have heard nothing more from them long ago I suspect. This was somehow all meant to happen just as it did. Life does that, you know. It happens as it is meant to, without change and without our permission most times. It's like time: no matter what we wish or demand of it, it moves on as it will, paying no attention to us.

He continued with his hope for me to gain from his experiences, but to not judge anyone too harshly. He knew that most people had a hate for him that he fully accepted, but he wanted different from me. He could accept hate from the masses, but from those he felt close to, he wanted not acceptance, but understanding.

I was trying to understand so much, but it was now feeling forced because of the lack of time left to gain more perspective from him. I would do my very best, but I begged him to not judge me if I could not find that understanding as he needed, but to know I would try.

I talked my father into another trip. This time, it was to Greentree Cemetery, where the empty coffin for Shawn was buried beneath the ground. I wanted to see what I felt when I looked at his stone, even if he was miles from where he actually rested.

The stone was simple but had a message that made me tear up. It said,

"May your life on heaven be easier than your life here on earth was."

I cried as I left the cemetery, and my father sensed I just needed a moment to let it out. I know he did not understand why I was so invested in all this, but instead of telling me to let it all go, he surprised me with news.

"Rain, I've been thinking a lot about your situation. I know this was a simple thing at first, and over time it's morphed into something both you and I would have never thought. I want to help you as much as I can, as it is a father's job, but after so much thought, I can only think of one thing I can do, and to be truthful, I am not even sure it's the right thing to do," he said.

He made me promise that if he could somehow pull this off, I had to keep this a secret from my mother for obvious reasons. Lying, as he said, was never a good thing, but if we told her afterwards, it was almost as good as telling the truth immediately. Almost.

"I have a good friend who works for the state. He called me a week or so ago about catching up over the family and work. I asked him if he could grant me a favor, and well, after a week of thought, he called me late last night and said that it was not easy, and I would owe him big time."

It was confusing me what exactly my dad was talking about, but he had my complete attention. I assumed it was something like a trip away after Michael was gone, or maybe a meeting with an old family member of another one of the victims, but that was not it at all.

In all the time I have known my father, there were more days than not that I cared little for what he thought or did. Don't get me wrong, I loved my dad, but we just didn't share that bond of understanding each other well at all. But this? This changed everything.

Chapter 35

* * *

My palms were sweaty, like I had a final exam and had forgotten to study for it. My throat felt like it was in my stomach, and my legs wanted to stay completely still when I told them it was time to move.

It was early morning, and I could hear the birds chirping, greeting us as my father and I walked out to his car. He turned it on and turned the radio down from where he had the volume the night before. This would be another ride for him and I, where we bonded as only he and I could. I felt proud that he was my dad, because never in a million years, would I ever imagine that he could pull anything like this off. Or that he would even consider anything like this, but for whatever reason he had, and he did.

As we pulled out of the driveway, I smiled to myself, a mixed of both nervousness and excitement and the chance to learn more about not just myself, but Michael as well.

The ride was strangely silent for the most part, but as we got off the interstate and drove down the long back road, he spoke.

"You feeling okay, Rain?"

I didn't know how I felt yet, but I smiled at him and said that I was fine.

The massive building came into view, and intimidation took over unexpectedly. I froze and asked my father to stop the car.

"Is everything okay? What is it?" he asked.

"Nothing. I just need a minute. I'm okay, really, I just need to get out for a second," I replied.

I got out of the car, took a deep breath of air into my lungs, and looked over to where the prison walls met the morning sky. It was almost magnificent, had it been built for any other reason. The location made it stand out like no other place. The mountains were to the east, and a hilly plot of acres and acres was to the west. If this were a wedding hall, or even a museum of some sort housing treasures from various artists from all over the globe or galleries of famous sculptures or long-ago artifacts, it would almost be heavenly. But it was far from heaven. As far as one could get. Behind those walls, slept men and women that had done things from petty theft to armed robbery, and even someone who were responsible for the vanishing of the unlucky thirteen from a small forgotten town in the mountains of West Virgina.

I was somehow going to meet with Tarvis Michael Richards. My dad had become my hero for the day, and I swore that I would never forget what he did for me and Michael. I mean, he had to be somewhat out of his mind as well for thinking this was a decent idea, but if I had to guess, it was that whole "I'll do anything for those I love," thing. This was so out of character for him, but he knew it was important to me, and if he thought about it well, which I am sure he did, Tarvis was going to die soon, so it wasn't like he would be able to cause me any issues after November.

I had written him another letter letting him know the news, but I doubt it got there before today. I was just so excited and wanted him to know, but it turns out he did know. Someone had told him that he had a young visitor coming in, and because he had been a model inmate for the years he called this home, certain guards had developed respect for him. Not for who he was on the outside, but rather for who he became on the inside. They were somehow able to separate the two different sides of Tarvis, but I guess when you see the same person day in and day out, you either like them or hate them. Lucky for him, he wasn't exactly hated here.

We walked in and I could hear the echo of everything taking place. Our voices echoed. Our steps echoed. I could swear my thoughts echoed through the entryway, much like they do in your own heart when the world around you is silent. For the distinct power the building displayed on the outside, it seemed anything but elaborate on the inside. A single window stood at the entrance, where there were a few uniformed guards talking and messing around with stacks of papers, as they wrote down whatever it was they did for their job.

I glanced over to where another glass door let the rest of the prison come into view and noticed more doors than I had ever seen in my days. Each seemed to hold back either those on the inside, or those on the outside, but they were clearly not welcoming at all.

My dad could tell I was feeling the pressure and nerves of this moment and grabbed my arm, saying,

"You are okay Rain. There will be someone with you each step of the way. There's nothing to worry about. And if you do feel overwhelmed and need to go? No one is going to think any less of you. This is for you, so don't make it about anything else."

He was right. I was the one in control here, because at any point in my visit, I could stand up, tell the guard I was ready to leave, and basically walk out the same set of doors I had entered from. Michael? He could not. If he was uncomfortable, the best he could do was to walk back to his cell, pull the door closed and sit with himself. It was hardly freedom if you asked me.

I was given a name badge, and realized that I had totally forgotten that to Michael, I was Olive. Instead, they wrote my first name out and I had not even noticed. But at this point, what difference would it make? It wasn't as if he would ever get out and hunt me down. He was weeks away from ever seeing anything other than his current perspective, and who knows what was coming next. I imagined whatever it was, it did not involve haunting me. Although, I guess I would never have imagined the voices and screams I have heard on the trail, and in my dreams either.

The guard's name was Roger, and he seemed like a no-nonsense man, who valued rules and consistency. You could see the other guards respected him greatly, so I imagined the inmates did as well. That, or they feared him, and at this point, respect or fear felt the same to me, so I was able to calm my nerves enough to smile at him.

"Hello, little lady. Listen here. Don't you worry about anything. I will be with you as long as you are here. Ain't nothing going to happen while I am here, okay?" he said convincingly.

He did put me at ease, so that now my concern wasn't for my safety, but more for how the conversation would go with Michael once I was face to face with him.

I had seen photos of the man when he was a much younger person, but I had to believe he changed over the decades. His diet was probably not one he would have eaten daily on the outside. The lack of sunlight would surely cause his skin to be void of the color it granted to you when you were free to feel its warmth. His hair, I imagined, would be thinning, if he even had it still. I would probably not recognize him at all, expect that he would be the one in the prison uniform, with possibly cuffs on his hands, and a guard or two next to him.

I waved to my dad, as he waited in the front entrance way. He allowed this to be my time, like when I met Rosemary. I think he didn't wish to be involved for a few reasons, but mostly because he knew this was my thing. If he felt strange about it at all, he may have pulled the plug and I may not have been as ready for that. I'm sure it was a tough spot for him.

Roger led the way with his hands, pointing towards the direction I needed to go, but he remained by my side as he did. Each time we entered a new area, I could hear the sound of what must have been the inmates on the other side of the walls surrounding us. As doors closed, they slammed against frames and seemed as if they were airtight. I could feel my anxiety rise more, but I just kept telling myself to remain calm and focus on why I was here.

We walked for what seemed like a mile, but really it was nowhere close. Roger told me that we were just about there, and as I looked to thank him, he smiled slightly as if he knew before I did.

The room we came to was closed off, with two guards standing on the outside, one on each side. They, however, were not smiling. They stood there as if they were guarding the president and their job was the most important in the world. Maybe for this place, it was.

Roger motioned for the two of them to step aside just a bit, so he could unlock the door and open the room up to us. I wasn't sure at this point, but I believed Michael was already in the room, or why would there be guards outside and the door locked if there was no reason? Keeping me out of that room was not as important as keeping someone in it, so he had to be there.

"Ma'am, I will be in the room with you the entire time. If at any point you feel the need to get up, please look at me first. If you find yourself ready to go, I ask you to just tap your hand on the table three times. This will be a sign that you are ready to go. Just stay seated, and I will handle everything. Does that sound fair?" Roger asked.

I nodded in agreement, hoping that I could remember

both of those instructions. I would hate to get those backwards and just need a moment to stand and catch my breath, and here he would assume I was finished and ready to leave. I didn't want that pressure, but I had to obey the rules while I was in their house.

He unlocked the door, took a quick glance inside, and then directed me to follow him into the room. I did as I was told and stood almost directly behind him as a child does with their parent when they are too shy to smile at someone.

"Tarvis, remain seated. This is Rain, and she's going to sit here and talk with you for a while. I do not need to remind you of the rules, now do I?" he asked, but really was telling.

He immediately replied that he understood. I could hear his voice calm, gentle but with a little depth to it. He sounded like any other man from Falls City or around the area, and I immediately felt a calmness over me.

When Roger fully entered the room, I could see he was pulling out a chair and sliding it to the left just a bit. He turned to me, told me to have a seat, and winked to remind me I was safe as long as he was there.

As he moved, I could see Michael was seated directly in front of the chair I would take, only a few feet away. He was a bit more worn looking than his photos, but not as much as I had expected. I would definitely walk by him on the street without giving a second glance for fear of what he was capable of doing. This did not seem like a man who had destroyed the lives of so many families. In fact, he could have been an uncle visiting for the holidays, or a father playing catch with his high school son who was preparing for a college tryout.

He looked at me with his soft blue eyes and nodded with a warm smile. As I offered one back, I quickly sat in the seat so as to not make that part awkward. Funny, in meeting the most famous serial killer in all West Virgina, one of my biggest fears was not having to do with him, but rather with my sitting in a chair and making that part feel stranger than it was.

His hands were handcuffed to the table, but they weren't as tight as I had expected. He could move them around some, which probably made this a little less scary for me and less embarrassing for him. I was so wrapped in my own story that I forgot that this could have been hard on him as well. I never asked for his permission, but I guess the fact he was seated here across from me was his permission.

He spoke his first words, at least his first that I have heard for myself,

"Well Olive, or Rain, whichever you prefer. It's an honor to meet you."

At that moment, I had finally realized how he knew my first name. For this entire time he had called me Olive, and I responded usually with Michael, even though for me, I knew his true full name. I just always felt like we should continue with how I had initially greeted him. And to call him Tarvis at this stage felt a bit disrespectful to all we had built. Anyone that knew him as Tarvis had a dislike for him. But when he was Michael? He was free of any hatred from others.

"It's nice to meet you as well," I responded cautiously.

Chapter 36

* * *

I thought back to my home and the comforts I had there. Whenever I was hungry, I could easily open the pantry up and grab whatever I wanted at whatever time I did, right out. When I needed my space, I could head to my bedroom, close the door, and lay on a soft, clean bed, with my laptop close by me, music and all the books I wanted, whenever I decided. If it was a warm day outside? I would just walk down the stairs, need no one's permission, and simply walk out the door, into the sun, and enjoy for as long as I wished.

But here, I even felt that none of that existed, even for me. Yes, I knew I could walk out when I was ready, but it didn't quite feel the same as home. For Michael? His life offered him very little control and even fewer comforts. And with the inevitable approaching for him, I wish he could at least have options with the sun, his privacy, and his ability to eat whatever he wished for a few weeks.

I knew he got a last meal and all, but why just one? He was about to die and he was able to pick just one meal? Not even a full day of them. What would he pick, I wondered? Was asking him too much or would it give him something to talk about?

We settled on Olive and Michael being what we would call each other. He agreed, it was how we were first introduced and why ruin that now with semantics, he said. I liked my name for the most part, but there was something fun about choosing a name that lent some grace to someone else at a time in their life when they needed it most.

We talked. At first it was a little strange, but we quickly settled into a rhythm that made it feel as if we had known each other for years on the outside. He even managed to smile a few times, which was not what I had expected of him, considering his position.

My mind kept focusing on the fact this would be my first and last chance to hear this man in the flesh, but I tried my best to make it not obvious.

For the first ten minutes or so, he asked about school, spoke of the bond I had discovered with my Mee-maw, and asked what had made me smile today. He was always worried I would forget to smile through each day, but I assured him I would not forget.

By this time, I had forgotten the guard, Roger, was still in the room with us. Michael and I were talking about nothing of great importance, so it did not matter. But I then felt the urge to ask more and dive a little deeper into the life he lived, the thoughts he now had, and what, if anything, he would be willing to share with me.

"I met with Rosmary, who was Shawn's mother. I am not sure if you remember her at all, but I felt a draw to meet with her," I said.

Michael sat a little more back in his chair, and responded,

"Yes, of course I remember who she is. She was a decent woman who had a lot of unfortunate hardships behind her and in front of her," he replied.

His response told me that he did not forget anything that had taken place, and that he was well aware of at least some of the victims' families and the collateral damage that was done by those acts of selfishness. I wondered if in some strange way, he felt he had provided a sort of justice for Rosemany, by performing an injustice for Shawn? It sounded bizarre, but could he have thought he was doing a good deed? That would not explain the other dozen wrongdoings, but it would at the very least shed some light on one of the deaths.

"Olive, if I may," he started, but then quickly stopped.

He seemed to have something heavy on his tongue, but the will to toss it from his mouth was held back as was his own freedom in the halls of this place.

"Michael, why? Why are you so relaxed when in weeks there will be nothing left to give? Why? Why are those families all suffering and yet you still refuse to give closure to anyone, including me?" I asked.

His look changed to one of confusion as he continued,

"What closure do you believe you need for yourself, Olive? There are days I am so grateful for having had someone such as yourself to write, but then there are other days where I can't seem to forgive myself for bringing you into something you ought not to be in. I wanted to help you, but perhaps I did the opposite, yet again," he said as he dropped his head.

The opposite of helping when he was trying to help stumped me again. Was he saying that the killings were for rightful reasons? If so, he was delusional beyond words. There is no justification for any of this. Not Shawn, not Pappy's friend Hep, and not even Michael. We all die, but to do so before God has decided, probably comes with severe consequences later on. I know so many people believe this man should die a long, painful and sure death. But what if they are all wrong? What if none of us has the right to decide who lives and who dies? Are they just as guilty and delusional as he was for his crimes?

"I've heard them, Michael. They cry on the trail, and they cry in my dreams, begging me to help them, and I can't. I can't help any of them. I don't know how to. I don't know why they even bother asking me for help. I have no idea what they want from me, or how to begin to get them what it is they want. That's the closure I need," I stated firmly.

By this time, Roger was leaning into me, and whispering that if I needed a second, I could leave the room and collect myself, but I was far too invested in my statement to take a breather and lose the momentum of the moment. I was determined and no longer concerned what he or anyone thought of me now. I truly needed something and if I had to beg? So be it.

He leaned forward, unable to do so fully because of the restraints, but enough that he was as close as he could possibly be.

"Olive, I believe you, and wish none of that for you. I've heard them as well on a few nights here, when no one else was around. When I ask what it is they want, I don't hear another word. It's as if they expect me to figure it out, but without aiding me. I believe you," he said.

Roger must have thought we were both crazy and basically out of our freaking minds. Two people in the same room talking about the ghostly cries that came out of nowhere and begged for help, but refused to say what help? If I was him, I would turn away and pay as little attention to this loony talk as possible.

But we weren't crazy. We weren't hoping to hear sounds and convincing ourselves that we heard what wasn't there. They were real, and the fact that more than one had heard the same sounds, describing them in the same way, from those who were either responsible, victims or perhaps close to where they had ended up, was almost supernatural.

Michael quickly changed the subject, as if he was telling me that he was finished with the talk of the dead. That he wanted no more of the memories he was trying to shake and instead wanted to travel down another path all together.

"Olive, your Mee-maw. Tell me more about her. What one thing did she share with you that you will always remember as you grow?"

At that moment, I knew immediately what the answer was and shared. It was the lesson of the pocket watch, and how it had so much life left in it, when others saw none. It reminded me in that moment of Michael and what was coming soon.

Would his death still bring some sort of usefulness to a world that refused to see any in him? Could I even find a purpose for good in his death, or would whatever good was left be lost like a secret that he would take with him? Could the pocket watch simply run out of the ability to tick?

"Michael, are you ready?" I asked.

He smiled as he always told me to do. That was not just something he did for me to give me guidance that he may not have believed in. His smile was real, genuine and without force. He smiled through a question that ninety-nine percent of the world would not be able to, but somehow, he had figured it out.

"I am almost ready, Olive. Almost. There are a few things I will need to address before my day, but when that day arrives, know that I shall smile until my heart stops beating. Don't you worry about that. They can take my possessions, and my freedom, and yes, the air from the very lungs, but they cannot, and will not take the spirit that is me," he said.

I wondered what he needed to finish, and when he expected to get on that. I know he had nothing but time in here, but that time was ticking away, and with each second of the clock, with each minute that passed by twelve, another chance to complete what was not finished, was gone.

"Can you let me know if there is anything I can do to help you finish whatever it may be so that you are ready? You don't have a lot of time to do much, and I want to make sure that at least you complete everything," I mentioned.

"No, Olive. This is something I need to do on my own

but listen to my words. I promise you this much. I will be finished and ready as I'll ever be. If there is anything left to be done, it was not meant to be completed. But I do have a favor to ask. Not now, though. In time I will let you know," he finished.

Again, I don't know if he had wishful thinking vibes in his head, or maybe he was refusing to accept the reality of the lack of time, as if it was his defense mechanism. He would be dead in just weeks, and that probably changes how your brain works. If you told me Rain, in three weeks' time, at three-thirty in the afternoon on a crisp but sunny day, your life is finished, I don't know that my brain and body would properly process and accept my fate until the very last few minutes when it knew, "Hey, this is really it. Say goodbye to life."

Then, as time seemed to pause in that room while we talked, it was apparent it had not. Roger tapped me softly on the shoulder, leaned in once more, and told me that he was sorry, but that it was time to go.

Michael knew. He seemed to understand Roger's body language and motions almost before Roger even spoke to me. It was what all those years here had taught Michael. Routine was your friend here, because it meant that your day was going to be just like any, except for the final. For Michael, routine was like the blood that flowed through his veins and pumped his very heart. When that routine shifts, so does his life. He will wake up one morning, for a moment feeling as if he needs to do exactly what he has done for most of his life. He may not even realize immediately the severity of the day. But when he does, everything will change. He won't need to brush his teeth if he chooses not to. He could tell the guards to screw off if that was what he really felt compelled to do. Breakfast? Up to him and really, did it matter? His body would never get anything from the short time he had left.

I know if I was on my last day, the last thing I would do was anything routine but somehow, I knew for Michael, it was still a part of his day that he would follow.

Chapter 37

* * *

My father said my name came from the morning I was born. He said that on the way to the hospital it had rained so hard outside, like cats and dogs as he said, that there was no other, more fitting name to give to me. I was either going to be named Rain, Cat, or Dog but my mom was the deciding vote. But that wasn't true. It was a stupid dad joke he told me over and over, or whenever he was around and someone asked me how they came up with it.

My mother told me she chose my name because it signified bringing water to build life. When it rains, all the flowers and trees that depend on it can thrive. Without it, they would die and never have the ability to grow. She felt that I was something needed in her life and had a purpose far beyond what anyone could see when I was born.

So she named me Rain. Looking back, it seems like a lot of pressure to live up to a name that almost demanded I be someone of great importance, but I wasn't anything more than a normal teen. I think either the drugs they gave her in the hospital spoke for her that day, or what she wanted for me, was a hope for greatness that all parents wish for their children, although it might not become a reality.

Still, though, I did like my name. It was unique enough that I could never find it on a souvenir keychain whenever we traveled, and although most people got frustrated when they could not find theirs, I embraced it. Sarah? A hundred of them. Ryan? God, every other one had a Ryan on it. Not Rain, though. Good luck finding a mug or keychain with that name.

When I chose the name Olive for Michael, maybe I was doing what my mother had done. I was giving myself that very same purpose she had wished for me, and that should make her happy that I did what she asked for. But I had doubts she would never understand.

And my dad? What would she do to him if she heard that he took me to the state prison to sit in a room without parental supervision to talk with a serial assassin that had nothing left to lose? I admired my dad for doing what he probably struggled with for a time, but I also wanted my mother to know more about me and how I felt. It was a battle raging inside of me, but at the end of the day, I made a promise to my dad and I intended to keep it.

School was a distraction from having this take over my life, but not having anyone to share this with was a frustrating feeling that I dealt with almost daily. I loved my friends but trusted none of them enough to believe they would not inform the school and have them step in to shut this off completely. With Michael having only a short time left, I could not risk it.

Then, as I arrived home just a week and a half from the end for Michael, I decided it was time. The letter Mee-maw had written to me, was finally telling me that I was ready to open it and here the final words she had for me. It was an emotional moment, but one I embraced fully.

She had been an interesting person for the time I knew her. At times I feared her, while most other times I misunderstood her. Not just for the strange phrase she used as if everyone should understand what in the hell she was getting at, but for the life lessons she tried to give to me in her own way. I believe as I get older they will carry even more weight and meaning for me, and who knows? Maybe I'll adapt a phrase or two of hers and use them on my own kids, confusing them enough to stop and think.

Rain,

There are things I find hard to say. Hell, even when I'm fixin' to leave this God awful world I ain't finding all the right words, but I'll give it a shot.

Mee-maw is dang proud of you. I know I wasn't always easy on ya, and that being around me when you were a small twig was anything else but fun. I was hard because life is hard. Ain't nothing about getting through this makes it feel easier, but a little toughness goes a long way.

You be good for ya mom and dad. I'm proud of your mama. She turned out nothing like me, and good on her! That dad of yours can be a sore on my ass, but he's good stock. He loves you and your mama and that's all I could have asked for. Even if he drives like an old lady.

I want you to remember what we talked about this past year. Find the good when others see only the bad. Ain't a lot of worth in the world other than how you treat folks, so if you are going to be known for something, make it for your worth.

I ain't sure how long my life is gonna be as these old bones are failing me more and more, but I hope that we get to sit and talk a bit more. It's one of the few things I have left that I enjoy. That and biscuits and gravy, but don't tell anyone about that. Ain't supposed to be eatin none of that no more. So keep it our secret.

I'll see you soon, Rain.

Mee-maw

That was the last words she ever said to me. I had no chance to sit with her again as she had hoped for. No time to ask her any more questions, or to hear a story about a broken watch or why she never remarried. She lived her life as she wished with what she had in front of her, and not what she did not.

If anything, I had to admire how she was brought into this world, how she lived it unapologetically, and how she left it. She never seemed to complain about much, other than the dang nurses and doctors that wanted her to change her ways, or my dad's driving. She was never going to give them what they asked for, so she saw it as a big waste of time.

I wonder if she knew she was never leaving that hospital. If she knew, would she have said more or would that last conversation be the exact same as if she did not know? I believe if she knew, she was never going to share that with me. It wasn't her way. She didn't want attention or for others to feel sorry for her at all. She preferred to be in a solitude state, surrounded by mountains that granted life to so many creatures, including her.

She did not mention Michael, or Tarvis as she called him, but I think she knew I would figure that part of my life out for myself. Maybe she didn't want to offer up her opinions or pressure me into feeling the way she felt over the way I did. I am unsure, but what I know is that she never judged me for the lessons I was learning and the way I was going about it.

I placed the letter in the top drawer of my dresser. There would be more times I would need to read over it, and I wanted it somewhere that I would see it daily, for those days I needed a little extra.

The days were passing by, and we as a family were getting ready for the holidays, planning the menu for Thanksgiving, figuring out what family members were still coming, and which would decide to do otherwise this year. I knew one person who would not be present, but I didn't get upset. I smiled instead, because I knew you could take her life from this earth, but you could not take her spirit. She would be here, and that was not debatable.

For Michael, though, he would not make it to another holiday. He would fall short by just days, but maybe to him it would not matter. He had no family visiting him to eat a turkey dinner. No laughing at an uncle who could not stand his wife and would tease her throughout the evening, while she rolled her eyes over and over for all to see. Maybe he could not miss what he didn't know anymore.

My dad figured I would struggle the week he was set to die. He seemed to be doing a little more than his usual. Each day he came home from the office, he would drop by my room and just ask if I was doing alright. Usually, I would act as if I couldn't understand why he would even bother asking, but lately I smiled at him and would say.

"Yea dad. I'm good. And you?"

He would also stop by the post office for me, picking any mail up and bringing it back with him so that I didn't need to guess when one was there for me. When there weren't any, he didn't say anything. It was his way of saving me from any disappointment I had.

Michael had been writing more often, and it seemed as if we no longer had the chance to do a back and forth question and answer system. Thoughts and questions were getting crossed in the mail, as he didn't want to not wait for letters to have an excuse to write.

As each day went on, and letters came in, he continued to battle with himself over what he wanted to say and what he would allow himself to say. I could feel his struggle, and even when I told him to just tell me whatever it was, he could not.

I heard when he told me there would just be questions that would never be answered, and even though I felt that to be a way out of telling the truth, maybe he was right. Maybe he didn't know all the answers, as many as people had wanted.

He never spoke in his own defense at the trial, and most would have thought it was because he did not want to slip up and give away his clear guilt, but I was feeling as if it was more him protecting the true answers that no one would ever know or be able to handle.

The internet was buzzing about Tarvis Michael Richards for the first time in decades. He was mentioned on local news stations, and through the grapevine as people spoke to one and other in casual meetings throughout the town. Most had forgotten him, and for those that had not, he was left in the distant past and all but forgotten. Many had sworn he was executed long ago, and for them this was a shock to hear he was still very much alive.

Alive as he was, he may have lost a part of his being in that courtroom when they announced their decision. Guilty. Guilty. Guilty.

But for a few short years, I felt as if he had found that lost piece of himself—as if it had returned as an offering of forgiveness from whatever or whoever was in charge of granting it. Had he forgiven himself, though, it was something I am unsure of. Maybe if he had, he kept that to himself, knowing it would not matter to anyone here on earth. Besides, would it make a difference when he was lying down on that bed, waiting for the nurse to administer whatever chemicals they placed in your veins so that your heart would beat slower and slower, until it just stopped?

My sleep was being interrupted more, as I desperately tried to stay up for just a few more moments so the time would feel as if it were granting him an added minute or two. Was he sleeping at all? Was he looking at the clock on his wall, wondering if he begged and pleaded enough, would he be able to stop it from moving?

But then, without any input from me, and without a say from Michael, the week came and went. He was on the final seven days of his troubled life, and now it would become real for everyone. The jail was putting the work in for the final preparations, running through tests and shifting around employees to ensure they were adequately staffed with the most professional ones they had. It would be absolutely important to know they could trust everyone with even the smallest of task so this went off without an issue.

I learned that there would possibly be some family of the victims in attendance if they chose. The Mayor of Falls City would also attend, although he was not associated with the original one who had pleaded with the state to send more help.

I asked my dad if there was any possibility for me to be there, explaining that it may be a small piece of comfort to Michael, having just one person there that offered anything near forgiveness. He said there was not a chance. The line had to be drawn somewhere, and as much as he appreciated what I was feeling, he could not allow his child to be a part of this.

That was crushing, and I hated that for me, and for Michael.

Chapter 38

* * *

Mom knew. She somehow either convinced my dad to tell her what all the recent secrecy with the day trips and talks he and I shared were about, or she had heard it from someone else who spilled the secrets.

She wasn't as angry as I thought she would be, but it did place some tension on my father and her. They got along mostly well, except for all the traveling he had done for work. She knew it was work related and important as usual, but she wanted and needed a little more help and attention at home.

Dad was quiet around me now, and I was hopeful that what I was going through was not a reason for his feeling down. We had finally come to the place where I saw him for the father he was, and I could not risk losing that.

At dinner that night, we sat at the table, which we rarely did anymore. Usually one of us was running somewhere, or my brother would throw a fit and ask to watch something and they would give in. Traditional family dinners were a here-and-there thing, reserved mostly for odd nights or holidays, and I had grown used to that. But now, for tonight, mom had prepared dinner, placed it on the dining room table, and laid out plates, cups and utensils.

My father sat down and looked at the table with his hands folded in front of him. Mom was serving the plates and adding drink orders to her chores before she herself would take a seat.

I could feel the energy in the air was off, and as everyone sat there, I knew whatever was going to be said was not going to be good for us. I swore I would not tell my secrets and protect what dad did for me, but I also was not going to sit there and let him take the blame. He was only trying to bond with me, and I appreciated that more than anyone knew.

Mom asked how everyone's food was, and dad just nodded in approval. I looked at them both, but neither was looking up. I picked at my asparagus with my fork, sliding it back and forth into the sauce from the chicken that accompanied it. I felt a sense of nervousness on top of what I was feeling already about the next week of events. But afraid to speak up, I just waited and played with my food. I didn't feel much like eating.

Then my mother, apparently waiting for the right moment to speak, picked this as it.

"Rain, your dad and I are going to take a little break, but we don't want to worry you guys. It's just to allow us time to figure out what we both need to do going forward."

I dropped my fork onto my plate in a purposeful manner that would solicit attention from everyone seated.

"You guys are getting divorced?" I screamed.

Whatever they said after that, I had not heard a single

word. Everything was going wrong in my life and no one seemed to understand I was hurting. Mee-maw leaves after she finds a likeness for me. The stupid school makes us do a project and gives me a convicted serial killer that I feel sorry for, and he's about to die next week. I have strange dreams of screaming and pleadings for help but no one is telling me how to help or what to do. And now, just when I am trying to keep my head above water and my sanity in check, this? They are so selfish, I can't stand it.

It has to be mom. She can't handle that dad is working all the time, but what does she want him to do, quit his job and stay home with her? She's probably more pissed off that he and I are getting along and that dad was the one to take me to see both Rosemary and Michael and she wasn't asked.

How could I? She was always overprotective and telling me what she thought I should do, and I am perfectly capable of making my own mind up.

I needed answers. Rosemary helped me understand more of what I was feeling and she confirmed that either I was not crazy for hearing the same sounds she could, or that we were both crazy and I had company. Either way, it was helpful and that was exactly what I needed.

Michael was teaching me that life becomes more precious with each passing moment, and although I haven't forgiven him, maybe he didn't need me to. But what I did know was that he always gave simple yet relevant advice and that mattered most. And he's being taken away now, and she could never understand that.

I was done. Done eating and done talking to both of them for the night. I could not stand thinking about moving somewhere else, and weekend visits with dad because he worked and mom didn't. I hated to think that everything was changing rapidly without my say, and it made no sense at all. We are family, and while we fight, we should also be fighting to stay together, not pushed apart.

Michael would probably understand me, but it was useless. I had written letter after letter, and I would bet that anything I wrote now would never arrive in time. I couldn't call him, and dad would not let me see him on the last day, so that part of my life was over and it was complete bullshit.

Why is it that adults feel the need to control and uproot everyone's lives to suit their own agenda? I could never leave someone I love. I could never tell my kids they could not do something if their heart demanded they do, and I could absolutely, one thousand percent, never make a decision that would see another human being die, no matter how terrible the crime .

It was growing colder outside, and rightfully so, as it was nearing mid-November and close to the holiday. But with everything going on, I had no idea if we were doing Thanksgiving now at all, or if we were, I assumed we had to act as if everything was just fine and dandy and fake smiles with my parents laughing like the world was right. Well, the world was anything but right. It was a gigantic mess, with no one working towards cleaning it up. My friends had all mostly experienced divorce and had stepfathers and stepbrothers and sisters. Some got along well enough, and others hated their step-people. I was not going to like anyone my mom or dad brought into our lives. This was their issue and not mine so how dare they ask me to accept someone cozying up to them and pretending to like me.

I feel asleep hard. It wasn't my intention but with all the crying I had done, my body told itself it was time to shut down. The dreams were vivid tonight. I saw my parents fighting at my school over a play I was in, and I wanted to run and hide but my legs would not go. All my friends were looking at me and it was absolutely embarrassing beyond belief.

Then I saw Michael, but he too was crying as he sat in front of a plate of food. It was a moment where I saw weakness for the first time in him, as if he was giving up and yet struggling to let go fully. He was all alone, and hardly touching his plate of food, although I cannot remember what it was.

After that, those chilling cries had resurfaced, and at first, it was just the faint sound of sadness, but then it became clearer as whatever it was got closer than I would have liked. I could hear words like never before, this time asking me kindly for help. In my dream, I could only hear them, despite how close they really were to me. I wasn't scared, though. In fact, this time I felt their pain over the fear I normally had. They weren't trying to hurt me but were gently pleading for me to set them free.

How? How could I set them free if I had no idea who they were and what needed to be done? They refused to answer me, which made this all the odder. I wanted to help and begged them to guide me to where I needed to go, but they drifted off into the loneliness of my thoughts, and with that, I was awake, in a hot sweat.

My blankets were soaked and when I tried to get out of bed, I could tell I was sick. My head was throbbing from top to bottom, and my muscles were tight and achy. Everyone was still fast asleep so I tried not to disturb any of them, but then I started vomiting all over my floor.

Mom raced in and immediately got me a trash can to throw up in. She went back to the bathroom and grabbed a towel from under the sink, warmly wet it, and brought it back, placing it gently on the back of my head and neck.

Dad then came in and asked what was wrong.

"I don't know, she's sick. I got her," mom said.

I think dad wanted to do more but knew this was what my mother wanted to be doing at that very moment. He had to allow her this, even if he wanted to step in.

Of all the weeks to get sick, this was the worst possible one. I had to believe it was stress-related, but mom kept saying,

"Honey it's okay, you just have a little flu is all."

I cannot be sick. This cannot be happening. People needed me. Michael needed me, although I had no idea of how to get anything to him. But he needed to know that I was with him, even in spirit, when his clock was up. No person should die, feeling as if they are alone and uncared for. And I had no idea if he knew I cared for his soul and begged God to let him be forgiven, even if no one else wanted to.

Mom stripped the bed of the sheets and blankets and told me she would bring me something to use until she could clean those for me. I just lay there on the floor, trying not to move too much as the slightest motion made me feel as if I would throw up even more.

I began to hate my life and wonder what I had done to deserve all this now. Was it because I was sympathetic to Michael? Or that I was supposed to understand the crying better and figure that out but for whatever reason, could not? Give me a break, I kept thinking to myself. Let me get better, get through this week, and then dump it all on me. I promise, whatever He has to give me, I will deal with it later, but as tough as I can be, I need a little grace.

I must've slept the entire day away, because when I finally got up again, my bed was made and I was back in it, but it was still dark outside, or dark again. My mother was downstairs and I could hear Christmas music playing in the kitchen. I felt it was always too early to play that before even Thanksgiving was here, but she would always say,

"Rain, when they make a playlist of all Thanksgiving songs, I will gladly keep the Christmas ones out of the kitchen until after."

Six days. That is the official countdown for Michael. Just six more days of life, and then he will be placed in a box, buried, and forgotten about, unless someone decides to write a documentary on him at some point. Six days of breakfast, lunch and dinners. Six days of reading the frantic letters I have written to him, and six days of waking up, and possibly, going to sleep.

In that time, I could have a vacation at the beach and be

home. Our team could win a game on a Friday and then play again the following week. It would be the number of days off from school over the Christmas break, which never felt like enough. Probably because six days are not enough.

And then, with each passing tick of the clock, and each time it completes a full turn around, the time shrinks.

Six-damn-days.

Chapter 39

* * *

I heard my sophomore English teacher say once that memories told us more about who we are than any words we could ever string together. I felt that.

It's the smaller moments I think about most in my life, and those are the times I would live over if I had a chance. Not the trips, although they were exciting and full of adventure in their own way for sure, and I don't wish to discount all the money and planning my parents put into those. But if you think about it, the moments where we have to pick between going left over right that lead us down a road we have never traveled before and would normally not have, or someone walking by us in the hallway of our school, smiling just to be kind at the time we needed that most, can change a lot.

I began to appreciate small moments more, and recently I believed I could keep memories of those closer to where I could access them whenever I liked or needed. They are mostly a comfort when comfort seems too far away, and the ability to sit in those thoughts, and feel almost exactly how I felt when they actually took place is pretty comforting.

I think an awful lot about the days remaining, and how I will look back on them as I grow older and build a very different life from the one I have now. Realizing I do not wish to have terrible thoughts as a reminder of what is happening, I try to focus on smiling through the frustration, sickness and unknown. Michael would appreciate that, and it would be the least I could do for him.

This flu is sucking the days from me as I sleep vital hours away that should be spent sending up prayers towards the sky that whatever is out there, accepts Michael for the bad that he has done, and the good he has tried to do. But I'm on this bed, and sometimes the floor when I have trouble pulling myself back in bed, struggling between freezing under layers of blankets and then sweating the last bits of water from my skin as if my body is bipolar.

My mother continues to bring in warm ginger ale that she stirs to remove any of the bubbles from carbonation, a packet of bland salter crackers and occasionally, a new wet cloth to place on my neck. None of which seems to be doing much of anything for me. I am dying. I feel like each muscle in my body is screaming at me, and my stomach is beating itself up over and over.

I don't handle being sick well at all, and when I say I am praying for death, I mean it at the time. But surely, I don't truly wish to die. I just want things to get back to where I can eat normal food and walk around the house without feeling like I am stuck inside the same air that probably started this flu.

Normally, I would just lay there, not seeing a light ahead leading to where I am back to the normal Rain I am. But this time, I know I will see a way to getting better. My body will slowly allow me to eat solid foods, and it'll get back to feeling the need to get up and walk around and feel fresh air against my face. That is something I am aware of more than in the past where dying felt like the only option.

But when someone is faced with dying, I am sure they would trade where they are for where I am, and I feel a bit selfish not understanding that entirely. I'm trying to be sympathetic to not only my situation, but to Michael's, and even to the families of the victims that have to relive those terrible moments for another day, when they watch the man responsible for their horrid disruption, close his eyes and vanish from this place as their loved ones had.

The difference is, though, that someone will know where Michael will rest I don't know if he will be buried at the prison he dies in, unable to escape its walls even in death, or if someone in his bloodline who has more mercy than most, takes him back with them and buries him in an unmarked grave so that he can rest in peace without the strange, fascinated, loony people visiting him in awe.

Dad came in and checked on me, but instead of dropping things off and leaving the room so that I could continue to sleep, he sat down next to me and talked. I can hear him, but I'm not sure if he knows that or not. It doesn't matter, though, as he isn't looking for back-and-forth as much as he is looking to perhaps ease my mind by easing his.

"Rain, I know life has been unbalanced for you lately, but I promise you, it will get to where it needs to. I won't promise it'll ever make sense for you, but it will take you where it needs to. I hate seeing you sick, and more so when you are concerned about so many other people. Don't concern yourself for mom and dad, though. We have struggled through many hardships in our marriage, and so far we are batting a thousand coming through those issues," he starts.

I am breathing as if I am asleep, because I know I'm too sick to talk about this in a way that I want to, but I am on his every word. He continues on,

"I'm proud of you, kid. Not only did you manage to make an old cranky and worn out, but loving woman happy at the end of her life, you found a way to offer respect and humility to someone who I don't know truly deserves it. You are somehow able to see things in others that others cannot see in themselves or anyone else. That is a true gift you have, and one I hope you never let go of. Be who you are, my rain drop, and nothing short of that."

I want to cry, but there is nothing left in me. I have sweated all my tears out through my blankets, and drinking any liquids doesn't sound like a very good idea at the moment because the second I do, it's coming back up.

Dad pats me on the back as if I was still his six-year-old little girl, but it's not annoying as it would be normally. It's precisely what I need from him, but I cannot even thank him for his words. Hopefully he knows me well enough to understand I appreciate him in this moment of time. Maybe

I haven't shown that enough to him or my mother, but I will as soon as I can shake this off.

He leaves the room, and I somehow manage to pull myself up just enough to pull one of those white crackers that I swear no one would eat if they weren't as sick as me, and take the smallest nibble I can possibly take. I cannot sit here feeling like this, so if medicine isn't going to fix this soon, I will find a will to figure it out, even if it kills me.

Five days. What is going through his mind now that he has just five days of twenty-four hours left to go? Is the realization starting to creep in, or does he look at this as another five days to be above ground, as he seems to have such a positive outlook on this situation for which he has zero say in?

I know one thing, though. Someone will know if his positiveness was all for show as his days count down. If it isn't for show, he will smile as they place the needle into his arm, unafraid of what comes next. But if he is hiding his true fears, oh they will come out. No one could continue to hide a fear like that from those around them for the remainder of their time. They would either break down in a crying fit, begging for just a little longer, or they may try to negotiate, perhaps disclosing what everyone has been after for years and years, thinking it may get to the right ears, and make a difference that it really had no way of doing.

On day five, I find myself finally able to take a small sip from the water bottle placed on my nightstand. The crackers that are now going stale from being opened and left out are still a welcoming break from an otherwise empty stomach.

At this point, food doesn't sound appetizing in the least, but something with little flavor and even less substance is just what I need.

I'm determined, and when I feel that, I want to find a will to do exactly what it is I wish. What I wish is to get through the next few days, to find my strength and stomach, and finish what I started. Otherwise, I don't truly know how I would feel, sitting here in bed suffering, while a man that I have learned to know and gain insight from, is breathing heavy, deep breaths, maybe trying to savor one over all the others.

Dad can see I'm pushing through, but he is also well aware of why I am.

"Rain, I know where your heart is, but trust me on this. Tarvis knows that you will be there in spirit, and that will be enough to give him a little calm. You don't need to rush yourself, kiddo. Get better, and when this is all over, we will talk about whatever it is you wish. This will all pass, I promise," he says.

He's wrong. It won't pass. A passage of time does not mean it gets lost in the air and floats away into nothingness. Not this. I will carry a little of this for my lifetime and remember the lessons both he and Mee-maw shared and the lessons I stumbled across on my own while trying desperately to under-stand a man that probably doesn't even understand himself.

And then, almost as quickly as the other days this week have come and gone, day five comes to the final hours, where the brilliant sun starts its game of hide and seek just under the horizon. I sip on the two-day old ginger ale, telling myself that we are done vomiting, and that tomorrow we are back to eating more solid food, even if we aren't ready.

I'm drained, and my body aches under the blankets that I've both had on my body and then thrown off me, but I am feeling like it's going to be a longer night of fighting to sleep, for good or bad.

I can hear my stomach growling in the hopes I'll hear it crying and feed it the nutrition it's so badly seeking, but I swear I need just another morning to appear before I take that chance. If I take a step back by rushing this, I will most certainly not make it through the next five days as needed.

I can't remember exactly what time it was that I dozed off, but I can remember how crazily my dreams danced around in my head. They were unlike the crying ones where I am on a trail enjoying nature and they show up begging me to hear them. No, these are the type of dreams that make me feel scattered and mentally off. Birds are flying towards my hair and pecking at the ends for no reason I can find. Fires are starting all over the mountains behind Mee-maw's property, signaling Indians from miles away to come prepared for battles that will need to be fought on the soil their ancestors have died on. There is a priest that is trying to shush the birds away as I start to cry, and he's growing frustrated with God, asking him why he won't grant him the strength needed to fend them off.

There's one Indian who stands out amongst the others. He's strong-looking, painted war stripes along his cheekbones and the top of his chest with vivid reds and greens showing off against the bronze of his skin. His eyes can see a thousand miles away, and he's patiently standing while everyone else is frantic. The priest sees him and asks me if I am afraid. I answer him,

"Should I be? What would he possibly want from me? I have nothing to give to him, so therefore I am of no use."

But the priest, he is afraid. I can see his lips quiver as he looks around him at the other Indians who are now beginning to close in. But I am still unafraid. I feel no desire to scream or run in a direction that will give me the best chance to escape.

I lock eyes with the chief, and his expression turns from one of calm, to one of regret. He knows he has a purpose for remaining there but seems to have doubts on why I need to.

I start to walk over to where he is, at the highest point to the trail in front of me. The priest begs me to stay where I am, but I will not. The pull is strong and I need to ask the Indian what I need to do to set the lost souls free. As I approach, the warriors that he has under his power, open a path for me that leads me straight to their leader.

In my mind, I should be frightened and questioning why I am without fear, but I cannot. There is such a blanket of calm covering me and reminding me with each step on the trail, I am where I need to be.

Finally, I arrived at his feet. He looks down at me and then looks over the valley below where we stand. He doesn't say a word but takes his hand in a sweeping motion out over the trees. I turn to look where he is directing his energy, and notice that there is an area filled with Japanese Honeysuckle from the edge of the trail and into the brush to the west.

Finally, his mouth opens and he speaks to me.

"Invasive as it may be, the honeysuckle has a reason to be here. It did not grow in this area on its own, but was brought over against its will, and forced to settle where its seeds were placed. It will remain here, long after it is picked and pulled from the ground in which it rests," he says.

I am trying to understand what he means, but I am having trouble following him. He stops talking, and motions for me to have a closer look at where he has directed me. I look at him and he nods as if I must do this and that it will be okay.

Strangely I trust this man, as if he is not intending to harm me, but to heal me. Maybe it's the flu I have had that he needs me to push from my body. Perhaps it's more about the mental healing I need from the struggles I have faced since meeting Michael. But I do as I am instructed and begin to walk through the picker bushes that scrape at my clothes, and the high grass that is allowed to grow as high and deep as it pleases.

When I get close enough to see what he needed me to, I can hear the faint calling that I have not heard in some time. The sounds of the crying begin but is quickly replaced with a strange request for help. As I lean in to understand better what it is saying, I stumble and fall into the weeds and begin to struggle breathing. My heart is racing and I fear I have made a grave mistake by trusting the chief and not listening to the priest that begged me to go the opposite way.

And then, I woke up. My body feels the stinging from the weeds poking and scratching at me, but there are no marks when I examine my skin. They feel like tiny needles have pierced my arms and legs without leaving a single mark.

It's three-forty in the morning, now four days and some odd hours from Michael's day.

Chapter 40

* * *

I tell mom that I want to try something else. Anything but crackers and warm ginger ale, please. Give me toast or oatmeal, but something that I can eat and keep down.

Thankfully, my body doesn't seem eager to reject it, and I finally feel as if I have turned a small corner, hopefully on the way to healing enough that I can shift my focus on the final four days.

The dream about the Indian and the warriors on the trail has confused me, because I didn't go to sleep thinking about any Indians at all. I know that sometimes when I am thinking of something and pass out for a night's sleep, whatever I had on my mind last, would invade my thoughts as I rested. That was a pretty normal occurrence and made sense to me, but this absolutely made little to no sense at all.

Michael was writing letters nearly all his days now. The guards would check in on him, and he would be sitting there on his bed with a stack of paper next to him, writing for hours on end. But he was not mailing them. Maybe it was about writing to the families with some insight into his sadness and hope for them to forgive him if they could find it in their hearts. It could have been that he had a lot to get out of his own heart and needed to write it before he had no chance to set it free.

His demeanor didn't seem to be changing much, to be as crazy as those working at the prison had expected. They had executed people before, and those men seemed to become entirely different people when the final weeks of their lives approached. Some would pray to God as if He was going to protect them after a lifetime of not believing. Others would grow angry, feeling as if they were being wrongfully judged for crimes they had never committed, despite the overwhelming evidence presented at their trials.

But for Tarvis Michael, he hadn't shifted either direction. For him, it was another day that he woke up with a consistency that still needed to be maintained for some sort of order to remain in his life. The only difference anyone could see in him was the letters. He had always written down thoughts, or maybe a letter here or there for some crazed person that swore they believed he was innocent or wanted his autograph to sell someday after he died.

He had a nicely stacked pile of envelopes on the corner of his bed, each with a name and address written across the front. They were stamped, and ready to be mailed, but he had not done so yet. Maybe this was him waiting until the very last second to send for some crazy sendoff, or it could have been a denial that he was going to continue to live, believing that life was never going to end, even though clearly, it was.

Being calm in the face of death takes someone with either a clear conscience or someone who has a mentally ill mind that believes he is not truly dying. I can't say I ever felt Michael was ill at all, and in fact after meeting with him, I was certain he had more than likely come to terms with the past, and understood he could not change any of it, so why fight it.

Dad was feeling down about how things were going, but I think that was mainly because he knew he had a chance to make things better, only he did not know how. It was a far different situation from what Michael was facing, so I knew he was fighting with himself over what do to, what not to do, and how to let mom understand this was not what he wanted at all. She seemed to be slipping away the more he tried to pull her in, and that confused his mind greatly. If she wanted him around more, here he was. If she needed him to take a bigger role in helping to raise us, that was exactly what he was now doing, but it felt like he was fighting a battle between hoping for the best and doing too little, too late.

I had two men who were both influential in my life, who both shared a great deal of knowledge and an understanding of both what and how I saw things, but one was lost and had a lifetime in front of him, while the other was at a perfect ease, and was dying in days. I wanted to help them both, but I was unsure I could assist either. This caused me a great deal of frustration and sadness, but I knew I could not give up just yet.

I thought back to Shawn, and how he was the final victim. I wondered why Tarvis Michael had not only chosen him, but had left something so incriminating, as if he either got lazy or slipped up. It didn't match the pattern of the others, where there was so little evidence, that had Shawn not been killed, who knows how many more would have gone missing.

Shawn had a temper and was oddly strong for a young man. He possessed a power that could have and should have been able to at least put up a struggle strong enough that Tarvis Michael would have shown signs of. But there were none. It seemed to baffle not only the authorities, but the jury as well. They did not come to a conclusion of guilt quickly. It took them a lot of debating from several members, who swore they had to get it right or they would not be able to convict a man.

I think because he failed to speak in his defense, that sealed the deal for the remaining members of the jury that were holding out. How could a man who was innocent, and faced such terrible charges and consequences, not say a word to save his freedom, and possibly his life? He had to have felt such guilt that to defend it seemed like a waste of a life. Guilty, by way of silence, was how the papers wrote it.

I sat up when my mother brought in some more solid food. The dream I had was intimidating to me, and caused me to feel as if there was a message there, I could not find the answer to. That put me in a mindset that scared me, and it showed. When mom asked what it was, I told her I just needed dad.

She was not happy with that answer and probably felt as if I was siding with him and pushing her away. Maybe I was, but honestly at this point I didn't know what end was up, and what everyone expected me to act like with all this damning going on around me.

So, she walked out of my room as if I had disappointed her to no end, and as she was walking down the hall, she called my dad to come up. I could not hear what they were saying in the hall as they were whispering, but it wasn't like the soft whispering you hear people do when they are trying to just keep others from hearing because you respected their need for privacy. It was more a whisper that had elements of frustration and anger, where I could hear the whispering tones raising up a level and then another, before my mom said,

"Fine. I don't care. It's always about you and you looking good. Do whatever you want."

I had rarely heard my parents argue, outside of planning a vacation somewhere where one wanted to go to the beach and one to the mountains, but they weren't arguments with hints of anger. They were mostly ones with differing opinions. This, however, had a substance behind it that I could feel in my bones.

So when my dad came into my room, I could see on his face the look of defeat based on defiance. He had lost something during that hallway conversation, but in exchange for that, he had gained something for me. I found that to be a tough spot for him, but he had choices to make, and if my mom was going all in with walking away, he was going to pick a few battles to where he could wage a silent war to gain a little of what he had lost.

"Rain, how are you feeling? Any better?" he asked.

"I'm getting there. I need to get better, dad. I have to somehow get something to Michael. Dad, I need your help," I replied.

He looked at me and smiled.

"Listen, you get better. Worry about that. Let me worry about the rest, okay?"

I had no idea what he meant but I trusted him. Maybe the guy he knew could get one final letter to Michael for me and I could finally let him know that even if he didn't want it, and even if I was probably not the person he was seeking it from, I was able to forgive him. I had to let him know before they decided time was up. It would be my last chance to give him some peace that he probably needed at this point in his journey.

Dad sat down and I told him I had a dream, for which I could not gain any insight into. He didn't judge me as I thought he may, but instead he sat there and listened. He hung on every word, showed a true interest when I felt as if I was babbling, and said not one word until I was finished entirely.

When I was done speaking, and honestly feeling like a freaking idiot after hearing what I said out loud, I pulled a blanket up to my face, embarrassed for all I had shared and waiting for my dad to tell me he had no damn idea of what my dream meant and how could he? But surprisingly that was not the reaction he gave to me.

"Well, honey. I think dreams can mean a lot most times, and nothing other times. If I had to guess, though, this was not one of times it meant nothing. Think about all you have invested in this whole Tarvis mess. You had a bonding moment with Mee-maw over a binder that for some reason, she felt she needed to share with you. You were never able to get more on that from her because she passed away before you were done. Then you met Rosemary, who probably hadn't talked about any of this in a generation of time. She led you to believe she had heard voices that maybe were in her head, and maybe weren't.

On top of that, I allowed you to sit with him, and to ask whatever it is you did. Why, I don't know but I just knew it was something you had to do, even if I had not been able to fully justify it for myself. Sometimes we just have these overwhelming feelings, and we either ignore them and wonder forever, or go with them and deal with the consequences, for good and bad," he said.

Mom knew. Maybe that was part of the reason she was leaving him. Maybe she felt like he placed me in a spot where things could have gone wrong for me but thankfully didn't. Not just physically wrong, but more a lifetime of issues because I had spoken to a man who was at one time the most hated man in all the state. And who could blame her for hating that? But it was not how it went. Dad knew, with his instinct, that had I not had that chance, I may never have forgiven myself. I had to get closure, and maybe he thought that meeting would do it. It did not, in fact, but it helped.

"What if your dream was telling you it was time to let go? In some odd way, the Indian chief could have been telling you to go, when you took it wrong. How would you know? In dreams, we learn lessons but sometimes there are strange oddities added for who knows what reason.

If it was not telling you to let go, it was surely telling you too not. Why? Well, maybe time will reveal that answer. I wish

I knew more for you honey. I really do. But that is what I got. I may not always make the best decisions, and I may struggle with those decisions long after I should if I had made better choices, but I believe sometimes we must go with our heart. What is your heart saying to you, Rain?"

I had to think about that. Being confused was hard enough, but I was still struggling to shake my sickness. Although, I was feeling much better and more aware than I was just a day or so ago. But what was it I needed to get my mind back to a place I loved? Because all this confusion and dreaming was causing me a lot of frustration and I needed it to simply end.

And just like that, I found myself understanding what I needed. I knew as soon as I paused long enough to see through the dream, after hearing the cries for help, and meeting with Michael. I knew exactly what I needed to do, and I needed Dad's help one more time.

Chapter 41

Three days. Seventy-two hours of time left in a human's life, and I'm over here worrying about getting better from a silly sickness, and that my parents sprung a potential separation on me. I felt selfish for caring so much, but I guess the hardest issues we face are just like those that anyone else faces, at least for how we see them in that moment.

But with each twenty-four hour passing, two things happened in my life. I first got that much closer to feeling more myself so that I could feel alive once again, and Michael got those same hours closer to not feeling so alive.

Perspective combined with time was fascinating to me. You could look at time in several ways if you could just sit and allow it to show you. What one person was losing in time, another was gaining. Seeing the start of a project for one was also similar in time to seeing the ending. Getting married to the love of your life one day would eventually lead to having to say goodbye at some point in time, and you had two options.

You could live each one as if it was a new day by their side or see it as one day closer to an eventual ending to what you once saw as the best moment of your life.

Mom and dad were there. They had found each other, fallen deeply in love and married, and each day for them was probably exciting at first. Then routine settled in, and those once treasured days of butterflies and excitement began to blend together and feel like every other one in front of them. There wasn't a great deal to look forward to with routines other than the same old same old, and that probably kills more marriages than anything.

If I ever get married, I hope it's to someone that refuses to quit. Someone that understands we have a certain number of days ahead, and each one we see as routine and mundane, is wasted. Eventually, we'll reach the point where half of the days we'll ever share have already passed—and we won't even notice. Mee-maw talked about Pappy as if he was still the love of her life, just as he was the day they married. For sure they had hard times, she would say, but she preferred a hard day with him over an easy day without him. That is the love I want at some point in my life.

Dad knew what I needed, and he intended to do what he could to help, even if that meant a bigger step back in his own life. He most likely saw it as a gift to me, and a way to break a routine in his own life, that by now felt as if that was all he had left.

I had to believe that by now my mother understood more of what was happening, and that my dad had already suffered for it. Yet he was ready to do it all again, if it meant they could take another step back—because, in his mind, it was somehow just.

"I did it, Rainbow. We are all set," he mentioned as he walked past my room.

Rainbow. He hadn't called me that since I was maybe five or six. I didn't need to say a word to him, as he knew without me having to, that I was thankful and knew how much he had done to ensure it was possible. I admired my dad in that moment more than I can ever remember admiring anyone. He knew what his daughter needed, and not just for her curiosity, but for her mental health. He could have easily said no, and that it was insane to think any of this was a good idea and what would people think if they knew? But instead, he saw a need for my soul to close a chapter that I never intended to open but desperately needed to.

I was going to visit with Michael one last time. It wasn't clear to me what I would be able to do and how long I would be able to stay, but I was granted the ability to visit with him prior to, and that would be my final attempt at quieting the cries in my dreams.

Hearing that news pushed me to heal quicker than I normally would have. I found myself leaping from the bed I had stayed in for days and moving things off my nightstand that reminded me of how sick I was. It was time to open my blinds and let the sun in, and the sickness out. A new day was upon me, and I wasn't going to allow it to go by wasted anymore. Enough was enough, and with only three days remaining, I had a lot of work to do.

On the news playing in the living room, there were updates on the coming execution, and where I normally paid the news no mind, I was glued to anything I heard that spoke of it. It was a much bigger deal than I had thought it would be, because it had been so long and no one seemed to care until there was something new to care for.

The woman mentioned that there were protestors standing outside the prison gates with posters in their hands, waving at the cameras and anyone that was within a distance to see and hear their message. Dozens of people on two sides stood their ground, each claiming they were right in their beliefs.

One side reminded everyone that murder was murder, and to put a man down was not going to sit well with God almighty. The other side, saw it as a long overdue penance that needed to be carried out, and would be so help them God. An eye for an eye type of view, if you will.

It looked mostly peaceful, but there were occasionally a few people who were a little bolder and louder in their beliefs on the side that swore he would burn in hell as soon as the execution was complete.

How anyone could celebrate death like this, I would never know. Even if he had done what they said he did, and even if he had decided this was exactly what he deserved, I would never be able to administer the final lethal drugs that ended another human's life. It was like playing God, and as my Mee-maw often said,

"God doesn't like anyone doing the work He has planned."

My thoughts were a bit scattered, and the idea of having

to drive through those protesting for and against, scared me a bit. I just wanted to see Michael once more without any drama or worry for my own safety. The news would clearly be there, and I was not looking to make a name for myself as the kid who believed a serial killer was anything but guilty. I don't know if he was or wasn't, but that didn't matter to me anymore. It was about human compassion and a hope that whatever comes next for that man, could have a little mercy if he truly felt sorry for all that had happened. But only he knew if he was truly sorry or not, and nothing I would or could say, made a difference.

Mom wasn't exactly ignoring me, but she was standing at a distance, both physically and emotionally. That made me understand she was not in agreement with my decisions, or what my father was able to once again pull off. I got it, but what she couldn't see was the turmoil I was facing inside that was eating me alive, and I wanted to put that to rest for good.

Two days. My notebook was ready, and I had looked over the binder a few more times, not really sure what I was looking for, but possibly for inspiration and a reminder to myself that lives were lost, and that was something no one could change.

I also decided to bring the old pocket watch, more as an inspiration for what I wanted to achieve here. If I could see the good in that dirty old watch, I could see the need for Michael to have his forgiveness, and maybe allow him to understand in the final moments he faced, he still had a way to bring something positive to those around him, and to the families of those that suffered and lost greatly.

Dad was quiet, and over the past day, had been running what he said were errands more frequently. Where he first tried to be around mom as much as humanly possible, he now shifted to giving her space and time to reflect on what her decisions could change in all of our lives.

I tried my best to stay out of their issues, but it pained me to think they were giving up on something without appreciating what their children loved about the dynamic of our family unit. I would forever be the child from a broken family, and I hated to think that there could possibly be a way to save this, and it was being selfishly overlooked because of some stupid ego.

That made me wonder. Had Michael been silent because of ego? Did he feel that if he had decided to defend himself, but because of overwhelming evidence been convicted still, it would have made him appear weak and afraid? He, for the short time I corresponded with him, showed me no fear. No sense of weakness whatsoever.

But I still had questions about Shawn I wanted to ask him. He may not be in much of a mood to talk about particulars, my father reminded me, so whatever you do, don't take it personally. Easier said than done, as I was the one who needed answers.

So I decided to write down all the thoughts and questions I had, not knowing how much time I would have with him with all the planning that was going on for that day, but I figured it was better to be overprepared versus not having anything ready and having more time than expected. What if he and I just sat there with nothing to discuss or go over, and for the rest of my life I would need to sit with the fact I had most of the last moments with him and did nothing with them, so he died wondering if he should have maybe asked someone, anyone else to be with his final thoughts.

I also prepared a few bible verses, unaware of what his true beliefs were, but again, it was always better to be safe and have something. If he would allow me to, I could recite a few to maybe ease his fears, but when faced with what he was going to see, he would need to be a believing man to understand it was all going to be okay for him somehow. I was still struggling with a God that would sit back and watch as his creatures decided who lived and who died, and did nothing to step in, but I guess that's why it's called faith. We have to believe there is a reason for everything that happens and in the end, we will understand it clearly.

I asked dad when he finally arrived back home, if he was okay. I hadn't asked my father that in forever, if I ever even did, but I knew he was struggling and seeing a man who always smiled struggling alone was difficult for me to watch. I didn't feel sorry for him, but rather frustrated that he tried too hard to make everyone happy, and if he failed, was it entirely his fault or was it that others had a say in whether he succeeded or not? There are many factors in living a completely happy or sad life, and for most, it's a balance they naturally get. For dad, though, he seemed mostly happy and rarely had a negative thing to say about anyone. But here he was, down on his happiness and acting as if he was perfectly fine. I knew him, and I could see, he was not.

"I'm fine, kiddo. Don't you worry about me. Let's figure this out for you and get you back on track. Sound like a good plan?"

Even in the sadness he hid, he still put me and my needs before his happiness, and maybe that was because when I was happy and content, so was he.

For some reason, the final two days went by as if they had blended together and no one told me. We got to one day, as if a vacation was ending and the time seemed to jump from the first day to the last one as we somehow had to come home when we swore we had not spent an entire week by a pool already.

I imagined that as the day came, and the last few faded into a distant memory, Michael was not the same relaxed person he had been. I could not begin to see a way he could still be calm, and ready for what was now, just hours away.

For some reason, I could almost imagine it was my last day, and instead of him sitting there on the edge of a bed, it was me who was waiting for them to come in and tell me it was time. My body felt a nervous energy it had never felt before, and I had to quickly shake the thoughts out of my head, but for the short few moments, I felt what Michael probably felt inside.

"Rain, you ready? Going to warm the car up. Whenever you are set, we can go. Take your time," my dad said.

It was time. My backpack was organized, but I knew they would probably not allow it to be brought into the prison walls. Hopefully they would allow just a few things in, if not the entire bag. It's not like I had a bomb in my backpack to break him out, but I guess rules are rules.

I double checked to make sure I was not leaving anything behind, then took a long look around my room where I had spent so much time researching and reading both on Michael and his letters, and then headed towards the garage.

Mom wasn't there that morning, which was odd to me, but I guess she didn't want to be any part of this, and that probably made it easier for all of us.

The car was warm, and the sun was out, as if it was guiding us along the interstate knowing exactly where we were going. I had nerves of course, but I also had hope that today would release me of any burdens I had that I had not asked for. Let today be a day of forgiveness for some, acceptance for others, and peace for those that beg for it. I know I probably needed a little of all three of those.

Chapter 42

* * *

The mountains of West Virgina are something I've seen every day of my life, but today on that ride, they seem to have something to say to me. I watch them as we drive through the land they stand proud over, allowing us a glimpse into their magnificent strength, eternal beauty, and the secrets they have been hiding for hundreds, if not thousands of years.

The stories they could tell if they were free to share, would be earth shattering and probably change how we view humanity as a whole.

Each mile we cross, I count down the time we have left in the presence of a man who has waited so many years for this day to eventually come and go. Not that he was waiting impatiently, but I am sure there were days he imagined it and what it would feel and mean to him.

As we get close enough to where I can see the gray of the prison come into view, the traffic starts to back up for what seems like a mile and a half at least. There are cars waiting in line, and it could only be for one reason. They are all here to either protest from one side of the opinion or the other, or to hear when the bell rings, signifying that Tarvis Michael Richards is officially declared dead.

My anxiety about having to wait in this line of cars is through the roof, but dad swears to me it looks worse than it is.

"We will be moving ahead shortly, so just hang in there," he promises.

Within a few minutes, the traffic begins to move forward, and I feel an entirely different reason to be anxious. We are getting closer to Michael, and I had never expected this much attention to be brought on a man that had left the free world so long ago. People probably should have just allowed this to happen quietly, and moved on with their lives, but they could not. It seemed as if everyone wanted to be able to say that they were there when he died, and they made sure they were in line.

At the front of the line, there were guards directing cars to a large field off to the left, and further behind the guards, were rows of cameras, well-dressed news people testing out their equipment, and further still, the entrance to the prison, where I assume only a few of those standing and driving here, would get past. Luckily for us, we would be one of them.

We parked and walked towards the guards who were directing everyone. At first they motioned for us to walk back towards where we came from, and then dad's friend who had gotten us in the first time came over and told the guards we were with him, then calmly walked us past all the people standing around and waiting. They looked briefly at us, unaware of what we were doing to get into the building. For all they knew, we could have been visiting any inmate in the entire prison, and they would never know.

The entrance was just as I had remembered, but there was a presence there unlike the previous time. People were in a more serious state, checking in with one and other and ensuring their demeanors were as professional as possible. This was a big day for everyone involved and would close a chapter in history that had begged to be over. Finally, it would be.

"This is Rain, you remember," my father said to the man who walked us in.

"Of course, Rain, it's a pleasure to see you. You father has told me a lot about you. You should both be proud," he said.

I was proud. My dad had not once, not twice, but three times, taken me to a place where I never expected him to. He treated me as a human with her own reasons, her own vision and her own dreams. I would not have guessed that he would be the one to see me through this, but next to Mee-maw, he was the only one I trusted enough to even ask.

The officer in charge had our badges with our names written out already at the front in an envelope all prepared. He handed them to us and told us we would walk through the two guards to the right of the doorway, and they would go through our belongings to inspect what he had brought inside.

Dad said he would be happy to go with me or sit back if that was what I preferred. I told him I wanted to do this on my own, and if that was okay, and to please let me. He nodded with approval and I began to walk over to where I would lay my belongings down for inspection.

They removed everything. My papers with questions, and the two pens I brought to write notes and possibly answers to all those questions I had formed. They took my water bottle from the bag and removed the pocket watch from its pocket in front of the bag.

"Paper and pens are fine, but this will need to remain," the guard said.

I tried to reason with her, but she told me while she understood, there were rules that absolutely needed to be followed. It would remain at her station until we were leaving, at which point I could retrieve it. I wanted to show it to Michael and tell him the story from Mee-maw, but I would not be able to do so now.

At least I was permitted to bring a pad with my notes, but they also kept my pens. I was told I could get one when I got to where I was headed, so I shook my head showing them I understood. They were intimidating for certain, but I guess when you work in a place where respect is needed, you find a way to earn it.

The echoes of the doors opening and closing felt louder than the first time I was here. I think it was because of the change in the mood of everyone here. They were expecting the families of the missing thirteen, or at least those that had family still alive that cared, the Governor, and a good deal of top people from the different law enforcement groups throughout the state. This was big, and no one wanted to be signaled out for being unprofessional. People could easily lose a job for messing any part of this day up as it was going to be reported to the entire state and surrounding ones as well.

Then, as I grabbed the few items I was allowed to take with me, I walked through the gated area, towards a different set of doors from the last ones I had gone through and entered an entirely different area of the prison.

There was a much larger area, with more tables and chairs than the small, single room we met in last time. The ceilings were higher, and the feeling was a bit more relaxed, partially because the room gave me more room to breathe, and possibly because this was now my second meeting with him, which naturally put me in a better headspace. I felt more prepared than the first time, having nothing to lose but my sanity if I could not get at least a few decent answers to allow those damning dreams that invaded my thoughts without permission, go like dust flying through a windstorm.

It was the same guard who greeted me from the last time. He smiled ever so slightly and said hello. He was all business no matter who was in the prison walls and how important they may be. I liked him as he felt like a man who would protect anyone that needed it. He seemed to fear nothing, and that must be a needed trait to have in a place like this.

"Rain, have a seat here. Tarvis will be along shortly. Just as the last time, I will be close by if you need anything. You remember the signals I told you the last time?" he asked.

I nodded that I did.

"Good. I will watch for those. If you feel you need anything, you just motion me over. And one last thing," he began.

I looked at him as he clearly paused, waiting for my full undivided attention.

"You be proud of yourself, kid. I may not agree with a man doing what they do, but when their times comes to pay for their missteps in this life, I believe they deserve a little humanity before they are sent off, and you are providing that. Well done," he finished.

There were two other guards to the right and left of the doorway that we entered in, and the main one took a stand about eight or nine feet from the table I was seated at. Fidgeting in place, I tried to calm myself enough so Michael would not feel uneasy as well.

Then, I could hear someone speaking on the outside of the door, and it opened with that same hollow sound I heard when I first arrived here. The guards at each end of the doorway turned in and took a step back to allow the other ones to enter. Michael was walking behind them, shackled by the wrist with a chain that wrapped around his waist, then down to his ankles, so he could barely move much at all.

I wanted to cry as I watched him struggle to walk in, as if he was being stripped of final dignity on a day where he would exist for only a few hours more. They could not give him that last sense of humanity, but he still seemed to understand more than I could the why.

When he was walked over to the table, he sat down and looked at the papers I had now spread out in front of him.

"Olive, what have we here?" he asked curiously.

I could feel all the words I wanted to say to greet him

and to throw at him in the hopes of finding that peace I was begging for were fading from my memory. Quickly I looked down, trying to find a way back to where I was just a moment before he entered the room. I wasn't feeling intimidated at all, but maybe sensing the reality of the moment had been greater than I expected it to.

"Whatever it is on your mind, it will all be okay, Olive. You are going to go home today, and when you wake up tomorrow morning, life will be there waiting for you to live. Don't you go getting wrapped up in the controlled chaos of today. You have done well, and for that branch you extended me, I am grateful," he continued.

My eyes filled up with tears I had not allowed to drop for longer than I could remember. There were plenty of opportunities to cry before this day, and other things to be upset over, but today was just different in ways I could not totally grasp.

"Michael, how is it that you can sit here so calm and unafraid? Do you not understand what is going to happen soon, and that everything changes from this point forward?" I asked confused.

He fidgeted with his shackles, as clearly they were affecting his ability to move his hands freely and comfortably.

"Well, being afraid doesn't change the outcome, now does it?" he said smiling.

"But how do you feel about this all?" I asked.

"I feel at ease. My life has turned left and right many times, and now, I no longer need to choose a path. It has been chosen for me, and whatever is to come, well, is to come without my say. I embrace a new chapter, and an ending to one I have had to live for far too long. It's time, Olive. It's time."

I could not understand the calmness that was in the room. His words hit me perfectly with peace and resolve, allowing my mind to open up once again, and for those thoughts of fear to hide away for the moment. I was ready. Ready to ask him those questions, and ready to tell him that even if not another soul on this planet could forgive him, I could. I had it even if he didn't ask for it or want it. That forgiveness was not only for him, but for me and the lost souls from decades ago. I felt as if they, too, were telling me he could die knowing they held no grudges any longer. Maybe that was true and maybe it was not but feeling that was enough for me to extend it to him.

I asked everything. All the simple questions like how he felt over the last few days here, to the ones I was unsure I would be able to ask, like was there any chance he would let anyone know where the lost were resting. Each question that came out was greeted with a simple nod of his head, showing me he absolutely understood what and why I was asking of him. While he did not offer any answers at the table, I felt like he had a desire to. Maybe it was a struggle he had come to face for himself. He could let the world know what they felt they should know, or take those secrets with him when he left.

"I wanted to bring you my Pappy's pocket watch Mee-maw gifted to me, as a final present for you, but the guards would not allow me to," I said.

"Well, they have their rules they must follow, and you cannot fault them for following rules. When we don't follow them, we end up in places we would rather not be. But thank you for the thought. It would have been nice to see it," he responded.

I smiled, feeling as if he genuinely appreciated the act over the gift.

Time, for some crazy reason, seemed to grant one last gift to us. It paused for a few moments, well, at least it felt as if it had done so. He had just a little more time with me than either of us expected, and for that, I was smiling.

But then came the words from the guard that I knew were coming but somehow hoped would not.

"Tarvis, it's time to go now," he said.

I quickly touched his hand, which I knew was against the rules, but what would they do to me? Lock me up? Tell me I would not be able to speak with him ever again? So I decided to break one of the rules, and told him,

"Michael, before you go. I have something to say," I started.

He was now standing up, ready to say his goodbye when I began.

"God has a plan for you, and for me. For you, I truly believe it is to learn all the things you have ever wanted answers for, and to give you a peace maybe you feel you haven't deserved but do. For me? I think he wanted me to do something that you may not want, but it is still needed."

He looked confused for the first time, and then I said it.

" I forgive you."

Chapter 43

∗ ∗ ∗

I did not attend the final moments of Tarvis Michael Richards. My father had to draw a line somewhere, and as much as I struggled with the decision, I think he was right. He told me,

"Rain, you do not want to hold the memory of a person in their final moment like that. It's better to remember them as you wanted to, not as you were told to."

But I told him we were not leaving the parking lot until I heard the bell ring. I wanted to know he was gone, and that I no longer needed to worry about him. I would then know his book was finished here, and that he was creating a new one somewhere far from anything that he had done.

I never felt that he was a good person, but I also never could come to terms with him being a devil either. He had committed terrible, unimaginable crimes, and for those, he paid the final payment. But there was a side to him very few would ever get to see and feel deep down to their soul. He wasn't unapologetic for what happened. He just never said it the way others would have preferred. I knew he hated that part of his journey, but he also knew that no spoken words would ever make it right, so he accepted that people wished for him to die, and he gave them that.

People were quieting down, including those who were protesting loudly just moments before. Both sides weren't giving respect to the other side as much as they were simply waiting. I had no idea of what people entered the room to watch Michael die, and nor did I care to know. They had their reasons, and they would need to live and die knowing what they saw and what role they played.

My dad tapped my head in a loving manner as we sat in the front of his car.

"Well, Rainbow, you done good. For the rest of your life, you will always know you gave a gift to someone that no one else on this earth could have. That's a moment to be proud of," he said.

I was proud, but sad that being proud came at such a great price. Had I never met Tarvis Michael, I would have cared nothing about this entire day. Maybe someone would mention it at school, or in passing a news anchor who was here outside now, would make a comment about him being executed, but other than that, it would have come and gone like the other three-hundred-sixty-five days of the year as routine.

This day was anything but routine, and even though I had a moment in there that time felt as if it stood still for us, it was not now. I was about to ask my father a question when it happened.

The bell rang out for everyone to hear. I could not tell you how many times it did, because once it started, I stopped. Stopped asking any questions and stopped thinking about everything. My mind shut down and I was paralyzed by the simple sound of ringing in the air, knowing what it meant.

Everyone was silent for a minute, and then when it stopped, when all the ringing was over and the people there had said whatever last words in defense that they felt were needed, people started to climb back into their cars, and went home or wherever they did to get back on with the rest of their lives.

Dad just sat there, not doing anything. He allowed me to have this time to myself, as much of it as I needed, without interruption.

I did not cry, though. It was a strange feeling to not feel the need to break down and let go. Instead, I felt a peaceful flow over me like a soft blanket of snow that covers the morning roads before anyone lays a hand on them. I smiled for Michael.

Today was a powerfully emotional day but a much needed day at the same time. People had some sort of closure they were waiting for, and Michael had what he had begged for over the years. He had peace.

Eventually, we started our drive home, and although most of it was a blur for me, I do remember how I felt about my dad on that ride home. He had gifted me more than he knew, and I swore to myself if there was anything I could do to save his marriage, I would. I wanted him to know I saw him and appreciated him for being who he was. I think dads feel unseen at times, and that hurt me for the first time. He was absolutely seen.

At home, mom was resigned to the fact that what she was adamantly against was now behind both of us. She would never be able to understand the importance of that for me, but I knew what it meant.

Could life go on as I had needed it to, and would those who cried for my help finally be at peace that they also surely deserved? I would not know until I knew, as strange as that sounded.

I could still hear the bell ringing in my head, even though a day later, it was far removed from ringing. I guess it was just part of the process when you have such an emotional time in your life. Things may go, but the sounds, smells and feeling of those moments stay with you for longer than you expect them to.

Michael was gone, and I had no idea what that meant for him. I assumed they would bury his body on the same prison grounds he had spent most of his adult life in, which to me seemed sad and cruel, even after death. He had finished his sentence, but had to remain on that property for the remainder of time?

His cell that he called home for far too long was most likely cleaned out, and whatever belongings he had to his name were probably tossed away, or sent to wherever he requested they be sent. He had very little, so that probably was done in a relatively short amount of time. Sad.

And then that would be it. The news would tell their stories, and after about a week or so, he would be removed from the memories of all. Not me though. I would keep the thoughts and lessons I learned from Michael for much longer than anyone else.

Though, in our last meeting, he did disclose a little more to me than others knew. He also made me a promise, that over time, I would understand more and see the truth that no one else could. I figured that meant that he could tell I would gain perspective as the weeks passed by and learn to see things differently. But that was not exactly what he meant.

A week later, when I was heading to the post office to close out my PO Box, I checked it just in case and saw a letter inside. The letter was addressed from the prison and looked exactly as the others Michael had sent. He was dead now a week, and still, he managed to write a letter just before and had it here waiting for me. I wondered why he had not simply handed it to me when we saw each other, but I guess he had his reasons.

I could not wait to get home to read what it said, so I opened it there in the lobby of the post office.

Dear Olive

Well, if I had to guess, this was not a letter you were expecting from me.

I sat down after our last meeting and decided to write you a letter to explain so much more that you will need to know going forward.

In the past few months or so, I've written to you a letter a day, and sometimes several more. Those were never sent out, and there is a perfectly good reason for that. I will explain.

By now, I am gone from this place, and there were

so many unanswered questions you had for me. I found that to be entirely unfair of me not to answer them, but I needed to wait until I was no longer here for very important, specific reasons.

Over the course of the next several months, you should be getting a letter a day, or close to that. Had you received them sooner, I could not guarantee myself that you would stand by silently and do nothing about the things I am about to tell you. I know you have a good heart, but you have a fighter's heart as well. I could not chance you standing up and defending my name, when it was not what I would have wanted or needed. I needed to be set free, and now I am.

If I could ask you a favor in death, it would be this. Keep all I share with you, between you and me. My name is not worth saving, and although I do believe I could have stood up more in my trial, there was an important reason I did not, and I would like to keep it that way even in my absence.

There is one other thing, Olive. I have signed a release to allow for my ashes to be stored away until a time when you are ready and able to take them. My final wish was that you spread them out high in the mountains, at a place that I will disclose to you later. If you could do that when and only when you are ready, that would be a great final gift to me.

T Michael Richards

A mountain of emotions took over my body, and I sat down there on the floor of the lobby, clutching the letter close to my chest and gripping it tightly. I had thought that somehow what I saw at the prison was it. There would be no more messages, and no more reading about what happened to who and all the rumors that circulated over time. I was done, but apparently, I was not.

He managed to trick me into believing that all of his secrets would die with him, buried beneath the ground where they would forever be sealed. All the questions unanswered remained completely unanswered, and I would have two choices in life; to accept that I would never know and drop it or to decide for myself what had really happened.

The postmaster came over to where I was seated, and asked if I had fallen.

"No, I'm fine. Really. Just need a minute is all," I said.

I would come back each week, no, every few days, whenever I could, to retrieve the letters and I hoped that somehow none of them would get lost and they all arrived in the order he intended them to arrive.

There was the question of how a man who was clearly dead, could get all those letters to me, day after day and without fail. I eventually learned the how of this all. That no-nonsense guard, who had walked me through each step of safety during my time visiting with Michael, the one named Roger, who had for whatever reasons known only to him, agreed to send the letters. Maybe he felt bad for me and thought it would make me happy to at least have them. Or it could have been the fact that he knew Tarvis Michael needed to face his punishment, but that after he did, he was no longer in debt, and the letters could and should be delivered as a gesture of understanding.

Whatever it was, he told Michael he would do that one last favor and let it go at that. Michael had a great deal of respect and trust for Roger, and in his position, what difference did it make? He had no other options, so he had to trust enough or not at all. So, he trusted just enough.

I trusted Roger and believed he would send each letter on a schedule he felt he could, and would not open any of the letters beforehand, as really there would be no reason to. Whatever he said in them, changed nothing going forward, and he, as a good man, believed it was the business of Tarvis Michael and me.

When I arrived home and dad asked how it went with the closing of the box, I told him I had not closed it after all. He looked at me confused, knowing I had fully intended to close that chapter, and apparently had decided against it.

"Dad, he's still writing to me," I said plainly.

"Wait, who is still writing you? Tarvis? How in the world is that possible, Rain?" he replied.

I told him about the letter, and that he said there would be many more. That he had written them over the months leading up to his death and would somehow ensure I would receive them all. I mentioned how he was supposedly going to answer some of the questions I had asked for him to, and even though I had no way of knowing which he would decide to answer for sure, I had to know.

I felt relief, even though I was being pulled back into a story I thought I had closed. It wasn't the same confusion as before, because now it wasn't about my response to him, as it would only be his message to me. That took off some pressure, and if he answered only a few of the questions, well, so be it. One more answer would have made it worth the wait.

As promised, the letters came and before opening any, I checked the postmark to ensure I was opening them in the order he had sent them to me.

At first, the letters were based on his early life, and how he had wanted more out of a world that seemed hellbent on keeping him down. He had found a little relief here and there but saw struggles in front of him for sure. But he remained positive, feeling as if at any point, it was all going to change overnight and he would embrace it and be on his way to great things.

The letters felt as if he was writing a book, and I was getting them a chapter at a time. His style of writing remained the same, as he gracefully detailed his travels, ambitions and struggles over each year he had free.

As they went on, I could see a change. It was sudden, and his writing felt choppy for the first time. It was as if he arrived at a scene that, even as the writer, seemed impossible to describe properly without a lot of great emotional pain. I had not known him to stumble over his words or to seem at a loss for words, but he struggled through some of the letters.

There was little about the victims, other than to say that when they had vanished, life in that part of the country was changed forever. He did not mention knowing the victims or watching them even for a moment in his travels, but he did say they were seemingly decent people who just ended up being in the wrong place, at the wrong time.

I wasn't sure how to feel about this. Was he hiding the fact that he murdered them, or was he trying to tell me something completely different, while dancing around the truth to protect someone else? It made little sense, and I had to wait until he alone was ready, or willing, to fix the gaps in his storytelling.

But then about twelve or so letters in, he mentioned the part where Shawn came into play. For some reason, he was more willing and able to discuss this one, who of course was his final victim. He knew Shawn personally, and that he did not hide. I wasn't sure he knew any of the missing, but this was interesting to me to hear at least one he did.

And Rosemary? He mentioned her more than the others as well. He knew of her struggles, and at one point, offered to help her on her home at a discounted rate, just to be a decent man. She accepted, and that is how they eventually met up. Was it his kindness and charm that let him in, where he would eventually take the life of her only son, or was there more to this?

A new letter would hopefully give me that as well, but once again, he shifted.

It was as if when he was just about to let more out and explain what no one else knew, he closed up and burrowed deeper into a place only he had room to go. His mind had thoughts of letting it escape from the hidden depths, but his heart was pulling the cords and telling him, no, not yet.

I wondered if he would ever find the strength, knowing

that once he left this place, he would never be able to take anything back, or explain things further once his writing stopped and the last letter was mailed. It wasn't about his legacy or proving that he wasn't the monster people had felt he was, but this was more about giving someone peace that he never expected them to need. A girl who he wrote a single letter in response to her high school project, had somehow been pulled into the trauma's that were silent for longer than she was alive.

Days went by, and the letters never stopped coming. Some were shorter, written in a haste that showed he knew his time was limited. They were always kind but seldom explained much of anything. Mostly, they told me to live a life worth bragging about, and to write my story however I saw fit, regardless of what anyone told me. He said that his story was written long before he was a thought in his parents' eyes. Michael felt that destiny was something most of us had to accept, but that for me, I could change that because I was different and capable of so much more than he ever was.

Then Christmas came again, and I felt a sense of loss that hadn't hit me in a while. The ability to reply to Michael was lost, and I felt an overwhelming urge to write to him and remind him that there had to be good in him, and that on Christmas, he should be smiling because someone believed in him. But he was gone, and I could not write to any place that he could receive it. The address I had memorized by now was useless as it housed a different person altogether.

The letter that arrived just days after we were finished

opening presents, as the excitement of the music and lights and sounds faded into a time when no one knew quite what to do with themselves, changed everything I had known to this point. And shock would never properly describe the feeling I had when I sat on my bed and read it to myself.

Chapter 44

* * *

There's a saying that people use often, and it says, "When someone tries to show you who they are, believe them."

Most times I hear it and ignore what the words actually mean, because people can hide who they are unless you are really looking close enough, and rarely do I care too. But in the case of Tarvis Michael Richards, I looked close enough without even trying. From the very beginning when I first encountered that man, I knew something was off. I felt that I had to write to him, even after hearing all the bad, terrible stories of loss and misery. Something told me to continue with my letters, despite what those around me would think or say if they only knew.

My dearest Olive,

I am unsure of how the timing of this one particular letter worked out, as it cannot be guaranteed that it arrives before Christmas as intended. If by chance it does not, well, then after it shall have to be!

I've done a lot of searching within myself as I stare at the paper before me and wonder just how much I can let flow from my fingers, before I stop myself yet again. I know I have led you to believe there would eventually be so much more to the story, and then I pull that away from you like a rug, just as you were expecting something very different.

And so, I will write as I will, as you deserve, and tell myself, "Self? This is how it must be done. It is okay. Olive is the one person that you can trust, and the only person who will take this with her the entirety of her own life without ever speaking a word." I trust you with this, Olive. I truly do.

I was alone in my bedroom and still, felt as if someone could be looking over my shoulder. I turned around and made sure I was completely alone, trying desperately to give Michael what he was asking of me. I could be trusted, I told myself, and whatever he had to say to me, would go to my own grave with me, even if it meant keeping the secrets that others felt they needed to hear.

The letter was three times as long as any other had ever been. His words had always caught my full attention, but with this one, I could hear his voice as if he was narrating the story to me from just a few feet away. I saw him sitting across from me, but unshackled now, free from the restraints that once held him closed off. He was able to say and do as he chose, free from judgement and rules.

Rosemary had known for longer than she cared to know.

When she met Tarvis Michael, it was not by chance as one would have liked to believe. She was a lost woman, desperate to break her own chains, and scared that if she did not, more would suffer needlessly.

She befriended my Michael and allowed him to do the small tasks that had gone undone over the years. Shawn had helped Tarvis on a few occasions and had done his very best to fit in as he had never done before, because Tarvis Michael had great patience.

But there was a side to Shawn that only Rosemary could see. Having known her son better than anyone else could ever know, she saw the dark secrets he hid, even when he tried to disguise them with lies that maybe another human would believe.

She was in a spot that no mother should ever find herself in. One where she had to decide the fate of her only son, who was all she had left in this world. He could never understand for himself the damage he had caused and surely would continue to if allowed. The lives of the lost were forever gone, but she could do right if she wished, by doing something that in her heart felt wrong but needed beyond words could ever express.

Shawn, although struggling with his temper and awkwardness, was trusted enough that people accepted how he was. There would never be a concern that he would ever purposely harm a single soul outside of his occasional anger issues that lasted only moments, and people were right on that. He had not harmed one, but twelve over the course of a few years.

Rosemary sat down with Tarvis Michael one morning, sobbing and shaking like a mother who is conflicted would, and begged for him to stop the madness. She knew that Shawn would never be able to understand what it was he was doing, and if he went to prison, he would be battered daily for being different than others. She could not spend the next thirty or so years of her life, wondering how her son was handling a life behind prison bars, a boy amongst men. He would survive, but only after suffering each and every day, and she would never allow that to happen.

Tarvis Michael sat and listened, in disbelief of what she was sharing that morning. Everything was changed after that conversation, and for Tarvis, he had to make a decision that he should never have had to make. He could give Shawn up, and end the vanishings right then and there, but subject a poor mother to a lifetime of regrets and concerns for her honesty, or he could make the ultimate decision and do as she asked, allowing her to somehow find peace in all this chaos.

He saw an opportunity to give by taking, and as much as he hated the thought of playing God, he had little choice. He wished she had never spoken those words or asked of him what would change his life forever, but she had. She had no one else to turn to, and she knew she could never finish this herself, either way.

So Tarvis Michael Richards went with Shawn on a hike to his favorite lookout, where you could see the lights below flickering in the early morning hours, as people got up, dressed and went on their way to work. The sounds below could not be heard, but you could feel them if you allowed yourself to. The people were living in fear, but while Tarvis and Shawn sat up high above, they were safe. They just did not know it.

The point at which the entire town could be seen, where the cliffs gave unique views into a world only seen from the heavens, was known as just that. Locals had called it "Point Eden," which meant heaven on earth, but it would not be labeled on any maps, and nor did tours ever go up to this point to grant curious folks a view of what so few had seen. This was a place that only few knew existed, as the terrain was slightly rough to get to, and the views, while magnificent, were earned, not given.

He did not stay there longer than he needed, as inside he was already conflicted with the decision he thought he had made. But in the end, after roughly ten minutes or so, before the light of the sun touched the tip of the mountains they were in, Tarvis Michael ended Shawn's life, which also brought an end to the vanishings over the small town below. He had allowed life to live but had to exchange two in return.

Shawn trusted Tarvis Michael because he was kind, gentle and understanding. He listened to Shawn when he spoke, and offered guidance where he could with patience and understanding no one else could.

While he never disclosed the exact location of the missing to Tarvis, he gave enough insight to allow his imagination to see where they were, and what had happened. That peak, where heaven began and the chaos of the world mixed in, was the final resting spot for those that could no longer speak. It was fitting that where it began, be where it all ended.

My mind raced as I fought with the thoughts of a man dying for all those lost lives, when he had actually saved more from going missing. Why had he not defended himself at the trial by standing up and exclaiming,

"I only helped! One man had to die so that all of you could live freely and without fear! Don't you see? I am not the devil you all claim I am!"

But he did not. He took what Rosemary had asked of him with him when he left. I don't feel as if he ever blamed her either. She had a decision to make—one that would change her life either way. And although Tarvis Michael knew what he was doing would be viewed as terribly wrong, he also believed that something good could come from something bad, even if not in his own life.

It was a sacrifice made, but still, he knew he took the life of another man, and when he was caught, he focused on that much. If they convicted him, then so be it. It was the penalty for taking the life of another, as no one has the right to play God. He accepted that, and for the years he sat in a cell, knowing that at some point he would be called to lay on that bed to die, he waited for peace.

Peace came, and so did forgiveness. I pray that before he died, he had learned to forgive himself as well. But I don't know if that was true or not. He said very little about his own sufferings and instead focused his time on ensuring that the secrets he had within him, died with him. There was no further need to involve Rosemary in any of this, and as for Shawn, he didn't know what he was doing. He should be remembered as a struggling young man, who was dealt a bad hand and did what he could with it. That was all.

Chapter 45

* * *

There would be more letters, until there were not. I remember the way the last arrived, and although I expected Michael to let me know it was the last, he did not. I think he felt like closing the book was unnecessary for us, as we shared enough words and thoughts to carry on long after the letters died.

My parents did not reconcile, despite the efforts I had put in, and that of my parents. They both tried by going to counseling, spending more time alone on dates which they had previously forgotten that part of life, and listening more than talking. But some things in life are just not meant to be.

I did eventually get the box of Michael's ashes, and during a warm spring morning, just before the sun came up, my father and I walked deep into the woods, past the trail hidden behind my Mee-maw's old house with the Japanese Honeysuckle patches all throughout, and over to Point Eden.

My dad had no idea why I chose this spot, but he knew enough to accept that this was where it needed to be. I sat there in peace, looking down below over the beautiful mountain, and imagined decades ago how a different view was seen by both Shawn and Tarvis Michael as they sat there that early morning. Somewhere here, the ashes of twelve souls remain trapped for eternity without care for time, and now Michael can join them as he saw fit.

The cries I once suffered through in my dreams and along this trail eventually died off, and I would not hear them ever again. I guess giving them Michael was all they needed to quietly move on with whatever it was they would be doing. I placed a simple wooden cross at the peak, and on it wrote the words,

"To all those lost, you are never truly gone. And now, your story is complete and you are free."

Tarvis Michael Richards was a simple man, just trying to live a life worth living. He had not asked for any of this, but he had made a decision that would change everything during the course of his life. Was he a bad person for what he eventually did or was he a hero for stopping what no one else could? I don't know for sure. I know that I never judged him after that day. He didn't want judgement from me. He only wanted someone to feel like he had worth, and he had worth beyond what even he expected to have.

I opened the box that contained the ashes of a man misunderstood, looked up to the sky and smiled, as he reminded me to do in all situations in life, both good and bad. His remains were cast out all around the ledge, so that he would always have the best view in all of West Virginia, whenever he needed.

And because time would continue on as it must, without our say and without our cries for different, I buried the pocket watch in the wooden box that his ashes had been placed —the same watch Mee-maw had given to me— because it would always have value no matter where it was, and what shape it was in. Just like Tarvis Michael Richards would always have value no matter where he was, or what shape he was in.

And as promised, I never told a soul anything Michael shared with me. Not even with my dad, who learned not to question me out of respect for the bond I had with Michael and the secrets we had between us. Some things we just take with us when we go, and that's just the way it is.

The end

**If you enjoyed this story, be sure to
check out the Authors other novels, available
on eBook, paperback, and hardback.**

When the Dandelions Sing

"When The Dandelions Sing," is a warm, heartfelt story about a young boy named Ronnie Jefferson McFarland Jr., who is trying to understand the meaning of the word "purpose", and what his purpose is in life.

His grammy, who nicknames him Jasper for some reason known only to her, and his grandad, give him valuable lessons through their own eyes, and a window to the past that sometimes gets overshadowed by bigger things in life, but never truly forgotten.

While Ronnie's momma struggles with her life, he leans on others around him to gain perspective and a sense of understanding. He learns that even after people leave his world, their impact remains, and he never stops learning from them. As it turns out, some of the best lessons in life come from those who seemingly have nothing left to give.

Ronnie learns that a family is not always conventional, but oftentimes made up of the people you choose for yourself, and who choose you in return. He discovers that joy can be found in the smallest of things and the simplest of moments...for even among a field of perfect flowers, the simple dandelion can sing.

"Everything has purpose, and everything, a meaning

beyond what we are even meant to understand. That's just the way it is. Purpose is not what we want it to be. It's simply what is meant to be."

Phoebe's Heart of Stone

In 1919, an unthinkable tragedy struck the blue-collar town of Alliance Ohio, and one particular family, the Bradway family, found themselves at the center of its terrible wrath.

In the wake of disaster, Carl, a father of six, was forced to make a decision that would affect both himself and those he loved for the rest of their lives.

Carl and his beloved wife, Phoebe, had worked tirelessly to build a life of love and contentment for themselves and their six young children. Though determined and deeply in love, the young family could not escape the horrible black cloud that haunted their family, seemingly hell-bent on taking all they had built together.

This story follows the shocking true-life events of a family who wished for the simple things in life, but instead faced a path riddled with misfortune that altered the course of each of their lives forever.

The Gift of Life, Plus One

Agnes is a young, unconventional little girl, who wants to be exactly who she is. Her father, Jon, struggles with the balance of raising his children the way he sees fit, while still allowing them to grow into the people they are destined to become.

When Agnes suddenly falls ill, her life and the lives of those around her are altered forever, in ways they never imagined. Both her father and mother, Amanda, are faced with challenges that will either break them, or save them.

Jon finds that when he drifts off to sleep, his mind often travels to a unique place where he is mostly alone with his thoughts, while discovering that accepting life is not always easy, but important to moving on to the next season of life.

"The Gift of Life, Plus One," provides the perspective that just because life doesn't necessarily go as we planned, it's exactly the way it was intended to go.

The Forgiving Path to the City of Springs

A young, often brash Michael Kelley is a tough, South Philly man with a dislike for anyone who cannot push through the struggles life throws your way. His past was riddled by tragedy and a poor upbringing, which he has allowed to shape him, for good or for bad.

He finds himself in front of a judge who offers him two options. Go to jail to serve his sentence, or agree to do community service within the city limits. He agrees to the community service, but has no idea of what is in store for him.

When Michael finds himself in the Mudflaps Tent Community for the Homeless along the Schuylkill River, in the very city he was raised in, he quickly wonders if he chose wisely. He loathes the homeless with a bitter rage for all they represent in his mind, and now must help those same lost souls.

But meeting two men, Von, who resides within the community but doesn't seem to fit in, and Marcus, who works for a nonprofit that helps the homeless and seems better suited to live there than Von, Michael quickly realizes he may have misjudged. Now he must decide if he can forgive others in his life, or if it's perchance him he needs to forgive.

The Forgiving Path to the City of Springs (98,700 words) is a novel told from the perspective of one Michael Kelley, and at times reflects on a horrible past he would rather forget, but cannot, or perhaps should not. This book gives a unique perspective on finding hope, learning to see deeper and clearer than your eyes allow, and ultimately, granting forgiveness.

Big Ish

There are men that walk this earth going mostly unnoticed and living peaceful lives while raising families, who slowly fade away when their time comes to an end as they breathe a final breath.

Then there are those few that cannot go unnoticed, who no matter where they go, cast shadows so large and dark that even if they wanted to hide, they could not. Nothing is balanced for them, and no one around them would feel safe if they dared to cross them.

Ishmael Heald was one of those men, who despite wanting to do right by others, never seemed to be able to. He fought with the force of three ferocious men and consumed enough alcohol to kill a normal human, all while existing in a life that seemed more fiction than an actual reality.

The loss of so much throughout his time and a constant battle from within that felt like the devil eating him away, filled his story with lessons that would last well beyond his death for this steel worker.

This is his story. He would have never expected to be remembered over a hundred years later for the life he struggled through, but he left a mark on this earth that cannot be, and should not be forgotten.

www.ingramcontent.com/pod-product-compliance
Lightning Source LLC
Chambersburg PA
CBHW020553120726
47903CB00001B/246